D1505270

DISCARDED

TRAIL TO VICKSBURG

TRAIL TO VICKSBURG

A Western Duo

Lewis B. Patten

Thorndike Press • Chivers Press
Thorndike, Maine USA   Bath, England

This Large Print edition is published by Thorndike Press, USA
and by Chivers Press, England.

Published in 1998 in the U.S. by arrangement with
Golden West Literary Agency.

Published in 1998 in the U.K. by arrangement with
Harold Ober Associates.

U.S. Hardcover   0-7862-0764-7   (Western Series Edition)
U.K. Hardcover   0-7540-3357-0   (Chivers Large Print)
U.K. Softcover   0-7540-3358-9   (Camden Large Print)

Thorndike Large Print ® Western Series.

The text of this Large Print edition is unabridged.
Other aspects of the book may vary from the original edition.

Set in 16 pt. Plantin by Rick Gundberg.

Printed in the United States on permanent paper.

British Library Cataloguing in Publication Data available

Library of Congress Cataloging in Publication Data

Patten, Lewis B.
     [Golden magnet]
     Trail to Vicksburg : a western duo / Lewis B. Patten.
        p.   cm.
     Contents: The golden magnet — Trail to Vicksburg.
     ISBN 0-7862-0764-7 (lg. print : hc : alk. paper)
     1. Western stories.   2. Large type books.   I. Patten,
Lewis B. Trail to Vicksburg.   II. Title.
     [PS3566.A79G65   1998]
     813'.54—dc21   98-5427

Table of Contents

Editor's Note

When Lewis B. Patten originally wrote the story he titled "Trail to Vicksburg," it found no acceptance among book publishers because it was set during the period of the Civil War. The typescript, as prepared by the author, is preserved among his papers at the American Heritage Center of the University of Wyoming at Laramie and was used for this first publication. Because the text was somewhat shorter than customary for a Five Star Western, it has been combined with Lewis B. Patten's earlier short novel set in Denver, Colorado during the early gold rush period. For the first book appearance of what was titled "The Man on the Stage" in *Best Western Magazine*, the title intended by the author has been restored. That story begins this Western duo.

THE GOLDEN MAGNET

I

THE MAN ON THE STAGE

This land had lain unchanged over a thousand years, marked only by the game trails, by the buffalo wallows, by the fleeting pause of an Indian village upon its vastness. Now a new scar lay upon it, a two-track road, winding ever westward toward the distant elusiveness of snow-clad mountain ranges. The coach that ran down this rutted road, raising a thin plume of dust behind, was no glittering, yellow-wheeled thing of beauty. Its hardwood sides had weathered to a dingy gray, and the grain stood out from the sandblasting of prairie storm, from the pitiless erosion of mud and water.

The painted legend of ownership, defaced by the same forces that had dimmed the glory of the Troy's first beauty, announced that it belonged to the line of **Forest Overland, Denver City, and Auraria,** or abbreviated, the F.O., D.C., & A. Four passengers rattled about inside the shell of the rocking coach, and of these only Cole Estes still held his temper in check, still could contain the irascibility and ill-humor that a week's jolting travel over the world's roughest roads could engender in even the gentlest of humans.

Another of these four was a young woman. She sat directly across from Cole, and she had fallen into a numbed and exhausted stupor. This merciful unconsciousness robbed her of arrogant imperiousness, of consciousness of her own dazzling beauty, things that were so prominent in her when she was awake. Her long lashes lay against smooth cheeks, and her full lips, relaxed this way, were soft and strangely inviting. Beneath the heavy material of her woolen traveling dress, firm and youthful breasts rose and fell evenly with her breathing. Her knee was warm against Cole's own. Sweat put a shine to her nose and cheeks that oddly increased her attraction for Cole.

He caught himself thinking thoughts about her that were not exactly proper. His gray eyes lost their hardness momentarily, but then he thought: *Sleep only shows her for what she might have been, not for the spoiled and willful brat she is.* His steady glance upon her and these thoughts of his must have penetrated her unconsciousness, for she stirred, moaned softly, and opened her eyes.

Cole tactfully turned his glance out of the window and stared moodily at the sameness of rolling grassland, of deep arroyo, of treeless infinity.

He was a big man and sat with an easy relaxation that cushioned him against the shock of the coach, slamming interminably down against reach and bolster. His face could have been called handsome or ugly with equal veracity. It bore no single feature that was fine, being too rugged and hard for that. In the aggregate it showed force of will, strength, and stubbornness. The eyes, gray and direct, could be unfeeling and brutal, yet at times during the journey they had rested on the young woman across from him with an almost unwilling gentleness and a lurking humor, as though her arrogance did not displease him nearly as much as it amused him. Except for this slight hint of gentleness, his was the face of an eagle, and wildness was its singular dominating effect.

He wore rumpled woolen trousers and a buckskin shirt, too tight across broad shoulders that revealed the flexing of long, tough muscles whenever he moved. His hair, cropped short, was curly and reminded you in color of a prime beaver pelt. Now he became aware of the low talk between the raw-boned Missouri farmer, Hobart, and

Schoonover, the merchant from Boston.

"Gold," said Hobart, "is all there is in this stinking country that is worth a man's time."

"Commerce is important," reiterated Schoonover pompously. "There is more profit in that than in grubbing a stream for gold."

It was an argument that had gone on, intermittently but steadily nevertheless, ever since the stage had left Leavenworth. Cole Estes felt a touch of impatience. He said: "Grubbing a stream for gold is productive, and commerce supplies the producers. Both are necessary. Let each man do what he is fitted for, and why argue it out hour after hour?"

The young woman, Norah Forrest, gave this talk her attention, obviously out of sheer boredom, yet she also gave the impression of keeping herself apart, and her air was haughty. She asked, needling Cole: "And what do you think you are fitted for, Mister Estes?"

He put his glance fully upon her, and his thought was plain on his face: *Fitted for taking some of that childish snobbery out of you, perhaps, if I had the time and the opportunity.* But he only said: "Fitted for what I'm doing, which is to ride this rattletrap into Denver and take the job that is waiting for me."

Already he found himself regretting the obligation he had taken on. He thought: *If this coach is a fair sample of Mike Forrest's stageline, then he did some tall lying in his letter. If his daughter is a fair sample of the women a man can expect to find in Denver City, then I would have done better to stay in St. Louis.*

Cole Estes was a stagecoach man, born and raised with the rumble of heavy wheels in his ears. Because he knew the business, and because he had demonstrated an affinity for a fight on numerous occasions, he was the one to whom Mike Forrest had come. He had known Mike in Illinois five years ago when they had both worked on the Illinois Central and Kansas Territory stageline.

There's a squeeze on me here, Mike had written. **The I.C. & K.T., driven out of business in Illinois by the railroads, have moved their headquarters here and are up to their old tricks of eliminating the competition, which in this case happens to be me. I've got a good deal here, Cole, a mail contract and a chance to run a line from Denver City to the mines on the Vasquez. I've**

got some pretty good equipment for a small outfit. But I'm too old to put up the fight it's going to take to beat them. There's a quarter interest in it for you, if you want to come, and we whip the big boys.

A postscriptum at the end of Mike's letter had stated: **My daughter's coming out here, leaving Leavenworth on the 20th of August. I worry some about her, traveling on my line, and I wouldn't let her travel on theirs. Maybe you could time your trip so's you could ride the same coach with her. I'd consider it a big favor, Cole. I'd know she was safe, then.**

So here he was, wet-nurse to a high-and-mighty squirt of a girl, heading into a trouble-shooting job on a line that probably wasn't worth the candle. He shook his head impatiently, still dimly aware of the steady drone of conversation within the stage.

The coach dipped into a cutbank, crossed a wide and nearly dry river bed, turning then to ascend the opposite bank. Turned thus, Cole had a glimpse of another stage, thundering along behind them, and this stage was as different from the one he rode as a Kentucky race horse is different from a shaggy Indian pony.

Under a thick layer of dust its wheels gleamed brilliant yellow. Neither dust nor mud had been able entirely to dull the gleam of its side panels, lustrous varnish that even yet threw back the gleam of the afternoon's brassy sun. A Concord Oxbow. A new one.

Automatically and without thinking, Cole scanned the road ahead, the road that wound along the precipitous river bank. Knowing all the tricks of stageline war, his thought could only be: *A perfect place for wrecking another coach.*

He shrugged and forced himself to relax against the seatback. Conversation had stopped within the coach, and both Hobart and the woman, who faced the rear, now pulled aside the curtains and craned their necks for a glimpse of the strange coach. Schoonover grumbled: "If I'd known they were this close behind us, I'd have ridden in that coach and been comfortable."

Norah stiffened and started to speak, her bridling anger plain. But Cole interrupted: "I've ridden them, my friend, and there's little difference. They're not made for comfort or intended for it, just to get you where you're going, alive if possible."

Schoonover grumbled unintelligibly. Cole said, his oblique glance on Norah: "I've a notion this lady is related to Mike Forrest who owns this line. Your blamed grumbling is getting her goat."

He became aware of the Concord's lead team drawing abreast, and suddenly the driver's whip popped sharply above their heads. Deeper into the harness they seemed to lunge, and in an instant their increased speed brought the second team into view.

Cole growled: "Devil of a place to pass." Uneasiness was a pressure upon him. His body bunched and tightened involuntarily against the seat, and he remembered his responsibility to Mike who expected him to bring Norah through safely simply by his presence in the coach with her.

A quick glance to his right showed how perilously near the bank were the wheels of the Troy. And then suddenly Cole was on his feet as he felt the front wheel of the Concord touch their own rear wheel. Leaning across Schoonover, he thrust his head from the window. "Pull up, damn you! You want to put us in the river?"

He got no answer, but he heard a laugh, mocking, faint, all but lost in the rumble of wheels, in the thunder of hoofs.

Alarmed thoroughly now, Cole pulled himself back and thrust his head and shoulders through the window on his own side

16

of the coach. Standing on the seat he could just reach the baggage rack atop the coach. Gripping this, he pulled his legs through the window, dangled a moment, and then began the swinging, climbing ascent. He felt the touch of the wheels of the other coach again. He yelled at the driver above him: "Pull left, you crazy fool! Don't let him pass you here!"

The driver, high-cheekboned and slit-eyed as an Indian, threw him a pitying and disgusted glance over his shoulder that said plainly: *I got to drive hosses that ought to be pullin' freight wagons. I got to ride stages like this one. On top of all that I got to listen to a loud-mouthed passenger tell me how to drive.*

These things, Cole knew, he would have said if he had time. Cole's head came up until he could look over the coach at the Concord. In the faces of both driver and guard he could see cold, impersonal confidence, and only then did Cole know surely that their plain intent was to put the Troy over the bank and into the dry river bed.

Crouched atop the swaying pile of freight and baggage, Cole half drew his gun, but stopped as the muzzle of the guard's rifle on the stage opposite swung to cover him. The man, a bearded and red-faced giant, shouted: "Put it up, or I'll blow you clear off of there!" Cole let his hand come reluctantly away.

The driver of the Troy, hunched and intent, drew his horses left, relentlessly, recklessly. Cole felt the Concord's front wheel lock with the Troy's rear wheel and heard Norah Forrest's shrill scream. The driver must have heard it, too, must have suddenly become aware of her, of his responsibility to her because she was Mike Forrest's daughter, for he tightened his reins. Unwillingness, reluctance were in the disgusted shake of his head.

Now, Cole thought, *the Concord would pull clear, knowing a woman was involved.* This must have been the driver's thought as well, for he kept a steady pull against his reins. As the Troy slowed, the Concord moved on, cleared their wheels, then forged steadily alongside. Cole turned sick with the realization that the safety of the woman meant less than nothing to them.

The driver of the Troy seized his whip, and it snaked out across the backs of his teams, popping violently. The horses laid into their traces, but this came too late. The coach was too ponderous, too heavily laden to show a change of speed in the split seconds that were left. Relentlessly the Concord drew alongside until it was fully abreast of the smaller coach. Cole knew the pattern of what would happen now. The driver of the Concord would crowd his horses roughly against those drawing the smaller Troy, forcing them off the bank.

Suddenly rage possessed Cole completely. He seized the whip from its socket beside the driver. It snaked out, but this time it was laid directly across the back of the Concord's guard. The man rose out of his seat, a harsh shout of pain breaking from his lips. His rifle fell into the whirling dust between the two coaches. Cole drew his revolver. The driver turned to yell at him: "Get the lead hoss on the far side!"

The Troy lurched violently. The driver sprawled out across the seat, fighting to hold his reins, fighting for balance. Cole felt the lurch as it started and flung himself down recklessly, and it was only this that saved him from being thrown clear. But in the instant it took him to regain his feet, to raise the Colt again, the Concord's teams were drawn roughly against his own horses, forcing them in a screaming, fighting tangle off the bank, a sheer drop of ten feet.

The coach tilted at an awful angle, and Cole was flung clear, still clutching his revolver. His last consciousness was of a terrible, rending crash as the old Troy toppled into the river bed, of Norah Forrest's terrified scream. Then he struck the hard-baked, sandy clay of the river bed and knew the whirling sickness, the brassy taste of descending unconsciousness. Before full blackness overtook him, he had the hazy remembrance of a flurry of shots, of distant, violent shouting.

II

THE STAGE WON'T BE COMING

Wetness along his whole side brought Cole to his knees, and he found himself in the middle of the thin stream that was all there was to Bijou Creek in the late summer. Not fully comprehending the circumstance that had put him here, he stared about dazedly. He saw the coach, lying on its side, its wheels still spinning. Dust raised by its falling had not yet settled.

He muttered thickly: "Couldn't have been out more'n a minute or two." He struggled to his feet, head throbbing and whirling. A steady, low cursing came from within the coach. Cole climbed to the top side of it and raised the door until it lay open, until he could look down inside. Hobart, the lanky farmer, broke off his steady cursing, and squinted up at Cole. Cole asked, his eyes glued to the still form of Norah Forrest: "You hurt, man?"

Hobart grunted. "Shook up, I think that's all." He struggled to his feet.

21

Cole lowered himself into the coach and pulled the inert form of Schoonover from across Norah's body. Blood oozed from a gash in Schoonover's forehead.

Now he knelt beside Norah Forrest. She lay tumbled in a heap against the door, utterly still. Hobart asked: "What the devil happened? It looked to me like they deliberately wrecked us."

"They did!" Cole laid his head against Norah's breasts and, as he felt their regular movement, sighed with relief. "Mike would never forgive me if she was hurt," he muttered under his breath.

He gathered her into his arms and stood up, laying her on the top side of the coach while he climbed out. Then he took her up again, carried her to a place shaded from the sun by the bank, and laid her down. Hobart followed him out, limping. "What about Schoonover?" he asked.

"Toss a hatful of water into his face. He'll come out of it."

Hobart limped back toward the coach to look for his hat. Cole tore a strip of lace from Norah's exposed petticoat and went to soak it in the narrow stream. Returning, he stared down at her for a moment. Her dress, revealingly low-cut, had fallen away from her shapely ankles. Her hair, not quite

22

black, was in complete disarray.

Sprawled out this way, her face smudged and dirty, there was an earthiness about this woman that Cole would not have believed possible. Her dress molded each curve of her body faithfully, showed its sensual, virginal beauty. He felt again a strong attraction. He said aloud: "There's nothing much wrong with you that the flat of Mike's hand once in a while wouldn't cure."

He knelt and realized suddenly that a thin film of sweat had dampened his brow. He bathed the dirt carefully from Norah's face. Norah stirred but did not wake. Suddenly, conscious of Hobart's glance, Cole stood up. His voice carried an unwonted hoarseness. "She'll come out of it in a minute," he said, "and then she can tell us for herself where she's hurt. Hanged if I want to poke around, looking for broken bones."

Schoonover sat on the sand beside the coach, looking like a five-year-old who was about to cry. Hobart asked worriedly: "How the devil we going to get to Denver City now?"

"The next station can't be over fifteen miles." Cole rummaged about in the sand until he found his gun. He removed the barrel and poked a scrap of his shirt through it. Reassembling the gun, he walked to the place, fifty feet away, where two of the horses lay, legs broken, in a welter of tangled harness. He placed a shot in the head of each and then came back, reloading the Colt from the powder flask he carried at his belt. "I'll go see if I can catch one of the others in a minute," he told Hobart. "You and Schoonover stay here with her. The Indians aren't hostile, but all this plunder, scattered out on the ground, would be one devil of a temptation."

The shots had brought Norah Forrest back to consciousness. Now she sat up, her eyes dazed and uncomprehending. A quick stab of worry turned Cole's voice unnecessarily rough. "Can you stand up?"

She nodded.

"Do it then. I've got to know if you're hurt before I leave."

For an instant she stared at him. Then stubborn and willful anger stirred in her dark eyes. "Just who do you think you are, anyway? I'm perfectly comfortable right here, and I have no intention of getting up!"

Cole went to her and stood for a moment, looking down. "Last chance," he grinned.

She did not reply. Haughty arrogance grew on her face. Cole reached down and caught her under her arms, bringing her to her feet. The arrogance left her, and her lower lip turned soft and trembling. Cole thought frantically: *Hell, she's going to start crying!* He asked contritely: "You're hurt, aren't you?" He was still holding her.

Wetness grew in the woman's eyes, but she fought this back, glaring. "I am not! I'm perfectly all right!"

Cole said, half smiling: "I think I ought to feel your legs for broken bones."

Norah yanked her hand loose and brought it sharply against his face. Cole laughed, tightening his hold on her. She demanded: "You let me go! Do you hear?" Her small hands beat futilely against his chest.

Cole asked: "Would you like to walk around and show me that your legs aren't broken?"

She nodded, glaring, her lips set in a firm, straight line. Cole released her, his eyes twinkling. Defiantly she flounced around a ten-foot circle. "There! Now are you satisfied?"

"Not entirely, but it's a good start."

Hobart, poking about in the rubble of baggage, suddenly exclaimed: "God! Look at this!"

Cole left the angry woman and went behind the coach. Half buried in baggage and freight lay the driver's body. His head was twisted at an odd angle, and the life was gone from him. A strong odor of whiskey rose from him. Hobart grinned. "Drunk."

Cole said: "He was as sober as you are. That smell is from his bottle. It broke in the fall." He shrugged impatiently. "It's getting late." He strode to the high bank and along it until he came to a place where he could climb out. A quarter mile away he could see the four remaining stage horses, quietly grazing, harness still hanging from them. Along the road toward Denver, though, not more than a hundred yards away, stood a gray horse, saddled and bridled, reins dragging.

Quick surprise touched Cole. He moved in that direction, speaking soothingly to the horse as he approached. When he was but fifty feet away, he fell abruptly silent, for now he could see the man that had ridden this horse.

Recognition stirred in Cole. He broke into a run, and the horse trotted nervously away, head turned so that his feet did not step on the trailing reins.

The man on the ground was short, stockily built, with a mane of shaggy hair, turning gray. One of his eyes had been shot away, and in its place was a horror of red and clotted blood. His other eye was open, staring and vacant. Cole croaked: "Mike, hang it, I told you I'd bring her to Denver all right. Why the devil did you have to come out to meet her?"

Moving again after the horse, he thought: *This is going to be tough on her. If she's got any of Mike in her, it'll come out now. If she hasn't . . . well, we'll see.*

Pushing the gray, Cole reached the stage station about two hours later. It was a hastily thrown up building of rough lumber, having but one large room downstairs, a part of which was curtained off, and a low-ceilinged loft where, Cole supposed, the women passengers slept. What furniture Cole could see was homemade, consisting of a long table, a bench on either side, a couple of packing boxes, and an empty whiskey keg.

Finding no one in the building, Cole came outside again and walked to the corrals where he found the station agent, currying a horse, one of six he had tied to the fence. He said: "You can turn them loose. The stage won't be coming."

"Why not?" Suspicion was in the man's tone which had a dry, nasal twang. Before Cole could answer, the man said sharply: "Who're you?"

The agent was a small man, stooped a little, and very thin. His skin was like brown wrapping paper that had been stretched too tightly over his face and hands and looked as if it might crack at any moment. His eyes, intensely blue, were narrowed and sharp.

Cole said: "Name's Estes. I was coming to Denver to work for Mike Forrest. A big Concord forced us off the bank, ten–fifteen miles back, and wrecked us. Mike got killed. So did the driver. I want a team and wagon to bring in the passengers and their baggage. You might, if you got two wagons, drive one and bring in the freight."

"Well, I'll be damned!" the agent breathed. "That blamed Oxbow went through here not an hour past. Killed Mike, you say? Hell, if I'd knowed that, I'd've blowed the driver an' guard plumb offa the seat!" The agent stuck out his hand. "My name's Castle. Davey Castle. Hardly ever see a lone rider on this road. Cain't blame a man fer bein' a mite suspicious, seein' how scarce riders is around here." He took off his battered felt hat and scratched his bald dome. Thinning hair at his temples was wet with sweat and plastered against his head by the sweatband of his hat.

Cole said patiently: "How many wagons you got?"

"One . . . rickety as the devil. An' a wobble-wheeled buckboard."

"When's the next stage?"

"Day after tomorrow."

"Could a man make it to Denver in the buckboard?"

The agent shrugged. "You'd hafta be lucky."

"We'll try it. You can send the baggage on the next stage."

Davey Castle, Cole discovered as they caught horses and hitched up, was a voluble man. He confided in lowered tones the reason he had left Maine, which was marital difficulties, and he even went into great detail to be sure Cole fully understood the difficulties and sympathized with him. "The wife was one of these big, buxom women," he finished. "Bossy as all get-out. But my gawd, onct a man got her in. . . ."

Cole interrupted: "I can imagine."

Davey laughed slyly. "You got a good imagination then, brother."

Cole climbed to the spring seat of the buckboard. He asked: "This thing belong to Mike?"

"Yeah. Why?"

"Mike must've taken some lessons in the art of lying. He told me he had some pretty good equipment."

Davey doubled up with laughter. He slapped a skinny thigh. "Mike must've exaggerated some," he admitted.

Cole touched the backs of the horses with the reins, saying: "The wagon'll be slower. We'll bring in Mike and the driver. You bring everything else, huh?"

Davey nodded, and Cole drove away.

Full dark blanketed the plains long before Cole Estes drove the buckboard into the station yard. Fatigue had long since silenced the grumbling Schoonover. Norah sat between Cole and Hobart on the spring seat, her face still and white. Behind, with Schoonover, rode the two bodies, wrapped in blankets. As the fat merchant tumbled off behind, Cole asked: "Can you cook?"

"What's the matter with her?"

Hobart grunted: "Go lay down somewhere. I'll do it."

Norah murmured: "I can do that much . . . if one of you would light the lamp for me."

Hobart said: "Sure. You come on in with me." He added over his shoulder to Cole: "I'll be out in a minute. Bring an extra shovel."

Cole drove the team to the corral, unhitched, and turned them loose. Then he rummaged in the lean-to behind the station until he found two shovels whose handles were unbroken. In this inky blackness it was difficult to find a place that might be suitable, viewed by daylight, for a burial ground. Remembering a tiny knoll to the westward, he started his first grave there. Hobart came out shortly and began one beside Cole's.

Cole was two feet down when he heard Norah's call to supper. He and Hobart ate their greasy side meat and potatoes in silence, then hurried back outside. When Davey Castle brought the lumbering, creaky wagon into the yard at midnight, Cole was just finishing, and Hobart was down to his shoulders. Cole said: "Deep enough," and climbed out, sweating.

He sent Hobart after the others. When they came, bringing lanterns and the buckboard with the two bodies in it, Cole said to Hobart: "I never went to many funerals. Do you remember what to say?"

Hobart, apparently a deeply religious man, nodded and said the burial service from memory in his deep, halting voice. Norah Forrest stood tearless and numbed beside him.

Walking back toward the stage station, with discouragement and utter tiredness in his muscles and mind, Cole thought: *You were crazy, Mike. No one could build a heap of junk like you've got into anything but what it is now . . . or worse. I'd do you no favor, or her, either, by trying. So I'll tell her to sell out and go back home, which is what she ought to do.*

With his mind made up, he slept as soon as his long body touched the hard, puncheon floor.

III

DENVER CITY

Across the trickle that was Cherry Creek, Denver City had a lusty air of brawling, uncouth growth. On every hand were the naked skeletons of buildings in the process of erection. From somewhere on Cole's left he could hear the high whine of a sawmill, and over the babble of voices, shouts, and ringing hoofs on hard-packed streets came the incessant chatter of hammers pounding nails, of handsaws, of sledge against iron stake. Perhaps a dozen buildings, being two stories high, stood out above the others. At McGaa Street a new bridge spanned the creek, and at Blake stood another, rickety and tilting in the middle.

From Wazee to the Platte, half hidden by cottonwoods, stretched hundreds of tents, wagons, and lean-to shacks. An Indian village was a sore upon the landscape north of the furthermost of these, and between the Indian village and the town were two wagon trains, drawn into rough circles.

Norah Forrest sat between Cole and Hobart on the spring seat, and the two of them wedged her in and kept her propped upright. Cole asked: "Where are your father's corrals? And where is the stage depot?"

"The stage depot is at the Quincy House. He never mentioned the corrals."

Cole halted the buckboard before a bearded miner near the McGaa Street bridge. The man stared at the buckboard, at its crooked wheels, and said before Cole had a chance to speak: "You didn't come all the way from Leavenworth in that contraption, did you, brother?"

Cole shook his head, a half grin softening the corners of his wide mouth. "Makeshift. Our stage was wrecked. Where's the Quincy House, brother?"

The man spat a stream of tobacco juice into the dust. He grunted: "Two blocks ahead, one to the right. Cain't miss it. It's just around the corner from the Elephant Corral."

Cole drove on and, at the designated corner, turned right. A huge, stable-ringed corral on his right proclaimed itself to be the Elephant Corral, and across Wazee and north a way was another, nearly as large, which was the Gigantic. At the western end of the Gigantic Cole saw a small sign with the letters, **F.O., D.C., & A** carelessly painted on it. Seeing no hotel, Cole swung right again on F Street and halted his team before a cream-colored, false-fronted building over which hung the sign **Quincy House.**

He caught Norah as she slid to the ground. He said: "What you need is about twelve hours of uninterrupted sleep. I'll go over what Mike's got in the meantime, but, if all the rest is like what I've seen so far, I want no part of it and neither do you."

He sorted her baggage out and set it on the boardwalk. Schoonover jumped down off the pile of baggage and shook himself like a fat terrier emerging from water. "I'll be at the Planter's House," he said pompously. "Have my baggage sent there."

Cole muttered dryly: "If you want a change of clothes before tomorrow, take it with you."

Schoonover started to protest, but Cole's steady glance upon him changed his mind. Grumbling, he sorted a bag from the pile and waddled up the street with it clutched in his hand.

Cole followed Norah into the hotel and set her bags down inside the door. Norah was at the desk in conversation with the clerk, a young man who lost no time in making himself agreeable. Cole backed out the door and climbed again to the buck-board seat. "Where you going to stop?" he asked Hobart.

Hobart shrugged. "Leave my stuff in the buckboard. I'll get it later."

The Gigantic Corral, while not so large as the Elephant, nevertheless covered nearly two acres. The corral was formed by open-front sheds on three sides, by two gates and an auctioneer's platform on the fourth. At each of the two corners nearest the gates stood small, enclosed buildings, one of which, Cole guessed, was a tackroom, the other an office. In the exact center of the compound thus formed stood a long water-ing trough, fed by a hand pump at one end. One of the sheds, fenced off by poles, con-tained loose, freshly cut hay.

There were buggies and buckboards, wag-ons and a welter of harness, but there were no coaches inside. Cole said: "Hell, the sign said. . . ."

Hobart pointed. "The sign's down there."

Cole stared. Parked along the western side of the Gigantic were half a dozen Troy coaches, all in a sorry state of disrepair. A corral made of poles, roughly a hundred feet across, contained perhaps twenty horses. Between corral and coaches stood a weath-ered tent and before this, on a folding stool, sat a bearded man, a short pipe between his teeth.

Cole snorted disgustedly. "If Mike wasn't dead, I'd give him a cussing! I've run across some liars in my time, but Mike tops them all!"

"There's always the mines."

Cole pulled the buckboard toward the tent. Suddenly it hitched and dropped. The horses started, but Cole held them in, cursing. The right rear wheel had come off the buckboard, putting the axle into the dirt. Cole called to the man before the tent: "Come and get it, my friend. It belongs to your broke-down stageline. Set my bags inside your tent, if you will, and I'll be obliged."

Without waiting to see if the man would comply, he jumped down and strode up the street, with Hobart hurrying to catch up.

For a block he walked in silence, fuming. Finally he asked: "Leaving for the mines right now?"

Hobart murmured in his easy drawl, "Ain't in too much of a hurry. A man ought to know where he's going before he leaves. But once he's in the water, he'd ought to swim."

"A sly dig."

" 'Twasn't meant so. Could have been

this man Forrest needed you so bad, he stretched the truth some. Strikes me that girl's going to need someone to look after her."

"You do it, then. I keep thinking how bad she needs someone to spank her, though I doubt if I could keep my mind on spanking if I ever got her turned across my knee."

Hobart ignored the jest. He paused uncertainly at the intersection, staring up Blake toward the towering and imposing shape of the Planter's House, a block away. "I got me half a notion to pitch in an' give her a hand myself."

Cole stared. Abruptly he laughed. It sounded harsh and caustic. Hobart stiffened angrily.

"If she was horse-faced and bony, would you feel the same way?"

Hobart's muscles bunched, but then he seemed to change his mind. He said: "Don't sneer at a man for the decent things he wants to do. I'm old enough to be that girl's father. I had a girl myself once that would be about her age . . . if she'd lived."

Shame touched Cole, but it did not soften him. "I'm sorry. But there's little chance for anyone, bucking a big line with an outfit like Mike's. I've seen the big lines work too often. Forget that girl and go on to the mines. She's got a mail contract to bargain with. She'll sell out and go back East where she belongs."

Hobart toed the dust aimlessly. "Maybe you're right." Together they walked in silence the rest of the distance to the Planter's House.

Night came down across this land, black velvet that began at the jagged peaks and rolled eastward. Lamps winked in windows, and tradesmen laid aside their tools. Working men plodded homeward, and the saloons began to fill. A flurry of shots could be heard in the direction of the McGaa Street bridge, followed by a ragged shout of pain.

Cole stood at his front window in the Planter's House and stared down into the street. A wagon loaded with logs lately arrived from the mountains passed, heading southeastward. Try though he would, Cole could not shake off his uneasy feeling of an obligation unfulfilled. Not more than an hour past he had called at the Quincy House with the thought in him that he would give her his refusal and be done with Mike's whipped and broken stageline once and for all. Norah, however, he was informed, was undoubtedly still sleeping, since no sound had issued from her room all afternoon. So he had left a note, brief but to the point.

Dear Miss Forrest,
Sorry, but I can't see it. Get yourself a lawyer and use your mail contract to bargain with. But sell out. It's the only way you can come out with anything at all.

Cole Estes

He saw a woman approaching along Blake, and even in the semi-darkness there was something about her movements that reminded him of Norah Forrest. He experienced an unwilling feeling of guilt and angrily shook it off. Still watching, he saw her pass through a beam of light that fell across the walk, and relief touched him. *Dance-hall girl* was his thought, for the woman's clothes were quite obviously not the sort Norah Forrest would wear.

He turned from the window. The sight of the dance-hall girl had vaguely stirred him, had made him remember the one remedy always successful in curing him of moodiness, of too much fatigue — liquor and a woman, in that order, for in this as in all frontier towns often a man needed the liquor to make him forget that the woman was hard and coarse and faded.

Moved from his thoughts by vague antici-pation, he took off his shirt and splashed vigorously in the tin basin that stood on a table against the wall. Straightening, reach-ing for the towel, he heard a small, short knock against his door.

"Come in." He walked toward the door, scrubbing his face and chest with the towel. When the knock came again, more strongly, he yanked open the door. His mouth dropped open. For a moment he stared, then humor entered his eyes and touched the corners of his somber mouth. With a towel-wrapped forefinger, he wiped soap from one of his ears.

"I saw you down in the street. I thought it looked like you, but decided it wasn't, when I saw your clothes."

A flush crept up to stain Norah Forrest's too-pale cheeks. She asked: "May I come in?"

Mockery was in Cole's gray eyes. "It's improper for a lady to enter a gentleman's bedroom even in this god-forsaken wilder-ness. People will talk."

"Oh, stop it! I want to talk to you. I got your note." She came in determinedly but kept her eyes averted from his naked chest and its mat of fine hair. Cole took his shirt from the chair back and slipped it on, deliberately watching her. He asked: "Where the devil did you get that dress?"

"I borrowed it from a girl at the Quincy House."

"A dance-hall girl?"

"I didn't ask what her profession was."

"Was it that obvious?" Cole was grinning openly.

Norah stamped a small foot angrily. "I didn't come here to discuss my dress, or a dance-hall girl, either."

"What did you come for?"

For a moment he thought she would leave. Anger sparked dangerously in her deep brown eyes. Her lips, that he remembered could be so soft and inviting, were not so now. Her firm chin was uptilted and very slightly thrust out. Arrogance was plain in her, as was the fact that she wasn't used to opposition and refusal.

With an obvious effort she controlled herself, even managed a tight little smile. "I came to thank you. You were very brave at the time of the wreck, and very considerate afterward."

Cole laughed outright at her obviously rehearsed speech. "And?"

"Oh, stop it! You're insufferable!"

"But you'd like to change my mind?" Deliberately he let his glance drop from her face to the dress, sheer and revealing and tight-fitting, to her tiny waist, flat stomach, full, rounded hips. In spite of himself he felt his pulses quickening, felt a lessening of his amusement.

"Yes, I would. If you are afraid you would not be paid. . . ."

Cole interrupted. "No, I've worked at staging all my life, and I know what can be done and what can't. If you are careful, you can come out of it with several thousand dollars. Then you can go back East."

Norah's small chin set stubbornly. Anger again stirred in her eyes. "I'll do no such thing. D'you hear? I'll not go back beaten. If you were not so. . . ." She paused, making a strong and determined effort to suppress her frustration.

"Cowardly?" Cole supplied, grinning.

"It was the word I had in mind. But, perhaps, I was wrong. Perhaps, you are thinking in terms of money and are waiting for me to make you a better offer than Father did."

"It might be interesting, but it wouldn't make me change my mind."

"Would a half interest in the line . . . provided you win . . . interest you?"

Cole shook his head.

Pure desperation shone for a moment in Norah's eyes, and this was puzzling to Cole. She took a step closer to him, managed a smile, and almost managed a provocative look. She asked softly: "Would I interest you?"

"Not if it comes as hard as all that." With complete suddenness the humor went out of Cole entirely. His hands reached out, caught her by the waist, and drew her roughly against him. His head bent, and his lips caught and held her own parted lips. For an instant she held herself rigid. Then, quite obviously remembering that this had been her own suggestion, she softened, but it was only the softness of acquiescence. Still Cole crushed her against him, his lips bruising and hungry.

All at once Norah's body arched upward against his. Her arms crept around him, and her fingers bit into his neck, the strength of her awakening demand in them. Breathing harshly, Cole pushed her away, his eyes still hot.

Norah searched his face, her expression wondering, and then she murmured, "You will help me, then?"

Cole laughed mirthlessly. "No. The sort of thing you're trying to offer can be bought anywhere in Denver City for much less."

Norah stared at him as though he had struck her. Then, as the blood drained out of her face, her eyes took on a look of untrammelled rage. Surprising him utterly, she sprang at him, and her fists beat against his face. "You . . . ! You . . . !" she screamed, apparently unable to find an epithet strong enough. "I might have known there wasn't a speck of decency in you."

Cole caught and held her arms in a rigid, inflexible grasp. Her helplessness seemed to infuriate her further. "You've used the wrong word," he told her. "What you have suggested does not require decency." The humor of this struck him now. He grinned down at her openly. "I have surprised myself tonight, but you did it so very badly. Now, go on back to the Quincy House and dress yourself like a lady. The first thing you ought to learn is to put the right label on your merchandise."

He had thought she was quite as angry as a woman could get, but now her eyes positively flashed. Reaching the peak of temper, there was possibly nothing left for her but tears. They began in a mistiness over her eyes that deepened until tears welled from their corners.

Suddenly she whirled and fled from the room, slamming the door viciously behind her. Conscious that it was growing late, that this young woman, dressed as she was, might be accosted in the street, Cole reached for his hat. But then he stopped and whirled the hat onto the bed, muttering, "Heaven help the man that bothers her between here and the Quincy House. He'll think he's tied into a bobcat."

IV

TONIGHT I'LL HAVE ALL THREE

Twice during Norah's block-and-a-half walk
to the Quincy House a man did approach
her, but both times, as Cole predicted, the
uncontrolled anger in her stopped them uncertainly before they had more than opened
their mouths to speak.

Norah could not remember ever having
been so angry. "Oh, I hate that man. I hate
him," she repeated to herself over and over
again.

But only partly was her anger directed at
Cole Estes. Partly it was directed at herself,
for she could not forget the way she had
responded to his rough and insistent kiss,
the way he had pushed her away as soon as
he had aroused her. She could forget neither
her own words — "Will you help me?" —
nor the tender, triumphant way she had
spoken them.

Her own honesty was beginning to assert
itself by the time she reached her room. She
paused before the mirror, gazing with grow-

ing distaste at the dress she wore, at her white, full breasts that were more than half exposed. She grew hot at the memory of his words, "Put the right label on your merchandise," and "What you're offering can be bought anywhere in Denver City for less."

He was no gentleman. He was at least not at all like the gentlemen she had encountered at school in the East, whom she easily controlled with an arched eyebrow, a mock frown. Though she did not know it, this experience, or lack of it, explained the youthful arrogance in her that was so irritating to Cole. Raised for the past ten years in an atmosphere where manners were emphasized more than courtesy, where the package was more important than the contents, she was only what they had made of her.

As she slipped out of the dress, she could not shake off the tarnished feeling that came over her. She flung the dress in a heap on the bed. "Damn him! Oh, damn him, anyway!"

"What's the matter, honey? Didn't the dress do the business?" A woman had come into the room, not bothering to knock, and Norah turned with startled surprise.

"Do you know what he said?" Norah asked indignantly.

"What did he say?"

"He said, 'Go back to the hotel and dress like a lady. The first thing you ought to learn is to put the right label on your merchandise.' "

For an instant Norah's visitor stared. Then a smile began at the corners of her mouth, in her weary blue eyes. Suddenly she began to laugh. Tears coursed down her smooth and beautifully translucent cheeks. She gasped: "I'm sorry," and collapsed into a chair, still laughing. "He sounds like quite a man, honey. What's he look like?"

Now, again, anger stirred in Norah, and her face took on an outraged imperiousness. The woman who sat laughing in such an unlady-like position in the big chair was taller than Norah by a full two inches. Instead of Norah's lithe youthfulness, her body had the fullness, the roundness of a woman's body. Her dress was a prototype in shimmering green of the dress Norah had flung on the bed, its purpose being to reveal rather than to conceal the full promise of her body. Her hair, cascading to her shoulders, was a rich, copper red that caught the glow of lamplight and flung back almost metallic glints. "What's he look like?" she repeated.

"Oh, he's tall. He's . . . so darn superior."

The woman, Sally Ambrook, murmured, "A good description. I could pick him out of any crowd after that. All men act superior, honey."

"Well, you'll probably see him, fighting, carousing around the place where you. . . ." Norah flushed, then said contritely: "Oh, I'm sorry. I didn't mean. . . ." Sudden awareness came to her of what Sally Ambrook was — a dance-hall girl — a *tarnished lady*.

Sally straightened in her chair and got up. "Nothing to be sorry about, honey. It isn't too bad a life, except your feet get awfully tired."

"Your feet?" Norah's face showed her puzzlement. "I thought. . . ."

"We dance with the customers, honey. That's all." Deep amusement lurked in Sally's eyes, but there was pity there, too, and regret for Norah's sudden and terrible embarrassment. "No wonder he finds it so easy to torment you, you poor kid. Now quit thinking and get to bed. You've had a tough time of it with your father and all. I've got to get to work or get fired."

Norah nodded dumbly, and watched as Sally moved gracefully to the door. When it closed behind her, Norah flung herself face downward on the bed, sobbing. A terrible feeling of loneliness oppressed her, like a leaden weight upon her spirits. This afternoon she had discovered, by a visit to Clark Gruber and Company, her father's bank, the true distress of the stageline's position. Riddled with debt, owning only worn-out equipment, the line had a mere three hundred dollars in the bank, less than enough for one week's operation. Aware fully that her father had sent her money for years at the cost of stripping his business, an awakened sense of loyalty to Mike had sent her to seek out Cole Estes, prepared to offer herself, if need be. Now, even this chance was gone before his coarse refusal.

She got up and blew out the lamp, removing the rest of her clothes in darkness. Then she flung herself upon the bed, sobbing into the pillow, and so fell asleep. But all through the night she was tortured by the recurring crash of the coach as it tumbled into the dry river bed, by the dreadful sight of her father, whom she had seen not at all for three years, a crumpled and lifeless figure in the dust.

Another figure was also in her dreams, Cole Estes, finding all her weaknesses with uncanny precision, and mocking her for them. Strangely, though, through all this his eyes were full of gentleness.

Denver's finest, the Gold Coin Saloon, was easily distinguishable by its sign, a four-foot reproduction of one of Clark Gruber and Company's privately minted twenty-dollar gold coins, that bore the legend across the top, **Pike's Peak Gold**, and a picture of a rather improbable mountain in the center beneath which were the words **Denver** and **Twenty Dollars**.

The building itself was a towering two-and-a-half story affair, festooned with scroll-work along its eaves and balcony. The tinkle of a piano, freighted from the East at pro-digious cost and effort, came through its open doors, rising tinnily above the well-bred murmur of talk and merrymaking.

Cole moved leisurely across the thick-piled carpet and found himself a place at the long, elaborately carved bar between two groups of earnestly conversing men. The talk centered on the gold fields of the Vasquez where, the previous year, Gregory had made his fantastic discovery.

"But what good are these gold fields doing either their discoverers or Denver City?" asked one of the men. "The miners are afraid to work more than enough to pay their bare expenses for fear of robbery. There is never a day passes on the Vasquez, or on the road between here and there, but what one or more men are waylaid and murdered for their gold."

The man beside Cole, a short-bearded, calm, and thoughtful man, replied without heat. "It is eventually going to become our responsibility to see that they have law and protection . . . if not law as we have known it in the East, then a committee of citizens who will track down these criminals and punish them. Surely you agree with that, General Larimer?"

"Then perhaps you will suggest such a possibility in your paper, Mister Byers. I have talked that idea for months up and down the streets of Denver. Everyone agrees that it is necessary, but nobody does anything about it."

Cole brought the flat of his hand down on the bar with a resounding whack. Byers, next to him, started. A bartender, white-aproned and bearded, came toward him. Cole said: "I'm here to drink and not to talk. But I would make a bet that, if I had a claim on the Vasquez, I would work it and heaven help the man who tried to rob me."

Byers said quickly: "You sleep like the dead after a day at a sluice box. And in the dark no man is a match for half a dozen."

Cole shrugged, but he was unconvinced. He poured a drink from the bottle that now sat before him and downed it at a gulp. Anticipation was a fever in him. The odd feeling of tension, that he had felt so often before, was in his head and in the lightness of his muscles. There were things that could ease this tension. Liquor was one. A fight was another. A woman was a third. Cole thought: *Tonight I'll have all three.*

A fiddler joined the piano player, and the two struck up a lively tune. Now the girls came down the stairs, hips swaying, eyes smiling. A murmur of appreciation rose from the crowd. Cole turned his head to watch the girls and felt a touch of surprise, for not one of them was over twenty-five, and, while their eyes were too worldly, none was coarse and none faded. Their white skin gleamed softly in the light from a dozen glittering crystal chandeliers. Quick excitement touched Cole. He poured another drink and tossed it down. The liquor was warm in his stomach, and he felt a loosening of his muscles, coupled with a strong sense of well-being.

A man in the group with Byers and Larimer chortled: "Man, will you look at that redhead!"

Cole looked. This one was tall for a

woman, and her hair was a copper red that appeared almost metallic in the soft light. Her eyes were a clear, smiling blue, and her skin was beautifully smooth and almost transparent. She was dressed in clinging, shimmering green that showed the mature roundness of her body. Cole asked: "What's that one's name?"

Byers shrugged. "They are all alike to a man of my age."

Another man in the party snorted. "A man never gets too old for a pretty woman. Her name is Sally Ambrook. But don't get any ideas, my friend, because she dances with the customers, and that's all."

"Then she'll dance with me," Cole murmured, and left the bar. He moved through the crowd and intercepted Sally Ambrook as she came off the bottom step of the stairs. His eyes were friendly, but they also contained boldness and a challenge. "Will you dance this first dance with me?" he asked. "After that, we will see, but I think you'll be dancing several with me tonight."

Her glance ran over him, and her eyes quickened with involuntary interest. Wordless, she laid a soft hand on his arm and moved onto the polished dance floor with him.

Afterward, they found a table, and Cole

ordered drinks from a white-jacketed waiter. Sally said: "So you are another of those who have come across the country to take a fortune in gold from the Vasquez?"

Cole shook his head. "I will take a fortune from somewhere, but it will not be from the bed of some stream."

Sally's glance was frankly interested. She asked: "How, then?"

Cole shrugged. "I haven't decided yet. Something will occur to me."

"There are too many men already in Denver and on the Vasquez waiting for something to occur to them. Usually what occurs to them is robbery and murder." Her disappointment in him was plain and put him immediately on the defensive.

"I'm not one of those. What is mine is mine, and what belongs to another man is his. Robbery and murder are the tools of cowards."

The waiter brought their drinks, and Cole laid a gold piece on the waiter's tray. As the man made change, Sally observed: "Already I have changed my mind twice about you. I hope I sha'n't have to change it again, because now I find myself liking you."

The waiter moved away, and Sally picked up her drink, set it aside, and then picked up Cole's. "You don't mind? The drinks they serve me are only tea. Tonight I feel the need of something stronger."

She was watching Cole with an odd intentness, as though she were looking for something in him and could not quite decide whether she had seen it or not.

Cole saw her eyes widen, saw her mouth half open to speak. He became aware that her glance had left him and was now fixed on something behind him. The chill of warning traveled down Cole's spine, and he came smoothly out of his chair, moving to one side swiftly as he did so.

Even as he turned, he brought the chair around in front of him. All of this was instinctive in Cole, a defensive action. Now he raised the chair to waist level, a bit startled and moved by half recognition of the man who came at him in such a clumsy rush. The chair leg poked this man in his middle, but he only slapped it aside with a long-reaching arm.

All at once Cole understood. This was the bearded and red-faced guard who had sat atop the Concord Oxbow and across whose back Cole had laid his whip. Cole said, his mouth drawn into a tight grin which had no mirth in it: "I'm glad you found me, my stage-wrecking friend, because I think I owe you something."

Behind the Concord's guard stood a half circle of his cronies, grinning their anticipation, and now one of these said: "Break his arm, Jake. Mess up his face some so Sally won't even want to look at him."

Jake made no effort to hit Cole. He swayed on the balls of his feet, arms hanging at his sides. He was an enormous man, whose chest and belly were one and made him appear top-heavy. His lips showed pink through the inky blackness of his beard. Abruptly and with confusing suddenness Cole moved, striking out with a long-reaching left. Jake's head snapped back, and he took a step backward to retain his balance, but the force of the blow seemed not to affect him at all.

Cole followed with a right, his weight coming forward and all the force of his shoulder behind his fist. Jake's nose flattened and spurted bright blood. But the man only shook his head and swiped at his nose with a sleeve.

This blow threw Cole in close, and he felt the huge paws of his adversary close behind him in the small of his back. He heard a voice: "You got him now, Jake! Break his damned back!"

Cole heard Sally's stifled scream and became aware of the deathly silence that had fallen over the room. Jake's arms, as thick as an ordinary man's legs, tightened inexorably, and Cole felt himself being forced backward. Jake's face was close to his own, the man's breath reeking of whiskey sourness and hot in his nostrils. Jake's lips were grinning, but it was only the grimace of physical exertion and had no humor in it.

Panic touched Cole. He had seen men like Jake work before, and had seen the broken things that were left when the inhuman power of their muscles had done its work. This panic gave him a strength he did not think he possessed, and for an instant he strained with all that was in him against the gradual and inexorable bending of his back. Throwing one last jerk into this effort, he felt himself come straight, his knees break their contact with Jake's. Explosively he brought a leg upward, smashing into the big man's groin, and he felt the fleeting looseness of Jake's grip, even as the grunt of pain broke from the man's lips.

Cole mustered all that was left of his strength and arched his back, twisting at the same time, and throwing his arms between himself and Jake to add further leverage. He felt himself break away and stumbled backward, falling. He rolled, even as he fell, and came smoothly to his knees, cocking his head and squinting upward. He saw Jake diving at him and drove himself upward. He felt the softness of Jake's belly, felt also the man's clutching hands. Cole grunted: "Oh, no! Not again. You won't get your damned hands on me again." He came to his feet, his fists lashing out, driving Jake away from him by their very force and regularity.

He panted: "Every man to his own style of fighting. Now, I'm going to cut you in pieces. I'll wear you down if I can't do anything else."

Again Jake stood, apparently completely relaxed, and his arms were loose and swinging slightly at his sides. Cole leaped in and snapped his head back with a left, following again with his viciously uppercutting right. Jake only stepped back and shook his head. Cole moved in again, darting back after each blow. He thought: *It's like hitting a stone wall. I'll break my hands on him, and I still won't put him down.*

So he put his attention on Jake's eyes, beating at the brows until the blood ran into Jake's eyes, blinding him. Helplessly Jake swiped at his eyes with his sleeve. A voice yelled: "Get your hands on him, Jake! You don't have to see him to break him up!"

Cole was circling, and Jake was stupidly trying to follow his sure-footed and lightning maneuvers. A man said hoarsely: "Quit runnin' from him, you slug! *Fight!*"

This voice came from behind him, and at the same instant he heard Sally's scream, felt the force of two hands on his back, shoving him violently toward Jake. Caught off balance by this unexpected push, he staggered forward, fighting desperately for balance. At the last instant he threw himself aside, but it was too late. He fell against Jake, heard the man's gloating grunt of triumph and felt the awful strength of the enormous hands upon his arm.

Excruciating pain laced along the arm as it bent under the tremendous pressure. Cole felt it crack, and blindness rose before his eyes in nauseous waves. His head was bursting with the pound of blood, of effort. But through his half consciousness he heard a voice: "Drop him, Jake! Damn you, if you want to brawl, do it over at the Criterion! I'll have none of it here."

He was conscious of Jake's release of his arm, of falling. Then, as he fell, Jake's heavy boot swung out viciously, connecting with the side of his head, blotting out entirely all feeling, all consciousness of the indignant murmur of voices that filled the huge room.

V

MEN WILL BE KILLED

As the fight started, Sally Ambrook had half risen from her chair, filled with consternation and with fear for the newcomer. Jake Rupp, in the short time since he had arrived in Denver City, had made a reputation for brutality, and this reputation was built upon the broken bones of lesser men. Realizing then, though, that there was little a woman could do in a thing like this, she sat back again, but tenseness filled her, and she watched with widened eyes and with increasing horror.

The more respectable element in the place moved away from the fight, with no eagerness in them to watch these two beat each other into insensibility, but there was another element that moved in, making a circle about the combatants, eventually shutting off Sally's view. She stood up and became aware of a tall man, elegantly dressed, who now stood before her. This was John Marple, owner of the Gold Coin. He was perhaps forty-five, his sideburns streaked with gray. He wore a short, carefully trimmed beard and a small mustache.

His voice carried no warmth at all as he spoke: "This fight over you, Sally?"

She shook her head. "Jake started it. There was something said about a wrecked stagecoach."

Marple's eyes, never warm, were now exceedingly cold. He muttered: "Damn him! I've warned him." He shouldered his way through the ring of spectators. Sally, following, felt a touch of sickness. Rupp had succeeded in closing with Cole and had the man's arm in the grip of his two big hands. Sally saw the agony on Cole's straining face. She touched Marple's arm. "Stop it! Please stop it!"

"You like this stranger?"

Sally nodded. "Hurry!"

Marple stepped closer to Jake. His hand, flat, came against Jake's bearded face, and his voice, sharp and commanding, snapped the words that Cole had heard.

Jake turned eyes that were somehow clouded and blank toward Marple. Marple repeated sharply: *Drop him!*

Jake released Cole's arm, and Cole slumped to the floor. The kick Rupp gave him was a last spiteful gesture of defiance toward Marple. Marple promised: "Some day I'll put a bullet into that stupid head of yours."

Sally looked at Jake Rupp, and an involuntary shudder ran through her. His eyes were nearly closed from the pounding of Cole's fists. His nose was splattered against his face and flattened. The whole front of his beard and shirt was speckled with blood and froth.

Marple's voice, still sharp, said: "Get out of here and don't come back!"

Jake snarled: "I'll kill him!"

"Not in here, you won't, because you won't be in here any more."

For a moment the eyes of the two men locked. Slowly the passion went out of Jake's heavy-featured face. His eyes dropped. "All right," he growled. Marple turned away, facing Sally. His eyes lost some of their hardness, though there was no tangible relaxing of his expression. "Now what?"

Sally heard the music start and felt the thinning of the crowd about her. Again the low rumble of conversation filled the room. Oblivious of her surroundings, Sally said: "He should have a doctor. His arm may be broken."

Resignation showed in Marple's face. He shrugged. "It is one after another, isn't it,

Sally? Each one is different, and you think you see what you are looking for in all of them . . . for a time. But it always turns out badly for you. They're weak, or they're cruel, or they're just plain bad. Is there never anything in me for you to want?"

"I can't help myself, John."

"All right. Go get the doctor. I'll have him sent upstairs."

Sally's voice was small and a little ashamed. "I'm sorry, John."

He gave her a twisted grin. "When will you learn that all men are alike? There is good in us all and bad as well. If you find gentleness in a man, you will find weakness with it. If you are looking for strength, you will find cruelty, too. What is it you want, Sally?"

Exasperation touched her because he had found the core of her own uncertainty. She countered with a question of her own: "What do you want, John?"

"You. Just as you are with no changes at all."

"But why me? What is it that you see in me that you cannot see in another woman?"

He shrugged. "I have all the answers except that one, and I won't give you empty flattery because that isn't what you want. I don't know, Sally. What a man sees in the woman he wants is too intangible to explain satisfactorily."

Sally turned, started for the door, but from the corner of her eye she saw a man bending over Cole, gently feeling his arm from which the sleeve had been cut away. She paused, recognizing the man, and went to stand beside him. "Is it broken, Doc?"

He grunted without looking up. "Just got here. Can't tell you yet."

A couple of Marple's waiters hovered a yard away, waiting. Sally asked: "Would it be easier to examine him upstairs?"

"Of course, it would," the doctor said testily.

Sally nodded to the waiters, and they stooped, lifting Cole easily. Sally walked beside them, steadying Cole's arm, watching his face all this time. John Marple's words were alive in her memory, and some of the weariness returned to her eyes. She told herself: *You have lived too much and have seen too much. What John says is true. The man you're looking for doesn't exist. You're clinging foolishly to a young girl's dream.* But her eyes, steady and soft on Cole's relaxed face, would not acknowledge her mind's reasoning. After they had laid him down on the silken-covered bed, she continued to watch him while the doctor probed at the arm, and at last she whispered, half trying to convince herself, "It will be different this time. It will be different because he's different."

Cole jerked and sat up. His injured arm came about with a brushing sweep that caught Dr. Fox in his chest and knocked him sprawling on the floor. Fox got up and said irritably: "The fight is over, so you can lay back, and let me finish examining you."

Cole looked at him blankly for a moment, then at Sally, then at the luxuriously furnished room. He made the slightest of grins. "If you weren't here, Doc, I'd think this was heaven. But the angels don't look as grumpy and sour as you do. Is it broken?"

"No. But the muscles are torn, and the elbow's dislocated. I'll put it back in, but you'll do no more fighting for a week and probably longer."

Cole murmured, "All right."

The doctor took hold of his hand and wrist. "It'll hurt. Lay back and brace your feet against the foot of the bed."

Cole groaned. "It hurts now."

"It feels good compared to what it's going to feel like." The doctor put a steady pressure against Cole's wrist. "It's time they ran Jake Rupp out of town. There's hardly a night I don't have to set a bone he's broken."

Anger set Cole's jaw rigidly. "I'll run him out of town, Doc. I'll do that much for you."

Fox snorted and laid back against the pull of Cole's arm. A long sigh escaped Cole's lips, and the muscles of his face strained and twisted.

Sally snatched his free hand in both of hers and buried her face against them. She heard Dr. Fox's brusque: "There. Give it a chance to heal before you go looking for Rupp again, will you?"

Cole's voice was unnatural. "All right."

Sally heard the door close, but she did not raise her head.

Cole said: "This hasn't been the evening I planned for us."

Sally brought up her glance, and there was a mistiness across her vision. She took her hands from his and rose. Cole swung his feet over the side of the bed and sat up. Sally came back with a woolen shawl and made a sling for his arm. Stooping to tie it, her flaming, fragrant hair brushed across Cole's face. She stepped back. "Now."

Cole stood up unsteadily, and this movement put him close to her, his face inches from hers. Sally felt a trembling expectancy, an almost girlish excitement. Her eyes showed some of this youthfulness, this wonder, this pleading, as she looked into his.

Cole's good arm went around her and drew her against him. Sally gasped: "Your arm . . . ?" She did not draw away. His head came down, and his lips found hers, which were soft and warmly eager. Molten fire ran in Sally's veins, and she rose on tiptoes, pressing herself against him. Again conscious of his injury, she drew back and whispered, "Your arm. I don't want you to hurt your arm."

"The devil with my arm!" Cole's voice was hoarse.

Sally smiled. Her soft hands went up and cupped his hard jaw. "Be careful when you leave," she pleaded. "I don't want you hurt again." She could see the cooling of his eyes, and her heart cried out: *I want you to stay! Oh, I want you to stay, but can't you see? You mustn't think I'm like the others, or you won't come back.* She inquired: "I'll see you again?"

He smiled at her, and the smile took from his face all of its somber moodiness, making it pleasant and warm. "You will. Of course, you will. And . . . thank you." He looked at her for a moment more, then turned, and opened the door. Sally watched his broad back from the doorway until he had turned around a bend in the stairway and disappeared from her view.

Now a deep depression settled over her. She thought: *He's not like the others, and he won't come back.* Some inner knowledge told her — *You can't hold a man by holding yourself away from him* — but she argued this fiercely and said softly aloud, "If I were easy for him, he would wonder if I were not easy for every other man as well."

Never yet had Sally given herself to any man, but tonight she would have given herself eagerly to Cole Estes. The thought kept running through her head: *He must be the one, because never before have I felt this way.* Deeply disturbed, she brushed her hair before going down the heavily carpeted stairs again.

Without pausing, Cole went through the crowded Gold Coin and into the crispness of this August evening. The shawl in which Sally had slung his arm exuded a faint fragrance that stirred his senses and brought her likeness vividly before his mind. With his free hand — his right — he fished in his pocket for tobacco, but, realizing that he could not use it one-handed, he tossed it disgustedly into the street. Anger began to stir in him, anger that increased as he

thought of the fight. He stopped at a tobacco shop and bought half a dozen cigars,
lighting one awkwardly in the doorway of
the shop.

Then he continued northeastward along
Blake. Reaching the corner of F and Blake,
he paused, puffing moodily on the cigar and
staring downstreet at the cream front of the
Quincy House. A tall, clumsily moving figure approached him from that direction and
presently Cole recognized the man as Hobart. He was hurrying, but, when he saw
Cole, he halted abruptly. "I've been looking
for you!" he panted.

"Why?"

"It's Norah Forrest. Some lawyer's down
there, trying to talk her into selling the
stageline. I thought. . . ."

"You thought I'd talk her out of it. Well,
I won't."

"You were a friend of her father's. You
ought to go down there . . . at least help
her to get the best kind of deal she can."

Cole shrugged. "All right. I'll do that
much. No use in letting them steal it from
her."

He walked in the direction of the Quincy
House, forced to hurry to keep up with
Hobart. Hobart told him jerkily: "I took on
a job, working for her, but I doubt if I'll do

her much good. I'm a farmer."

Cole felt a touch of obscure anger. "You'll do her no good at all. Why couldn't you keep your blamed . . . ?" He closed his mouth and lifted his shoulders resignedly. *Babes in the woods,* he thought. *They'll be broke in a month if they try to stay in this business.*

There was a small office in the lobby of the Quincy House, situated between the desk and the outer wall. The door stood ajar, and it was toward this door that Hobart led him. As they entered, a man rose, graying, slim, a short man, whose smile contained the professional unctuousness of an undertaker. He smiled and nearly managed to cover the fact that he was irritated. "Ah, Mister Hobart," he said, and, looking at Cole, "I expect you are Mister Estes. Miss Forrest spoke of you as having been a friend of her father's."

Cole took the lawyer's hand. Norah stared at Cole's injured arm, plainly thinking: *So you have been brawling?* She explained: "Mister Thurston is representing the Illinois Central and Kansas Territory and wants to buy out father's stageline."

Thurston raised a hand, palm outward. "Pardon me, Miss Forrest. Not the stageline. Only the mail contract . . . and the franchise between Denver City and Leavenworth."

Suddenly Norah rose. Her face was white. Cole could see the weariness in her, but her chin was firm and her glance steady. "No. My answer is no. You couldn't even wait until my father's body was cold before you started your grab for what had been his, could you? Do you know that the people who hired you murdered my father and tried to murder me?"

Thurston's face assumed the expression one uses with an erring child. "An accident, Miss Forrest."

Norah clenched her fists. "We'll see what the authorities have to say about that."

"There are no authorities."

"But they shot my father!"

"Did you see it happen? There are Indians on the plains, Miss Forrest. It must have been the Indians."

Cole felt a stir of pity for Norah, so overmatched in this contest. But Norah had not finished. She cried: "Get out of here! Tell them I'll go broke before I sell to them! Father sent me money for years . . . money he could not afford. He stripped his business so that I could have everything I wanted. I didn't know it, then. I know it now. Do you think I'd sell out his life's blood to the same murderers who killed him?" Her voice rose in pitch.

Pure admiration sent a tingle down Cole's spine. He caught Thurston by a skinny elbow. "You hear all right, don't you, friend? She said git."

Thurston snatched up his bag and scurried angrily out the door. Cole breathed, "You sure know how to say no. There's little doubt in him about that."

He turned his glance to her, but the magnificence that had been in her a moment ago was gone. She sank back into her chair, and there was hopelessness in the sag of her shoulders. She put her head down into her hands. "What am I going to do?"

Hobart made a step toward her, but Cole said: "Wait a minute." He was thinking of the words in Mike's letter — "a chance to start a line to the Vasquez" — and he was thinking, too, of the conversation he had overheard in the Gold Coin earlier that evening. Up to now he had seen no hope for Mike's stageline, but coupling the two things in his mind had started a whole new train of thought. He continued: "Miss Forrest, if I were to take on the job of trying to pull this stageline out of the hole it's in, would you back me up, or would you buck me all the time?"

She looked up. Tears blurred her eyes, but she wasn't crying. There was sudden hope in her eyes that made Cole feel ashamed. She stated: "You could do it your way."

"All right. I'll see if you mean that. To-morrow I'm going to the I.C. and K.T. and tell them you've changed your mind. What did they offer you?"

Norah hesitated, seemed about to protest, but then said: "Three thousand."

"I'd hold out for five." He watched her closely for a moment. Surprise touched his tone as he asked: "You're not going to give me an argument about this?"

Wordlessly she shook her head. Again admiration stirred in Cole. "Then I'll tell you what I've got in mind. At present there's no stage running between here and the Vasquez. The miners are afraid to work their claims more than enough to pay their bare expenses for fear of robbery and because there is no way for them to send their gold to Denver. Your present run between here and Leavenworth is going to have to be given up anyway, because you can't hold it without thousands to throw into its defense. They'll drive you clean out in a month if they put their minds to it."

"Then why do they offer to buy at all?"

"Because, if they force you out, there might be a stink. You could go to the Kansas Legislature, who granted the franchise, and you could go to the Post Office Department, who gave you the mail contract. They figure that three thousand is a pretty small amount to get you out without a squawk, and it is. If the franchise and contract aren't worth ten thousand, they aren't worth a dime." He waited a moment for her to speak and, when she didn't, went on: "Five thousand will give you something to work on for a while. It'll buy men to ride guard on the Vasquez run. And more than that, it will be making them pay for something you know you have to give up anyway."

Hobart interjected: "But is there enough money in a short run like that to make it pay?"

Cole grinned at him. "If you had a claim you could take a hundred dollars a day out of, but you know the chances were at least even you'd be killed for it before you could send it out, how much would you pay to get it safely to Denver? Five percent? Ten? Twenty-five?"

Hobart whistled. "Plenty."

"So will they. We'll charge them ten percent. We'll show the toughs we can be tougher than they are. And we'll be fighting the I.C. and K.T. with their own money because, when they see what we're doing with the Vasquez run, they'll sure as hell want to horn in."

Norah sat upright, her eyes sparkling. In this moment her arrogance was entirely gone. The way she looked at Cole, the way life returned to her, gave him a warm feeling of strength and confidence, but experience had taught him that no venture, particularly one in which your antagonists were strong and well organized, was easy. He cautioned: "It's dangerous. Men will be killed. But . . . it just might work."

Then Norah came across the room and put a hand on Cole's arm. She said: "I've made up my mind. I will sell and go back East. There is nothing important enough to me to have men killed for it, and I know father would have felt the same."

Cole said: "Every day, or nearly every day, some miner on the Vasquez is murdered for his gold. Nothing worthwhile is ever done by evading a fight. If the miners stop carrying gold themselves, the toughs will let them alone and concentrate on us. But there's a difference. We'll be ready and a match for them."

Hobart added his assurances to Cole's,

and at last Norah was convinced. Cole put his hand on the door. He said: "Good night" and went out. His mind was busy with the riddle that was Norah Forrest. He had seen only her shallowness at first, but now he was beginning to see other things as well, things that come out only under the pressure of adversity. He thought: *Mike would have been proud of her tonight.*

VI

THE CITIZENS' COMMITTEE

A dozen miles west of Denver City, lying between the long, ridged hogback and the hills that marched away toward the divide, stood a new building called the Mount Vernon House. Built of native, cream-colored sandstone, it served as post office, roadhouse, general store, and saloon, and lay beside the Ute Trail, where it entered the dark, winding Apex Cañon on its way to the Vasquez. Lamps winked from its windows as Fritz Woerner and Edgar Pense mounted their horses at the corral. Fritz yanked his cinch tight with unnecessary violence. "Gott damn it, Ed, I tell you it's shorter if you go south an' break through Hog Back Mountain there."

Ed Pense shrugged. "All right. You go that way. I'll go the other. I'll bet you a bottle of the best rot in Denver that I beat you in. Mind you, though, if your hoss is sweated up, the bet's off. I'll meet you at the Gold Coin."

Fritz Woerner swung into his saddle. "It's a bet." He was a short man, roundly built without being fat. The hairs of his beard were stiff and stood straight out, giving him a look of almost ludicrous fierceness. His eyes were a pale, washed-out blue. He swung away at a trot, heading south. There was no road here, just the tall grass that swished against his horse's legs. The deeply bright stars above afforded only a small amount of light, and Fritz let the deep-chested bay pick his own trail.

Disgust with this country was a thing deeply rooted in Fritz Woerner. Full of hope early this spring he had come West with the rush and had since tramped the Vasquez, Chicago Creek, and had even crossed the vast expanse of South Park. He'd found, where there was gold, all of the claims taken. Elsewhere he found no gold. Finally, broke, he went to work as a miner for day wages that hardly paid more than his expenses. But out of this, he had saved enough for the bay horse and enough for slim provisions along the tedious ride back home.

Now the land began a long, steep slope, and after another thirty minutes Fritz came to a rushing, turbulent stream where it broke through a monstrous gap in the long, seemingly endless ridge called Hog Back Mountain. Here the way was narrow between the steepness of rocky ridge and roily water. And here it was darker. Suddenly a shot blossomed in the blackness ahead, and a voice rang out, thickly accented and touched with madness. "Get back, you murderin' thieves! Followed me, did you? Well, you got it all, and there's none left!"

Fritz reined about frantically in this pitch dark. The voice faded into mumbling nothingness, and there were no more shots. Behind a jutting shoulder of yellow limestone, Fritz paused, thinking: *If I go back and take the other way, Ed'll beat me in, and it'll cost me the price of a bottle.* He squinted up at the rocky steepness of Hog Back Mountain and muttered, "A full half hour it vill take to climb over that." Experimentally he shouted: "I dunno who you are, friend, but I vant nothing you haff. I'm travelin' this way because of a bet that it's shorter than the other, and you delaying me iss going to cost me the price of a bottle."

He got no answer. An odd tingle, partly fear, partly superstition, traveled down his spine. He began to wonder if this had not been imagination. Trembling, but determinedly, he reined his horse again into the defile. Its hoofs rang loudly against the crumbling rock along the trail. Twice in a hundred yards, panic almost controlled Fritz, and both times he reined the horse to a halt but did not turn around. At last, he came out onto the plain, and it was here, in brighter starlight, that he saw the horse, a dim shape against the relative lightness of the plain.

The animal appeared to drowse, not bothering to graze, but, as he neared, Fritz could see that he was saddled, could see his reins trailing. Very tempted to spur out onto the plain, Fritz controlled himself and called cautiously: "Man, are you hurt? Do you need help?"

His voice, unnaturally loud, echoed back from the walls of the defile, from the sheer steepness of the ridge across the creek. But Fritz got no answer.

He rode to the drowsing horse, and the animal lifted its head, staring at him without interest. Close like this Fritz could see all the evidences of hard riding on the animal, from the dried sweat foam that covered him to the utter weariness that kept him rooted to this spot, uninterested even in the lush, drying grass that surrounded him.

Fritz thought, remembering the strange words: *Now, what would I do was I being chased and rode through here?* Looking back toward the defile, he saw a huge rock that had broken from the rim ages past and rolled to the bottom. He murmured, "I'd git me behind that rock."

Dismounting, he advanced cautiously. But not until he was a scant ten feet from the rock did he see the elongated, prone shape of a man behind it. He called, softly, but with the hoarseness of his fear: "Now, don't start shootin', mister. If you'd like to get to Denver City, I reckon I kin help you."

No movement stirred the man. Fritz advanced farther and, at last, could kick the rifle that lay beside the man out of his reach. Then he breathed a little easier. He knelt and turned the man over. Becoming bold, he struck a match and cupped its flickering flame above the stranger's face.

Blood ran from the three-inch gash along the man's temple and had dried and clotted in his beard. His lips were a swollen, purpled pulp, and one of his eyes was completely swelled shut.

Feeling a stickiness on his hand, Fritz examined it, found it covered with thickened blood. He struck another match, held it higher, and found the stranger's right sleeve red and thoroughly soaked. Now Fritz dropped his head and laid an ear against the man's chest. A slow, steady heartbeat brought him instantly to his feet. He said aloud: "You'll bleed to death if that ain't stopped. I'll need a fire to see by. Wonder if they're still after you, or if you got away?"

Taking his chance, he kindled a fire from dead and dry twigs he gathered. Then he cut away the unconscious man's sleeve with his knife. A bullet had smashed the bone, had torn a two-inch ragged hole when it came out. But the bullet had missed, miraculously, any arteries. Fritz tore strips from a blanket he found tied behind the man's saddle and bound them about the arm. Then he led the stranger's horse over. He hoisted the limp body into the saddle, tying his feet and uninjured arm beneath the animal's belly and the man's belt to the saddle horn.

Holding the reins of the led horse in his hand, he mounted and set out across the rolling plain toward Denver City. He should, perhaps, have been thinking of this life he had saved. Instead, he was thinking with characteristic thriftiness: *I'll tell Ed the bet is off. By gott, he can't hold me to it.* But there was no conviction in him. Ed would say, grinning wickedly: *Pay up. I got here first, didn't I?*

John Marple was irritated when they brought the bleeding, dirty miner into the

Gold Coin. But, quickly seeing that perhaps this would afford a chance to unify sentiment in Denver City behind a vigilante movement, he ordered two tables brought together and had the man laid there, while the grumbling doctor, roused from his bed, worked feverishly over him.

Standing in the forefront of the circle about the makeshift operating table, John Marple, tall and without emotion, asked: "Anybody know him?"

He looked closely at the man on the table. The stranger was tall, nearly as tall as John himself. Bearded and badly beaten, there was still a certain handsomeness to his craggy features. The throng stirred, and a voice, far behind him, said: "Let me through. Let me look at him."

John turned and saw a perspiring, clean-shaven fat man, trying to force his way through the crowd. He called again: "Let me through."

As the fat man came out of the press of bodies, Marple asked: "Know him, friend?"

The fat man approached to the doctor's shoulder and looked down. Then he turned. "You are blamed right I know him. I should know him. I played with him as a boy in the old country. His twelve-year-old son is up in my hotel room right now."

Marple asked: "Who is he?"

Apparently not hearing, the fat man asked indignantly: "What kind of a country is this, anyway? George Osten is an honest, hard-working man. He had a claim on the Vasquez that he's been putting fifteen hours a day to working. You want to know why? Because his family is still in Luxembourg. He has not seen them for five years, and George Osten is a man who loves his family. All that five years he has worked, he and the boy, trying to make enough money to send for them, the wife and the other four children. But it is no good. He does not speak English too good and can only take jobs that pay him a little bit. His wife gets sick and cannot work, and the money he sends back goes for food. Then comes the gold rush. George tells me . . . 'It is chance to make enough to send for them,' and he made enough. He had it when he started for Denver. But he does not have it now."

A low growl arose from the packed crowd. The fat man, red of face and perspiring freely, shouted: "Somebody else have it now. Somebody maybe right here in this room." He stabbed an accusing finger at random. "Maybe you. Maybe you."

The men he had singled out flushed and started forward, but John Marple put himself in their way. He said: "He's naming no names. He's trying to tell you that we ourselves don't even know the men who are robbing us."

A voice from the crowd called: "Then let's find out. Let's find out and string 'em up!"

John opened his mouth to speak but halted as he felt a light touch on his arm. The doctor, gruff and sour, whispered, "No use in me stayin' any longer. He's dead."

Marple said: "All right, Doc." He raised his voice. "Doctor Fox says the man is dead. We've been talking law for a long time now. Are we going to keep talking, or are we going to do something?"

It started as a murmur that swelled in seconds to a roar. Marple raised a hand. "I am not proposing mob rule. That is worse than no law at all. What I am proposing is that a committee of citizens be formed, citizens about whom there is no doubt whatever. When a crime is committed, they, or a posse selected by them, will ride until they catch the culprits. A trial will be held. The guilty will be executed. The innocent will go free."

"I'm for it, John," someone said.

"Me, too," said another. "Let's git busy."

The fat man made himself heard above

the uproar, climbing clumsily onto a chair. "That will not help him," he shouted indignantly. "What am I to tell his boy?"

John caught the man's arm and pulled him down. He said: "Osten will be avenged. If it is possible, his son will have his money." Again he raised his voice, and it carried the length and breadth of the room. "Drinks are on the house. While you're drinking, talk over your selections for the members of the citizens' committee. Then we'll vote. Where's the man that brought Osten in?"

He saw the short, round man with the bristling beard and pale blue eyes coming out of the throng. With the feel of his success strong within him, John Marple could still think: *It is a good thing, this law by the people. But for a while it will be overzealous, and the innocent will suffer with the guilty.* He asked: "Where did you find this man?"

"South of the Mount Vernon House vhere the creek breaks through Hog Back Mountain."

"Then we'll send out a posse in the morning with an Indian tracker. If anyone knows anything that might help, it is his duty to report it. We will let these toughs know that it will be harder from now on."

He glanced up and saw Sally Ambrook on the balcony. She was watching him in an odd way that made him feel self-conscious. He dropped his glance and moved out of the crowd and about his business. He had lighted the fire. It would burn now, without him.

VII

RIDE OUT, STRANGER!

Cole Estes walked into the offices of the
I.C. & K.T. Express at eight in the morning.
A graying, sharp-featured man with spectacles
came toward him from behind a long
counter. Cole said: "Jess Dyer still run this
outfit?"

The clerk nodded.

Cole asked: "Is he here yet?" When the
clerk again nodded, Cole said: "Tell him
Cole Estes is here."

The clerk shuffled to a door on the far
side of the room, stuck his head inside, and
mumbled something unintelligible. Then he
turned. "He says to come on in."

Cole went into the inner office and closed
the door. A man rose from behind a desk
— a man grown fat with success — and
gave him a genial smile, waving him toward
a chair with his cigar. Cole noticed today,
as he had often noticed before, that Jess
Dyer's smile was a mere habitual contortion
of his facial muscles. His eyes remained as

cold and hard as polished quartz.

Dyer boomed: "Cole, blame your eyes, what you doin' 'way out here? Haven't seen you for years . . . not since, let's see . . . 'Fifty-Six, wasn't it?"

Cole nodded. "You haven't changed, Jess. It looks like you'd let a man like Mike Forrest alone, seeing as he worked for you for nearly fifteen years."

Dyer guffawed. "Business, my boy. Business. Never let the opposition get their breath."

"Did you know your toughs murdered him?"

The smile left Dyer's face. "Don't get smart with me, boy."

Cole shrugged. After a moment he said: "I came out here to give Mike a hand, but you beat me to him. Now his daughter's here, as you know. Last night she turned down your offer for her franchise and mail contract. I talked her into accepting it."

The geniality — the surface geniality — returned to Jess Dyer. "Fine. Fine, my boy. You won't regret it."

Cole finished: "At a slightly altered figure." He let his eyes rest deliberately on Dyer's and they were cool and penetrating and contained a certain challenge.

The smile left Dyer's face. His eyes turned

shrewd. He asked: "What figure?"

"Five thousand."

Dyer appeared to consider. "And she'll leave the country?"

"She likes it here. Are you afraid she'll hang Mike's killing on you?"

"I told you once not to get smart with me, Cole. Remember it."

Cole felt his anger stirring. He said: "I've got a few thousand saved. I'm stubborn enough and mean enough to throw it into her line and take a whack at beating you."

"I'll break you."

"Sure. But it'll cost you a hell of a lot more than five thousand to do it."

Dyer shrugged and smiled reluctantly. "All right. You win. Five thousand it is." He went to the door, shouted: "Childs. Bring in those contracts . . . and five thousand in cash."

Cole said softly: "Gold."

Dyer yanked his head around and scowled. "You drive a damned hard bargain." But he shouted into the outer room: "Gold."

Cole said: "Miss Forrest is waiting in the lobby. I'll get her."

"Damned sure of yourself, weren't you?"

Cole nodded.

Dyer stared for a moment, and then he

laughed. "How'd you like to work for me again?"

"Isn't Jake Rupp tough enough for you?"

Jess Dyer snorted and for the first time seemed to notice Cole's injured arm. Looking at it, he said: "Tough enough, but not smart enough. Go get this girl, Cole, and when we've finished with her, we'll talk."

Cole brought Norah Forrest into the office with a final caution: "Take his money, sign the contracts, and let it go at that."

Jess handed over the contracts and a heavy small canvas sack of gold coin. While Norah signed the contracts, Cole counted the money. Then he leaned back in his chair. Norah was reading the contracts, and she turned to him with a puzzled air. "It says we must abandon the run between Denver City and Leavenworth, but . . . ?"

Cole said quickly: "That part's all right. They're buying the franchise."

He took the contracts from her and read them through. Satisfied, he said: "They're all right. Wait for me in the lobby and we'll go over to the bank with the money."

Norah gave him a sober glance, then signed the contracts, and went out silently. Cole closed the door behind her. "What did you want to say to me?"

"About that job . . . ?"

Cole interrupted. "Jess, now that I've got the money for Mike's girl, I'm going to tell you something. I liked Mike Forrest, and I like his girl. I have never liked you, and I don't like monopoly. You're going to pay for killing Mike. I'm going to see that you do pay for it."

The full hardness of Jess Dyer's character manifested itself. His eyes narrowed until they were mere glittering slits. He chewed his cigar for a moment and stared hard at Cole. Finally he said softly: "You've pulled a fast one, haven't you, boy? You've got me to pay for something you were going to have to abandon anyway." He blew a cloud of smoke into Cole's face. "Get out of the country, Cole. Get out while you're still alive."

Cole beat down the anger that boiled in his head. He rose. "You've played at being God for so long you think you are God. You order a man killed, and he gets killed. But you're only a man, Dyer. You can die as easily as any other man. Remember that."

He lifted the sack of gold from the desk. Before he went out, he spoke again. "This is a new country, where every man has an equal chance. There are no entrenched interests, no monopolies. There are a lot of men, like myself, who will fight to see that none get established. Keep Jake Rupp off my neck, Dyer, or you'll be looking for a new bully boy."

He closed the door behind him and stepped out through a side door into the lobby of the Planter's House. Norah Forrest rose and came toward him. The anger on his face seemed to give her reassurance. Cole asked: "Doubting?"

She dropped her eyes. "A little."

Cole said: "He offered me a job."

Arrogance flickered across Norah's face. She began: "Of course, if you. . . ."

Cole interrupted, grinning wickedly: "You going to fire me already?"

"No, but. . . ."

Again Cole interrupted: "I made my decision last night. I didn't want to start a fight that was useless, that there was no chance of winning. There is a chance of winning this one. But you'll need more faith in me than you've got now, because I'm going to do some things you won't like."

For half a block she walked beside him in silence. Finally she asked, her tone rising: "Why can't people let each other alone? Why does there always have to be fighting and killing?"

Cole shrugged, having no ready answer for this. But he said: "There will be a sort of law here before too long. Vigilante law."

"And that will mean more killing."

"It will. It may mean the deaths of men who are innocent. But there is one failing found in law, as you and I know it, that is not found in vigilante law. It does not discriminate against a man because he has no money or no influence. It does not favor the rich."

They came to the bank, and Cole followed Norah inside, introduced her, and waited while she deposited the money to the stageline's account. At the door he left her, saying: "I will have to ride to the mines and persuade the miners that we can bring their gold safely to Denver."

Norah asked: "Can we?"

"Maybe. If we can't, you will go back East broke, and I will be on the run from the vigilantes. But, if that happens, at least the miners will be no worse off than they are now."

He left her then, looking somewhat bewildered. An auction was in progress at the Elephant Corral, and Cole bought himself a horse, paying a shocking price but getting a good animal, a long-legged, deep-chested gray, whose mouth said he was five years old. Saddle and bridle for the horse cost him about a fourth of what the horse cost.

Satisfied, he crossed Cherry Creek at Blake, turning toward the mountains.

While it was not at all necessary, he rode the ferry across the Platte and paid his toll cheerfully, meanwhile making the acquaintance of the ferryman, a huge, bearded man named Rostov. With the exception of this ferry the road was free then, the ten miles to Golden City, and thence south to the mouth of Apex Cañon where the toll road began.

Cole had his dinner at the Mount Vernon House, so named because of the proprietor's inordinate admiration for George Washington. Then, paying his toll of ten cents for the distance between Mount Vernon House and Elk Park, he set out, alternately walking and trotting the gray.

The way was steep here, and Cole was thankful for the care and time he had used in selecting the horse, for the gray took Cole's crowding on this grade without undue heavy breathing or sweating. This was a land of towering yellow pine, of belly-deep grass, of sheer granite cañon. Aspen thickets made light green patches against the deeper green of the pines. The road kept rising, and at four Cole reached Elk Park, continuing westward to Cresswell, a way station, post office, and saloon.

Leaving, he again paid a toll for the shorter distance between here and the Vasquez, and at dusk dropped down the steep grade into the deep cañon of the Vasquez.

Along this stream winked tiny flares, those of the miners. Cole rode along the road in darkness, coming at last to a fire where half a dozen men hunkered, eating beans from tin plates. He dismounted and approached.

Suspicion brought these men around, facing him, forming a solid wall of hostility. They were all bearded, all ragged and dirty, and reminded Cole more of wild animals than of men. One asked roughly: "What you want?"

Cole felt at a distinct disadvantage. He said: "Name's Cole Estes. I'm starting a stageline from here to Denver City to haul gold mostly. I'm hiring guards and booking shipments."

The hostility in these men was unchanged, but one of them asked: "You guarantee delivery?"

This was the crux of the whole matter, Cole knew. He asked a question of his own by way of reply. "When you ship gold from Denver to New York, does the line guarantee delivery?"

A man growled: "Ain't interested. Ride out, stranger."

Cole turned, bitter discouragement touching him. But a new voice said: "Wait, Joe. This could be a good thing for us all."

Cole swung back and looked at the speaker in the flickering light from the fire between them. He was a tall man and very thin. Not a whit cleaner or less ragged than the others, he nevertheless showed an intelligence not apparent in the others, and his speech was that of a man of education.

Cole said: "No stageline goes further than to guarantee that due care will be used in protecting shipments. And no stageline's guarantee is better than the men behind it. I could promise a guarantee, but, if a large shipment were lost and the line liquidated, there would still not be enough to replace the loss. I'm offering you something better than what you've got . . . which is nothing at all. Not a one of you can sleep soundly. Not a one of you but what is afraid to take your gold and start for Denver. And when one of you does take the chance, he is risking not only his gold but his life as well."

The tall man said: "We'll talk about it." His voice had an air of finality. Again Cole turned. He mounted his horse, continuing downstream. He could feel the unwinking stare of the six against his back and thought: *There's nothing in this world that's worth living in a cave like an animal and fearing all other men until it becomes an obsession.*

He was almost clear of the circle of firelight when an odd feeling of uneasiness possessed him. He almost yanked his head around to look back, but then he thought: *It's only something that I've caught from them. There's so much fear in them that some of it's rubbed off on me.*

He rode another ten feet with the uneasiness increasing until it was a plain tingle in his spine. Not used to ignoring these signs, these hunches, Cole suddenly reined his horse to one side, driving the spurs deep into the animal's sides. Behind him, flame blossomed from the muzzle of a rifle, the racket of the shot reaching his ears an instant later. A smashing blow drove itself against Cole's shoulder, catapulting him from the saddle. He heard the shouting of the men that had been at the fire and then the drumming of a galloping horse's hoofs against the ground.

Not understanding, he drew his revolver, muffling the click of the hammer as he drew it back by holding it between his arm and body. His left shoulder was numb, sticky and warm with the free-flowing blood. Cole heard the voice of the tall miner: "Looks like they didn't want him freighting our gold. And it's too late for us to change our minds now."

Cole called: "Not too late. The light was bad for shooting, and he only got my shoulder."

He got to his knees, still feeling little pain from the shoulder wound, still aware of the numbness in it. He caught his horse and walked toward the approaching men. As his arm swung at his side, the pain came in waves to the shoulder, making these men blur and swim before his eyes. The tall man caught his good arm, steadying him, and led him to the fire. Cole sat down, with no strength left in him at all, and the tall man cut away his sleeve with a knife. After that, there was the searing heat of red-hot iron against his shoulder, which, mercifully, he could stand for only an instant. But through this all he had the feeling that hostility had gone from this group. He heard Joe's ragged voice, just as he lapsed into unconsciousness: "If they want him dead so bad, Vance, mebbe we should want him alive."

Cole awoke once during the night, wrapped in blankets beside the dying fire. For a long while he lay there, staring at the bright, star-studded sky and listening to the steady roar of the Vasquez as it tumbled through the cañon toward the plain below. He dozed then, and, when he awoke again, it was full daylight and nearly a score of men stood around him, looking down. Cole stumbled awkwardly to his feet.

The tall one, Vance Daugherty, said: "We've talked it over, and we'll try you out, twenty of us at five hundred dollars apiece."

Cole felt a new surge of hope. He asked: "Any of you want to hire on as guards? Pay is sixty a month and beans."

Vance Daugherty said: "I'll ride the first half dozen trips, because I'm the one who has talked for you. Now fill your belly with beans and coffee and go get your coach."

VIII

TOO LATE

At nightfall, Cole splashed across the Platte and ten minutes later dismounted at the Elephant Corral. "Feed him good," he told the hosteler. "He's earned it."

He swung around the corner and headed uptown, thinking: *First step is a bath, then a feed. If I feel like it by then, I'll have Doc Fox look at my shoulder.* There was an unaccustomed lightness in his head, and the shoulder and arm throbbed mercilessly. Cole raised it with his right hand and slipped it into the sling Sally Ambrook had fashioned from her shawl. Even yet a hint of Sally's fragrance inhabited the shawl, and Cole smiled a little, remembering her.

As he passed the Quincy House, the door swung open and a voice called: "Cole . . . Mister Estes!" Cole paused, turning. Norah Forrest came onto the walk clad in a dark blue dress with a high collar of white lace. Even in the poor light cast from the windows of the Quincy House, she saw the cutaway sleeve of his buckskin shirt, the dirt and blood on his clothes, the shadow of weariness in his face. Her hand came out and touched his arm lightly.

"You've been hurt."

"Not bad. The bushwhacker's aim wasn't very good."

Concern turned her face sober, her lips soft. Fear touched her wide eyes. "Supposing his aim had been good? Oh, Cole, it isn't worth it. It isn't worth it at all. Please, let's give it up. I have enough money. You can find something to do that will not put your life in danger."

Surprise ran through Cole, and he said: "You've changed already. It is an old saying that the frontier is tough on women and horses. But I like you better for the change it has made in you."

She laughed unsteadily.

Cole went on: "There are several reasons I'm doing this, and it surprises me to realize that money is the least of them."

"What reason could there be except money?"

"Mike, for one thing. I owe Mike something. Now that I'm started, I find I owe something to the miners on the Vasquez who have put their trust in me."

Norah's eyes dropped, and disappointment put a shadow across her face. Cole thought: *It would not have hurt to tell her she was one of the reasons for doing this . . .* and he realized suddenly that it would have been true.

Norah asked: "You were successful in persuading them that you could transport their gold safely?"

He nodded. Suddenly full awareness came to him of how entirely alone was this girl, how courageously she was facing her loneliness. On impulse he put out his right arm, circled her waist, and drew her to him. She did not resist but, instead, was passive, waiting. Cole bent his head and touched her lips lightly with his own. Drawing back, he said: "It's a rough town now with no place for a girl like you. But that'll change, and you'll be less lonely."

A smile crossed Norah's face, a smile that was older than her years. Standing on tiptoe, she kissed him fully on the lips, then turned, and fled back into the door of the Quincy House.

Cole stood for a moment, looking after her, and then, half smiling, continued toward the Planter's House.

Later, bathed, shaved and fed, a clean dressing on his shoulder, he sought out Hobart, finding him in the lobby of the

Planter's House. He sat down so they could talk. Hobart had been busy while Cole was gone. He had sent a rider eastward to Leavenworth, calling in all of the way-station keepers, with instructions to bring all movable equipment and horses. He had hired carpenters and wheelwrights to put into shape what equipment was in Denver City. He had a coach ready for Cole to take in the morning and a driver to hold the reins. Cole said with satisfaction: "You may be a farmer, but you're more than that."

Hobart flushed.

Cole rose. "For some reason tonight the thought of a bed is more welcome than the thought of a bottle. Good night."

He made his way through the crowded lobby and fifteen minutes later, with a chair propped against the door, was asleep.

Dawn found Cole atop the tall seat of a Troy coach, a shotgun held snugly against the seatback by the pressure of his body. Beside him rode the driver, Elston, red-haired, freckled, and salty, and below in the coach rode Hobart. A drunk tottered on the walk beside the McGaa Street bridge, his maudlin song halted while he stared. A swamper tossed a bucket of dirty water into the street from the door of a saloon on

Fourth, narrowly missing a man slumped against the wall. The swamper raised a salutary hand as the coach rumbled past, and Cole waved back.

The sun poked above the rim of the eastern plain, laying its copper glow against the jagged line of peaks to the west. On the naked range behind them a thin layer of new snow lay, and Cole remarked to the driver: "They'd better get busy on the Vasquez if they expect to get their gold out before the winter sets in."

"Plenty of time. There will be two full months and a part of another before frost stops 'em."

Drawn by six mules, the coach ran along the dusty road, climbing steadily, and, before mid-morning, reached the Mount Vernon House, where Cole paid their toll of a dollar and a half that would carry them as far as Cresswell, west of Elk Park.

Now the mules slowed, laboring against their traces as they pulled the weight of the coach up these steep and rocky grades. The coach swayed and strained against its bullhide thoroughbraces. So narrow was this road that a dozen times they were forced to pull far to one side to let a wagon or buckboard pass. Men, riding saddle horses and mules, were numerous, and all stared, for this was the first coach they had seen on this road. Occasionally Elston would pass a heavily laden wagon, a freighter bound for the placers on the Vasquez with beans, sugar, coffee, and miner's tools.

With his left arm useless, and giving him pain with every jolt the Troy took, Cole was forced to cling to the seat with his right hand, bracing his feet against the floor-boards, and even then there were times when he thought he would be flung clear.

They had their dinner at Cresswell, though it was well after noon when they reached the place, and following this Cole rode inside the coach where he could better brace himself and spare his arm, which was now torturing him to an extent that it blurred his vision and made his head reel. In late afternoon, brakes squealing, they rolled down the long, steep grade into the cañon of the Vasquez.

Vance Daugherty waited with a score of others beside the burnt-out ashes of last night's fire. As Cole climbed out of the coach and approached, he said: "They have changed their minds a dozen times since you were here. They are wondering why they should be the ones to get this plan started, to take all the risk, but I have finally convinced them that conditions will get no better unless someone is willing to take a chance. You and I are gambling our lives. These others have finally agreed to take a chance with their gold."

Cole thought he noted a change in this man since he had last seen him, a certain lack of straightforwardness he had not previously noted. He said: "A vigilante movement has started in Denver City because of the murder of a man named Osten who tried to carry his gold to Denver alone. Eventually his murderers will be known and punished. In the meantime it will be a good thing to let the murderers know that Osten was not the only one who was not afraid of them. Someday a man they try to kill will recognize them and live to tell of it, and that will be the chance for the vigilantes to start their cleanup."

Now each man stepped forward to place his gold in the coach's strongbox. This was not gold dust and nuggets carried in pokes but solid chunks of gold that had been fused in the campfire. They were like gleaming pieces of slag from a blast furnace. Each was tagged with its owner's name. When the box was full, Cole closed the lid and snapped the padlock on it.

Hobart and Elston heaved it inside the coach. Cole climbed inside and checked the loads in his Colt. Elston climbed to the seat, sorted his reins, and Hobart climbed up beside him. Vance Daugherty had disappeared, but he came running alongside as the coach got under way and pulled himself in through the door. As he did this, his swinging coat banged against the side of the coach with a thud, as though he carried a pocketful of rocks.

Once inside, he hauled a bottle from his pocket, grinning. "It will be a long ride into Denver City, and this will help pass the time."

Cole felt a stir of anger. He growled: "This is no party but a serious thing. We are sure to be jumped somewhere along the way, and a man with his wits addled by liquor is no good in a fight. Put the damned thing away."

His appreciation for the support this man had given him was rapidly turning to dislike. There was something furtive and insincere about Daugherty that grated against Cole's sense of what a man should be. And, instead of showing anger, as most men would, Daugherty only shrugged, smiled, and settled back against the seat.

Tension began to build in Cole as the coach began its long climb out of the cañon. The road wound interminably back and forth in switchbacks to reduce the grade, and on first one side and then the other the cañon yawned below them, the roar of the Vasquez slowly diminishing as they gained altitude.

At sundown they came to the top of the hill and started down the eastern side. Now Cole could relax somewhat, for here began a long, wide valley through which a tiny stream wandered, and there were no places where they could be ambushed. Out of a corner of his eye he studied Daugherty, wondering about this man.

He said: "It's unusual to find an educated man working a placer. Gold seekers are usually those who have found only failure in their daily lives and are always looking for something to remedy that failure quickly."

Vance Daugherty gave him a twisted grin. He replied: "You think that because a man is educated he's unfamiliar with failure?"

"I had that thought."

Daugherty laughed bitterly. "It's what all men think who don't have an education." His thin face, covered lightly with graying whiskers, showed Cole self-derision, even what appeared to be self-contempt. He added: "Success or failure is determined by what is in the man, not by what he has been taught. Even on the Vasquez I was able to pan only about half as much as the others. But, hell, why talk about me? There must be more pleasant subjects, surely, to pass the time."

Something about Daugherty's words puzzled Cole, but he could not decide what it was. The coach came off this grade, out of the lush meadow, and commenced to climb into heavy timber. The coolness, the dampness of the air here came through the windows of the coach and brought with it the light, pleasant smell of pine. Cole grew tense again, for here, with the coach slowed on the grade and with abundant concealment, an ambush was possible, even likely.

Cole stuck his head close to the window, peering into the increasing gloom ahead. Above him the driver's whip snaked out, popping over the heads of the mules, and Cole could hear Elston's salty stream of curses. Once he glanced about at Daugherty. The man sat stiffly on the edge of his seat, and his face had turned white. His eyes had a peculiar, fixed look, and his hands were held against his knees and could not stay still. Cole said: "Relax, man. It is no use worrying about the thing until it happens."

Turned vaguely uneasy, he drew his Colt and had it on the seat beside him, holding it down and still with his leg. In his mind he was going back over Daugherty's words of a few minutes ago and trying to put his finger on what it was in them that had so puzzled him. Suddenly he yanked his head around to stare at the tall man. He growled: "You said you were able to pan only half as much as the others. Why *were?* Aren't you going back?"

Abruptly now Elston's voice rose atop the coach, and a gun yelped ahead in the timber. A strange voice shouted: "Pull in, driver, or I'll drop you off that box!"

Cole snatched the Colt from under his leg and poked its muzzle through the window. He heard the movement of Daugherty behind him, ignoring it for the moment, and snapped a shot toward the flash in the heavy wall of timber. He heard Elston's whip lay itself sharply against the mules and felt the coach leap forward.

Hobart's shotgun roared above him, and its flash illuminated for an instant the timber and the half dozen horsemen within it. Cole put a shot into the midst of them and was rewarded by a man's harsh yell of pain. Again the shotgun roared, and now gunfire blossomed in the timber. Bullets tore through the thin panels of the coach.

Cole half turned to Daugherty to ask:

"What the hell's the matter with you? Ain't you got a gun?"

He caught the man's movement, rising from the seat on the opposite side of the coach, but instead of moving across to the other seat, the man came directly at him. Cole yelled: "Watch what you're doing, damn. . . ." Then he saw Daugherty's upraised arm, saw the long-barreled pistol in the man's hand. He threw himself forward, but, even as he did, he knew he was too late.

The barrel of Daugherty's revolver came down against his skull, bringing an instant of whirling pain and then utter blackness.

IX

STRING 'EM UP!

Dawn was a flaming spectacle of fiery cloud and pale blue sky. The Troy coach stood hidden in the timber no more than two hundred yards from the road, the lead mules tied to a tree. Fidgeting, they sought to lower their heads to graze, but they succeeded only in getting enough to whet their appetites for more. The coach rocked gently back and forth with their movement, and it was this that brought Cole to consciousness and then out of the coach, staggering and blurry-eyed. The first thing he noticed was the overpowering reek of whiskey that rose from his clothes. His confused brain fought for remembrance or understanding of the circumstances that had put him here.

At first he thought: *I must have been on one lulu of a drunk. But how the devil did I get out here?* Then pain brought an exploratory hand to his head. His fingers ran gingerly over the lump there, and slowly he began to recall. He remembered the chest full of gold that had been in the coach. He remembered the attack, the treachery of Vance Daugherty. He growled: "Hobart . . . and Elston? Where the hell are they?"

He made a circle of the coach at a shuffling run that brought dizzying waves of sickness and further pain to his head. Then he headed back along the plain tracks the coach had made in the tall grass, coming at last to the road and to the two silent, cold bodies, lying there, sprawled grotesquely in the dewy grass.

Cole sat down, his stomach contracting spasmodically. He retched, gagged, and almost fainted.

Down the steep grade toward the Vasquez he heard a shout and, plainly then, a man's steady cursing, the creak of an axle, and the metallic jangle of harness. Suddenly it came over him of how this would look. Cole Estes, reeking of whiskey, vomiting, his driver and guard dead on the ground. *God,* he thought, *I've got to have time to think this out.*

He staggered to his feet and, fighting against the pain in his injured arm, dragged first Hobart and then Elston into the timber where they would be hidden from the road. Just in time was he able to hide himself, watching from concealment the passage of an empty freight wagon as it passed on its slow and rumbling way toward Denver City. He held his breath as the wagon lumbered past, keeping an anxious eye on the driver lest he note the signs of disturbance in the grass, but the man was too preoccupied with cursing his mules to give more than a passing glance to the wayside.

As the sound of his cursing faded on the clear morning air, Cole went again to the coach. The chest in which the gold had been locked was splintered and gaping on the ground a dozen yards away. Inside the coach lay Cole's revolver, untouched, and an empty whiskey bottle, one Cole now recognized as the bottle Daugherty had waved at him as he entered the coach on the Vasquez.

Why didn't they kill me too? he asked himself, and for a moment considered the possibility that they'd thought they had. But he shook his head. *They wouldn't be that foolish,* he concluded. *It's got to be something else. If they thought I was dead, why pour whiskey over me?*

It came to him then, and he knew that this was Jess Dyer's way of revenging himself against Cole for the five thousand he had paid out unnecessarily. Dyer had felt killing Cole would afford him only a nominal vengeance. But this . . . ? Cole considered what would now happen. He would drive the coach on into Denver City, carrying the bodies of Elston and Hobart but no gold. He himself would reek of whiskey, would show every evidence of having been on a monstrous drunk. Who, then, would believe his story? Would the miners believe him, those who had lost their gold? Would Norah Forrest believe him, she whose doubt of him had been all too apparent after his interview with Dyer? Her tenuous faith in him would shatter all too easily.

Would the newly organized vigilantes believe that Cole had been sober, that he had been slugged by Daugherty, whom somehow Dyer must have reached and bought in the time it took Cole to return to Denver for the coach? At the very best Cole could expect to be driven from the country, accused of having betrayed everyone who trusted him. At worst he should expect to decorate the handy limb of a cottonwood tree.

The desolation of utter despair washed over him. The only apparent evasion that occurred to him now was mounting one of the mules and fleeing the country. For a short instant he considered this, but then his jaw hardened, and his eyes turned cold. *That is what Dyer wants me to do,* he knew. *Then he'll have a free hand to come in here with his own line.* He began to understand what Daugherty's stake had been: the ten thousand in gold that the coach had been carrying — less, perhaps, the five thousand Dyer had given Norah Forrest — and safe conduct to Denver, maybe even to Leavenworth, with his share of the gold.

Cole thought desperately: *There has got to be someone in Denver who will believe me.* He retrieved his gun from the floor of the coach and began to load it awkwardly from the powder flask at his belt. The shawl sling, used lately only to rest his arm when it was not in use, caught his eye and he pondered: *Sally, I wonder . . . ?* He called to mind the steady clarity of her blue eyes, the softness, the womanliness that was in her.

Fully aware that his story was thin, that it would be difficult for anyone to believe, he nevertheless also knew that this was a chance he had to take. He had to have sanctuary somewhere from which to start his search for Daugherty, who was the key to this thing.

Desperation turned his hands awkward and clumsy as he unharnessed the mules and turned them loose to graze. He thought: *If Sally will not believe me, at least she will not betray me to the vigilantes.* He mounted one of the mules bareback and set out along the road to Denver City at a steady trot, alert for other travelers and ready to leave the road at the first indication of their approach.

It was full dark when Cole came out of the Cherry Creek bottoms and made his cautious way to within a hundred yards of the brightly lighted front of the Gold Coin. Here he found a darkened space between two false-fronted frame buildings and took up his wait for Sally. She would pass within a yard of him on her way to work, unless by some remote chance she came to work by a different route, or unless she was driven there tonight in the carriage of some admirer.

His inactivity and his helplessness made Cole rage inwardly. Every hour that passed meant that Vance Daugherty was putting more miles between himself and Cole Estes. A dozen times during the next hour Cole shrank back into the darkness to avoid discovery by a passerby. This furtiveness further enraged him, and he was in a vicious frame of mind when he finally did see Sally turn the corner and come toward him.

She was dressed tonight in brilliant scarlet, her flaming hair done softly in a bun low on her neck. Over her dress, concealing its scantiness about shoulders and breasts, she wore a light wrap. Cole noticed again tonight, as he had noticed before, the indefinable grace that was in her as she walked. As she drew abreast of his hiding place, he murmured, "Sally?"

Startled, a hand went to her throat, and she poised for an instant like a frightened doe, ready to flee the instant she placed the source of danger.

"Sally, it's me . . . Cole Estes."

Not moving, she asked: "What's the matter? Are you hurt?"

"Worse than that. Will you help me? Will you listen to me?"

There was no hesitation in her, but there was quick fear, and this seemed inexplicably combined with pleasure that he had chosen her to ask for help. She said: "Go back to the alley . . . to the back door of the Gold Coin. Wait there. I'll come as soon as I can."

Then she was gone, moving rapidly toward the beams of light that fell across the walk from the windows of the Gold Coin. Cole walked through the velvety dark, stumbling over scrap lumber, and shortly stopped before the Gold Coin's back door. He waited only an instant. Then the door opened, and Sally whispered in the darkness, "Come on. Take my hand or you'll stumble."

He closed her small, warm hand within his own, and she led him up a stairway and out into the dimly lighted hall on the second floor. "One more flight," she whispered, and again they climbed stairs. Sally opened a door, and only then did she speak normally as she drew him inside. "Are you in trouble? Is someone after you?"

"Not yet."

Sally struck a match and held it to the lamp that stood on the table, lowering the rose-colored shade over the flame and turning it low. She looked at him, and her face mirrored compassion and something else, something that put the innocence of a young girl into her eyes. "You've been hurt again."

Cole was now very conscious of his appearance, of the dirty stubble that covered his face, of the dried blood that matted his hair, most of all of the reek of whiskey that still clung to his clothes. But these things seemed to matter not at all to Sally. Softly perfumed, she moved near to him. Suddenly he closed her in his arms, and she pressed herself against him, raising eager and slightly parted lips. She said wonderingly: "You're in trouble, and you've come to me. Why

122

didn't you go to that other girl . . . Norah Forrest?"

"You'll know when you hear the story." Cole released her and stepped back. His face turned bitter. "I wouldn't believe it myself if I didn't know it was true."

He sank into a chair upholstered in tapestry, the weariness of the last two days beginning to make itself felt. "I started a run between here and the Vasquez. I persuaded some miners to ship their gold to Denver, but the stage was held up before we got to Cresswell and the gold stolen."

Sally interrupted: "That's easy to believe. There're hold-ups all the time."

"You haven't heard it all. The driver and guard were killed. I was inside the coach because it was easier on my shoulder and arm. With me inside the coach was a miner who helped persuade the others to take a chance with their gold. Instead of fighting, he slugged me and poured whiskey over me." Cole's voice rose involuntarily, "They killed the others, but they didn't kill me. They tried to make it look as though I was drunk and didn't put up a fight."

Cole was angry. He was angry because of what Dyer was trying to do to him, but more than that he was angry because of Elston and especially because of Hobart, who'd been expecting help from inside the stage and had gotten none. He watched Sally closely, waiting for the shadow of doubt upon her face, but he saw only surprise.

She said softly: "I have seen you only twice, and yet I believe you. But a woman's heart and the minds of men are different things. The vigilantes are new, and this will be the first crime committed since their organization. You mustn't let them find you."

Cole's mind was running ahead, and he spoke his thoughts aloud. "If I was Dyer and had put Daugherty up to this thing, I'd sure as hell not want him found. I'd kill him, or I'd hold him somewhere, but I'd not let him out of Denver City until this thing was settled."

"Then you've got to find Daugherty."

Cole answered her bitterly: "And how can I do that? If I stick my head out of this door, they'll grab me. They failed to catch the men who killed George Osten. Do you think I'll get a fair shake if they catch me? It's too easy to say . . . 'He's lying! String him up!' "

With no hesitation whatever Sally said: "You can stay here. I'll bring you food."

"Marple helped organize the vigilantes. He'll find out and turn me in."

124

"He'll be quiet if I ask him to. He'll believe you because I believe you."

Cole glanced at her sharply, beginning to understand Marple — and Sally as well. He said: "I've no right to ask this of you." He stood up.

She came close to him and slipped her arms about his waist. She explained, her eyes still and honest, "John Marple is in love with me, but it hasn't been like that for me. Can you believe that . . . ?" Halting, she dropped her eyes. Color ran across her cheeks.

Ignoring the pain in his arm, Cole brought her roughly against him. Her arms slipped up to his neck, and she raised her lips to his. Excitement and passion were inexorably combined with tenderness as Cole felt the eager pressure of her. His face buried itself in her fragrant, flaming hair, and his lips found the soft hollow where her neck and shoulder joined. Sally gave a small, helpless cry. Then, suddenly, Cole's passion ended as quickly as it had kindled. He pushed away from her, breathing hoarsely. "No, by God! It's the man who should be giving, not forever taking." He strode to the window and scowled, looking into the street.

Sally's eyes upon him were dark and unreadable for an instant. Then she smiled, and Cole did not see the shining pride that came in a flash to her face and left as quickly, to be replaced by a woman's unending doubt. The words — "Is it Norah Forrest?" — were never uttered. Sally stood for a moment, watching him, and then she said: "First of all, you will need a bath and clean clothes. Then we'll see what can be done about finding this Daugherty. John will help us there. I know he'll help us."

She was rewarded by Cole's look of puzzled gratitude. He said: "Another woman would have been angry."

She turned away so that he couldn't see her face. But she was thinking: *Another woman would not love you so much that nothing mattered to her but what you wanted.* She closed the door behind her and went to find John Marple, knowing in her heart that this was all wrong, that no woman had the right to ask of a man who loved her what she was now going to ask of John Marple. Yet, there was no hesitation in her at all, for she was a woman not plagued by uncertainty once she had decided what must be done.

X

THE LONG MOMENT

Wearing his perpetual scowl of bitterness, the scowl which he had worn since the night George Osten's body had been buried, Karl Osten slouched down Blake toward Cherry Creek. He was a tall and towheaded boy, thin from denying the voracious and unending hunger of youth, the hunger that was never satisfied because there was never quite enough money. His first sharp grief at the loss of his father had lessened, but there were times yet, like today, when sudden awareness that he was entirely alone would turn him sullen and defiant.

Wandering alone in the creek bottoms had its way of easing his tortured thoughts, for he was yet boy enough to find the small creatures who lived there of extreme interest. There were minnows in the shallow pools; there were frogs, rabbits, squirrels, even an occasional coyote or deer, though these were to be seen only at dusk or in early morning. There was peace in the soft voice of the creek, in the quiet rustling of the cottonwood leaves overhead. Here, alone with his back to a tree, anything became possible to Karl, even the money for passage across the sea to bring his mother to this new country, even the discovery and punishment of his father's killer.

So down the creek Karl wandered, his path zigzagging aimlessly, and at noon he halted and sat down, hungry but reluctant to return to the small shack that he now occupied together with his father's friend. Nearly hidden in willow brush, he was startled as a man walked past, carrying a sack over his shoulder. The man was bearded and dirty, but it was his furtiveness that made Karl shrink out of sight until he had passed. It was the same furtiveness that aroused the boy's curiosity and drew him along behind the stranger at a safe distance.

A quarter mile westward, very near the place where Cherry Creek flowed into the Platte, the man entered a small log cabin and closed the door behind him. Karl's curiosity was waning, but, nevertheless, he sat down and concealed himself in the brush to watch.

This cabin was small, hastily and carelessly built. Where its oiled-paper windows had once been were now rough boards, and weeds, grown high about the door, indicating that it had until very recently been abandoned, perhaps by a miner gone for the summer to the mines.

Karl gave it his fleeting attention and then lay back to daydream of the things he would do when he found his father's killer. He was a helpless and lonely boy no longer, but a man, grown tall and strong. Muscles bulged inside his tight shirt, and a gun swung at his hip. Respect showed in the faces of the people he passed on the street, and in his imagination he heard a man murmur, "That's Karl Osten. He's found out who murdered his father, and he's going into that saloon to kill him."

The saloon doors banged open as he thrust his way inside. At the bar, a lone man whirled, his face losing color and turning gray. Karl snarled: "Murderer!" — waiting, knowing the pattern of these things, knowing that the man had to fight.

Like a cornered animal then, yellowed teeth showing, the man at the bar flung a lightning hand toward his gun. It came out, spitting flame. Bullets whined close to Karl's head. Smiling grimly, Karl drew his own gun and fired. The man let out a scream and dropped. . . .

Down at the cabin a door slammed. Karl

started and sat up, realizing suddenly that his forehead was bathed with sweat.

The bearded, furtive man was leaving, the sack, empty and dangling from his hand. This puzzled Karl. He had no way of knowing what had been in the sack, but, whatever it was, it was now inside the cabin.

The man passed him, fifty feet away. As soon as the sound of his movement through the brush had stopped, Karl rose and walked cautiously toward the small and deserted cabin. For no apparent or tangible reason fear touched him as he drew close, made him hesitate, nearly made him turn away. But the daydream of courage and strength was yet with him, and he forced himself on.

At one side of the cabin a board had been torn away from a window, and it was to this opening that Karl went. Crouching beneath it, he heard a sound within the cabin that sent a chill down his spine. His breathing turned loud and hurried. Carefully he raised himself until he could peep inside.

A man sat in the center of the room at a crude table, eating, his back to Karl. He was a tall man, thin and somewhat stooped. His clothes were ragged, yet there was, in the way he ate, a certain elegance that reminded Karl of people he had seen eating in the Planter's House.

Food, then, had been in the sack. Still, it was puzzling to Karl that this man would be here, apparently well and unhurt, having his food carried to him so far and in such a furtive manner. He backed from the window, worrying at his puzzlement with only a part of his mind, with the rest thinking of his own dinner, now an hour delayed, and feeling the increasing pangs of hunger.

Shrugging lightly at the peculiar actions of men, he left his place at the window and started his long walk back toward town. He hurried because he was hungry. He had not gone two hundred yards before the bearded one stepped from behind a tree, querying roughly: "Where you goin' so fast, snoopy?" He reached a long arm out to grab him.

Instinctively Karl began to run, dodging the reaching hand nimbly. The man lumbered along behind him, fast enough in his clumsy way, slowly closing the lead Karl had gained by his surprised first spurt of speed.

Karl resorted to dodging, to diving into thick clumps of brush and trying to outthink his pursuer. But the bearded man seemed always just a thought ahead of him, and the lead he had narrowed even more.

Panic touched Karl. His chest heaved and fought for air. His breathing grew fast and hoarse. His legs became weights, and his throat was on fire.

He scrambled out of the creek bottom at Blake, the man now only fifty feet behind him. Recklessly he cut in ahead of a lumbering wagon, and behind him the man had to swerve. By this maneuver Karl gained ten feet. He crashed through a cloister of men on the walk, bowling one to the ground, and his pursuer lost another several feet in avoiding their outstretched and irate hands.

Ahead, the splendor of the Gold Coin loomed, and Karl saw a woman alighting from a carriage. He dodged, but she stepped into his path, and he knocked her against the carriage driver, skinning his nose when he fell himself. On hands and knees he saw his pursuer approaching, slowing because of his sureness, his face ugly with rage and streaming sweat.

Karl yelled: "I ain't done nothin'! I just looked in an old cabin window an' seen a man eatin'. But he started chasin' me."

Sally Ambrook smiled. The coachman growled: "You little hellion! I'll learn you to go runnin' around, knockin' ladies down!"

Karl howled: "Please! I didn't mean to. Don't let him get me!"

He stumbled to his feet, but his yelling

had taken all of the breath that remained to him. He knew he could run no more.

The bearded man seized him roughly, and cuffed his mouth with the back of a hairy hand. Sally's voice was icy. "Take your hands off that boy!"

The carriage driver moved close, interfering in this because of Sally. "You heard her, mister! Let him go." The inevitable crowd began to collect. Hating his own weakness, Karl began to blubber, fear and exhaustion both contributing to the sobs that tore at his throat.

Sally said again: "Let him go!" Now men from the crowd moved forward to enforce her demand. The bearded man snarled viciously, but he released Karl's arm and backed away.

Sally caught at Karl's sleeve and murmured, "Go inside until you're rested. Then we'll see what this is all about."

Sally Ambrook followed the weary and panting boy into the cool dimness that was the Gold Coin at midday. At first her interference had been prompted only by pity for this boy's fear and exhaustion. But then a small memory had stirred within her, and recognition of his pursuer had come. The bearded man had been present the night Rupp had fought with Cole Estes. He had been one of those cheering Rupp on. Perversity and antagonism had thenceforth controlled Sally, but, as she listened to the boy's hurried and breathless story, she began to wonder if he had not unwittingly uncovered the thing that might in the end defeat Rupp and Dyer and save Cole. For his description of the man at the cabin tallied with Cole's description of Daugherty. Too, it seemed odd that one of Rupp's cronies would be carrying food to a hidden man, unless that man were Daugherty.

Quick elation made Sally hurry the boy upstairs, made her tremulous and hopeful, after leaving him in the room with Cole, while she returned downstairs to get the boy some dinner. Later, when she brought a plate of steaming venison for the boy into Cole's room, the boy had obviously already told Cole what he had seen. Cole was excited and jubilant.

"Sally, this is it!" he said to her, as she took the plate to the boy who was sitting at the small table. "They've got Daugherty down there at that cabin now, but they won't keep him there long. I've got to get to him before they have time to take him somewhere else."

Sally set the plate down before the boy, smiled her encouragement, and watched him as he began to eat, timidly and slowly at first, but with increasing ravenousness.

Cole said: "Hang it, Sally, you're not listening."

She gave Cole her full attention now, feeling his excitement touch her with its contagion. He was buckling on the Navy Colt and belt. Depression and defeat were gone from him, and in their place was this new enthusiasm and strong male-animal recklessness.

She said: "It's full daylight. How will you get there without being seen?"

"I don't give a hang if I'm seen. All I want is to get my two hands on that. . . ." He paused. "Once I get to Daugherty, then the vigilantes can have us both." He moved toward the door.

A sudden fear chilled Sally, and she pleaded: "Let John go with you. Wait until I can find him. Please! Do at least that for me."

He shrugged, his disappointment plain, but he also realized just how much he owed to this woman. "All right. But hurry. Rupp won't waste any time getting to Daugherty once he realizes that we know where he is."

Sally ran from the room. Five minutes later she watched as Cole and John Marple mounted horses in the alley behind the Gold

Coin and spurred recklessly toward Cherry Creek. Sally Ambrook had learned to care for herself in a land full of violence. She had been often afraid, but never quite so afraid as she now was. Trembling, she closed the door, and for a long moment stood with her back against it before she climbed the stairs.

XI

THEY'LL BE BACK

Marple led the way, never leaving this alley until he came to the creek. A steep path led downward here into the creek bottoms, and the two turned their horses and spurred them westward along the wide and sandy bottom that had been formed ages past by the rampaging waters in springtime.

In his careful and cautious way Marple managed to avoid the tent settlements that lay scattered in the cottonwoods, and Cole was suddenly thankful for the man's company, knowing that he himself would have forgotten caution entirely in the urgency of the moment.

There was no mistaking the cabin to which Karl had referred, for it was the only permanent building within half a mile of the place where Cherry Creek entered the Platte. In a fringe of cottonwoods a hundred yards away John Marple halted, holding his fidgeting horse with difficulty. He warned: "He may have a gun, so we'd better leave the horses here and go in on foot."

Cole grinned. "I've got a better idea. We may need these horses. You stay here while I go in. When I'm inside the cabin, you tie the horses. I know Dyer's careful way. Knowing that Daugherty's presence here is known, he'll lose no time in moving him and hiding him somewhere else."

There was a certain unspoken antagonism between these two. Cole recognized it for what it was, animal rivalry over Sally Ambrook, masked but lightly by a civilized control. Marple nodded his grudging assent.

Sun beat downward, hot in this airless and brushy bottom. Sweat dampened Cole's shirt, and excitement stirred him as he made his swift but careful way from tree to tree, from brushy pocket to brushy pocket. At last he stood but a short stone's throw from the cabin door. If not for the need to extract a confession from Daugherty, Cole would have called to him now, would have fought it out across this narrow stretch of grass that lay before the cabin door. Realizing, however, that vindication for himself lay in Daugherty's spoken words, he cat-footed across the clearing. Coming to the door, he flung it wide and entered with a rush, gun in hand.

Daugherty, reading an old newspaper that

he had spread out on the table, sprang to his feet, whirling, entirely surprised and unprepared. Seeing Cole, his hand snaked foolishly toward the gun at his side, but Cole rushed forward and brought his own gun barrel smashing down across Daugherty's wrist.

Daugherty howled with pain, and a grin of pleasure crossed Cole's twisted and enraged face. His hand went out toward Daugherty's undrawn gun. When the man dodged, this time he brought his own Colt smashing against the side of Daugherty's face. Daugherty staggered. His hand went to his face, came away sticky and red with blood.

Cole said harshly: "The gun. Hand it over and be careful, or I'll give you this one again in the same place. Marple will be here in a minute, and then you're going to talk. You're going to tell everything you know, and you're going to tell us exactly what happened the other night."

"They kidnapped me! They slugged me, and I couldn't help you! I swear that's the truth. I swear it!"

Again Cole swung his gun. The barrel and the cylinder smashed again into the bloody side of Daugherty's face. As Daugherty staggered, Cole yanked the man's gun from its holster and flung it, sliding, across the floor. His voice was cold. "The trouble with thieves is that they think honest men are soft. I'll show you how soft I am. Are you going to talk, or do you want this again in the same place?" He heard the door close behind him and swung his head to look at Marple. "He'll talk, but don't interfere." Now he asked of Daugherty: "How much did they pay you to slug me on the stage?"

Vance Daugherty hesitated, but, as Cole advanced with the gun in his fist, he babbled: "Two thousand, but it should have been more. There was thirty thousand in the box."

"Who paid you, Rupp or Dyer?"

"They haven't paid me yet. And they got my gold along with the rest."

"Who held up the stage?"

"It was Rupp. He's the one that's been robbing the miners on the Vasquez. He's the one that killed Osten."

Cole laughed harshly. "You're a fool! Do you think they'd let you live, knowing that about them? Do you really think they'd give you back your gold or pay you for slugging me? There's only one reason that you're alive now, and that's because you might be useful as a witness against me."

Marple interjected a question: "Where does Dyer fit in?"

Daugherty replied: "He's behind Rupp. When he's driven Estes out of business, he'll haul the miners' gold, but there'll still be enough of it stolen to make the hauling profitable. And he'll raise the rates for hauling it to twenty percent."

Cole grinned, asking Marple: "Heard enough?"

Marple nodded.

Cole turned toward the door, yanking Vance Daugherty with him. The horses had wandered as far as the first fringe of brush. Marple moved ahead now, toward them, and, as he did, a bullet thumped behind Cole and Daugherty into the soft log wall of the cabin. The report made a flat and vicious sound in the still, hot air.

Cole growled to Daughtery: "Run, damn you, but don't try to get away. If they don't get you, I will."

Daughtery drove across the open clearing, his legs pumping furiously, but he tripped as he neared the brush and slid on his face. When he came to hands and knees, the bloody side of his face was encrusted with sand, and his face was twisted with pain. There was no pity in Cole. Pity was killed by his thinking of Elston and Hobart, dead because of this man's treachery and lust for gold.

Cole entered the thicket with a rush, as bullets ripped into the ground behind him, kicking up their spurts of fine sand. Marple was holding the horses, prancing and frantic, and Cole said sharply to Daugherty, pointing to his mount: "Hoist yourself up, and fast!"

Daughtery scrambled into the saddle, and Cole snatched the reins from Marple, leaping up behind Daugherty. Marple mounted his own horse easily and swiftly, and this way they pounded into the open and up the bank southward, angling across the grass toward the road.

Behind, half a dozen riders boiled out of the bottoms, firing over their galloping horses' heads.

Daugherty yelled, his voice rising on a note of terror: "They'll kill us!"

Cole shouted into his ear: "Hell, nobody can shoot straight from a running horse. You just better hope that none of them gets the idea of stopping and using a rifle."

The distance into town, so long to a boy afoot, was a matter of minutes to men atop galloping horses. At the Gold Coin they yanked to a sliding halt, piling off and releasing the horses to move off upstreet uncertainly, reins dragging. Cole shoved Daugherty into the door, crowded Marple after him, saying: "Watch him. He'll get away if he can." He turned then, his lips splitting into a savage grin. As the pursuers rounded the corner, he brought up the smooth-worn Navy Colt and let a shot rip downstreet toward the creek. A man yelled and came tumbling from his saddle.

This brought the lot of them to a chaotic halt, and their shooting from the backs of their plunging horses was no match for Cole's steady aim. Cole fired again, dropping a second man. His third shot went through the neck of one of the horses, and the animal went down, pinning his rider beneath his twitching body.

As quickly as they had come into it, they whirled from the street and went out of sight. Behind, they left two still shapes and a yelling, struggling man, trapped beneath a dead horse.

Cole backed into the Gold Coin and heard Marple's worried voice: "They'll be coming again. We've got the thing that'll bust their gang wide open. I'm going out to round up the vigilantes. We'll never have a better chance to clean out Rupp's crew."

He ran through the door, but a shot ripped into the frame wall beside him, and he ducked swiftly back. Cole said: "They didn't run. They're covering the door from the corner with rifles. Try the back."

Together they ran through the big room, and now Daugherty followed, craven and thoroughly frightened. Sally met them there at the door. "The alley is full of men. I barred the door."

Cole shrugged.

Marple said: "The vigilantes'll hear the shooting."

Sally was more realistic. "Half of the men in the alley belong to the vigilantes." Her face was stricken and frightened, and it held her knowledge of how this would end. Confusion was allied with Rupp's forces. The vigilantes would be disorganized, easily persuaded that this attack was for the sole purpose of killing or capturing Cole Estes, whom Marple was hiding in the Gold Coin.

Marple asked: "What will they do now?"

Cole looked at Sally, so soft and wide-eyed, so filled with fear. He would not say what was in his thoughts, but he knew how ruthless Jess Dyer could be. Here was one way of eliminating all of the opposition in one terrible operation. Jess Dyer would not overlook it. Of that Cole was certain. Coal oil and fire would do for Jess Dyer what the guns of his toughs could not.

It was an accurate prophecy. Presently flames were licking at the walls of the towering and imposing Gold Coin. The walls were dry and fire-hungry. Heat forced the four up the stairs, but it was not until they reached the third floor that Cole remembered Karl Osten.

"Where's the boy?"

Concern sent Sally running from room to room. When she came back, there was puzzlement in her expression, but also there was elation and gladness that in some way the boy had been spared this death by fire. "Poor kid. He must've been afraid even of staying here. He must've run out the front door while you were trying to leave by the back."

The fire in the lower portion of the building now made a steady roar, and the rising heat was becoming unbearable. Minutes only remained to them, Cole knew. He went to the window and began firing methodically into the street. Useless perhaps, but it was very necessary to him that this should cost Dyer something. He saw the look that passed between Sally and Marple, and suddenly self-blame flooded over him, because it was he who had brought them to this. Swiftly he began to rip bedsheets into strips, knotting these strips together into a long rope. He would die by a bullet, perhaps, before he could reach the ground, but at least he would not die helplessly.

XII

THE RIGHTEOUS ANGER

Karl Osten had known by the very urgency and concern that was in Cole Estes that his discovery of the man in the cabin had an importance greater than any that was at first apparent. He was grateful to Sally for rescuing him from the bearded man, yet she was a stranger and, as such, could not entirely quiet the fear that was beginning to consume him. He sensed that there was real danger in the thing he had discovered. To the strongest of mortals danger is most easily faced from familiar surroundings.

As soon as Sally went downstairs when they heard the sound of shots in the street, Karl followed quietly. When Cole and Marple hurried to the back door with the fugitive he had seen, Karl slipped out the front. He dodged a bullet sent at him from a man hidden around the corner, then he was out of range across the street. He had gone little over a block when he noticed a man following him, closing the distance between them rapidly. Karl ducked into a narrow passageway between two buildings, ran, and, when he came to the back alley, turned and lost himself in a pile of empty crates and rubbish. Crouching there, he saw the man come into the alley and shortly saw him meet with two others who had entered from either end of the alley. The three stood, talking quietly, and Karl caught the words: "He's hiding here somewhere. You two cover the ends of the alley, and I'll look around. Rupp'll nail our hides to the barn door if that kid gets to the vigilantes."

Trembling, Karl waited. He could hear the man poking around in the rubbish pile, drawing nearer. A rat scurried past him, pausing momentarily to stare at him with beady, unwinking eyes. The man kicked a can, and it rolled to within inches of Karl's feet. Jumping up, he leaped atop the piled crates, fell, felt the man's clutching hand. Then he slipped away, darted up two flights of open stairway, and ran into a dim hall. A door was open into a room to his right, and he went through this, coming to a window that faced onto the roof of an adjoining building. A drop of ten feet yawned below the window, but Karl lowered himself until he was hanging by his hands, and then dropped. Gravel crunched under his feet.

Above, he could hear the sound as his pursuer pounded into the hall.

Karl ran, and then crouched behind a chimney half way across the flat roof. He trembled as he heard the man's cursing voice from the window, and he waited in terror for the sound that would tell him the man had dropped from it.

The sound did not come, and he heard the man's retreating steps, heard a door slam, heard baffled and obscene cursing, muffled by distance. Below in the alley one of the others called: "Get him, Sam?"

Sam yelled down: "Hell, he's here somewhere. It's a ten foot drop out of this window. Come on up here an' give me a hand."

For what seemed an eternity, Karl crouched there, unmoving. His legs turned stiff and began to tingle from poor circulation, yet he would not move. He could see the towering Gold Coin across the street, and, after what he judged to be several minutes, he heard voices again in the alley. "That kid just disappeared! Let's get the hell out of here. As long as Rupp don't know he got away, we'll be all right, so don't say anything."

It was then that more shots sounded in the street, mingled with the frantic pound of galloping hoofs. Taking his chance, Karl crept to the edge of the roof, peeping over the low parapet to look into the street. He saw Cole Estes drop two men and a horse with three deliberate shots. Still Karl waited. He saw Rupp's men run into the street from both ends, and he saw the blaze of the fire and, once, Sally's white and frightened face at an upstairs window.

To Karl this suddenly abrupt daylight violence was shockingly unreal, and fear for his own life brought a quick trembling over him that made his teeth chatter. Fear had touched him before while he was being chased. But it had not been this icy and raw fear for his life. In panic, he ran to the back edge of the roof.

He scanned the alley from one end to the other, but he saw no one, for the excitement in the street had drawn everyone there. A lean-to shack provided a quick and easy way to the ground, and five minutes later Karl pounded into the tiny one-room shack on the eastern outskirts of town.

The fat man forced quiet and coherence into the terrified boy by sternness and patience. When he had the story, he took down the long flintlock rifle from the wall. "Come with me, Karl. We will see what the vigilantes will do now. If they will do nothing, then at least you and I can do our bit against these murderers." He handed Karl the pistol that had been his father's and led the way at a swift and panting walk toward town.

There is something grimly terrible about the righteous anger of honest men. Cole saw them coming, in tightly compact groups from either end of the street, as he swung himself from the window and began his sliding descent to the ground. With his head level with the window, he told Sally: "If it will hold my weight, it will hold yours. Wait until the shooting stops and then come down."

The knots slowed him, and bullets cut viciously into the frame walls beside him. Concentrating only on speeding his descent, he heard the vicious chatter of gunfire as the vigilantes opened up on the concealed, sniping toughs. He felt a slamming blow against his left arm, the burn of pain, and the wetness of blood. The arm lost all of its strength in a single, numbing instant, and Cole slid unchecked for a full five feet until his right hand caught on one of the knots. In that short instant a scream rose from the street below. Holding on, sweating, Cole glanced around, saw the upturned and terrified face of Norah Forrest.

Her scream was not heard by himself

alone. He saw the monstrous and long-armed figure of Rupp running, saw him seize the girl, saw the brief struggle and the brutal blow of Rupp's fist that turned her limp and silent.

Rage flamed in his brain, and he released the crude rope, dropping the last ten feet and feeling the shock of falling, the momentary dizziness as he hit the ground. Rupp was fleeing, the form of Norah tossed across his shoulder.

From the window above he heard Sally's scream: "Cole!" He yanked his glance around, tilting his face upward. Sally was sliding down the rope, and above her John Marple's face was a mask of horrified concern. Cole glanced around once more, the awfulness of indecision tearing at him. Rupp had disappeared, and his disappearance with Norah Forrest gave Cole the answer he had been seeking, but, loving Norah or not, he could not leave until Sally was safe on the ground.

He waited then, catching her in his arms before her feet could touch the ground. In an instant John Marple was down, and Daugherty came immediately behind him. Cole released Sally, who gave his face an instant's searching, then turned wordlessly to Marple. Marple tossed Cole a triumphant look, closing Sally in his arms, and Cole grinned. Then he whirled, running, heading for the Planter's House and the offices of the I.C. & K.T. Express. Norah Forrest was Rupp's hostage, but, when Rupp left the country, he would want his gold, and he would need a coach in which to travel.

Cole fought his way through the ranks of vigilantes, through the crowd of curious on-lookers. Fire-fighting equipment was moving up, ladders, wagons loaded with tanks and buckets, and this further slowed him. There was in Cole a feeling of time forever lost, and desperation turned him frantic. For the moment Norah was useful to Rupp, for she guaranteed his escape. Later, when he had made good his escape. . . .

At a tearing run Cole rounded the last corner, and even from here he could see the still form that lay on the walk before the Planter's House. Upstreet, a coach swayed and rocked as its galloping horses took it swiftly out of town, heading eastward along the road toward Leavenworth.

Cole paused for a brief instant beside the body that lay on the walk. Jess Dyer, in death, still showed the evil and ugliness that had been so apparent in him in life. Cole was reminded of his own words to Dyer: "You can die as quickly as any man." He knew that Dyer had never believed it until perhaps the last moment when Rupp fired the fatal shot.

Beside the body lay a small trunk, spilled open, its contents plainly Dyer's clothes and personal belongings. Cole muttered, "You were skipping with the gold, and Rupp caught you. Now he's got the gold, and he's got Norah, too."

The rack before the hotel held half a dozen drowsing horses, and Cole picked a tall and glossy black, swinging into the saddle as the horse broke into his run. His left arm had scarcely the strength to hold the reins, but he would need his right for the revolver. His heels drummed on the black's sides, urging the speeding animal to even greater exertion. The coach was only a speck ahead, lost in its rising dust cloud.

The grain-fed horse began to sweat, but Cole slowly closed the distance between himself and the coach. While he was yet a hundred yards behind, Rupp opened fire with his rifle, using it one-handed from atop the Concord.

Cole, helpless to return the fire because of Norah inside and because of the uncertainty of shooting from the back of a running horse, was forced to face Rupp's deadly fire with only the swerving of his horse from side to side to throw it off. Then the gap had closed until he was directly behind the coach and sheltered from Rupp's fire by the Concord itself. Still there was no sign of Norah.

Cole drew slowly ahead on the right side of the coach and, peering inside, saw the sprawled and unconscious form of Norah, half on the seat, half on the floor, being pounded mercilessly from side to side by the rocking of the coach. He drew farther ahead until he could see Rupp, his hands full now with the bolting teams, but holding them with his left hand only, while his right turned a revolver toward Cole.

The flame and smoke from Rupp's gun were acrid and blinding in Cole's face, but the bullet had missed him. Cole raised his own gun and, as the sights wobbily centered on Rupp's naked and hairy chest, snapped off a shot.

The big man howled, a roar of mingled pain and shock, stood up on the seat, and pitched off directly in front of Cole's galloping horse. Cole felt the lift as the black soared over Rupp and was nearly unseated by the shock and surprise of it. The coach had drawn ahead in this short instant, but Cole drummed on the black's wet sides and forced him abreast.

This was the vicious part — Norah unconscious, terrified, with runaway teams drawing the lumbering coach, Cole himself with only one good arm. He holstered the Colt, swung his right leg over the black's neck, braced it momentarily against the saddle, and leaped. The black veered away, and for a split second Cole hung in mid-air, the whirling, grinding wheels of the coach directly beneath him, reaching and hungry.

He felt his hand, his right hand, close on the seat rail. His left met it, but his feet were dangling and touched momentarily the spokes of the front wheel. Slowly and painfully he drew himself up, and at last sat atop the bounding seat.

The reins, dropped by Rupp as he had stood up, dragged now on the ground between the teams. Cole leaped from the seat, landing astride one of the wheelers, and, clinging to harness, leaned far to one side, finally grasping the trailing reins.

He straightened then, hauling back with all his strength. Slowly, slowly the horses came under his control, until he could draw them to a full halt, could climb back into the seat, and set the brake.

He was down then and into the coach. Norah, bleeding slightly from her bruised mouth, was stirring and moaning, but she clung to him and drew herself close.

There was time for relief and time for thankfulness. The Osten boy would have his father's gold. The vigilantes would have Daugherty and the remainder of Rupp's gang. The time for hunger and for love would come later, when Denver City was peaceful again.

TRAIL TO VICKSBURG

I

Jeff Hueston let his horse pick a careful, skillful way through the thorny tangle of Texas blackjack, towering high above his head. He could see less than a dozen yards, but he could hear what he could not see — cattle coming to their feet ahead of him, pausing momentarily in silence to listen and to sniff the air like wild animals, then crashing away along the narrow tunnels they had made through the thorny, nearly impenetrable thicket of brush.

There were smells in Jeff's nostrils, familiar smells, the hot, steamy smell of the sweating, hard-working horse between his knees, the smell of saddle leather and of cattle droppings in the trail, the dusty smell of the thicket itself this hot October day. And there were the things that he felt, the scratches made by the brush on his face and hands, the heat of the sun upon his back, the almost intangible excitement he felt because the time was now so close at hand.

Jeff was a tall young man, seventeen last month. He was old enough, he thought, to join the army of the Confederacy, the way his brothers had. He was old enough to fight, old enough for the excitement of it and the glory. He was old enough to be a part of it. But they wouldn't let him go. They couldn't, his mother and grandfather said. Someone had to work the ranch. Someone had to try and get enough money together to pay the taxes. If they weren't paid, there wouldn't be a ranch for his brothers to come home to when the fighting was over.

Jeff didn't want to stay. But, he supposed, doing this was the next thing. His brothers had written that the soldiers of the Confederacy needed food if they were to fight successfully. They needed meat, and meat meant Texas beef, if a herd could be gotten through.

Jeff's mouth firmed a little as he raised an arm to ward off a thorny branch. If one herd could be driven to New Orleans, others would follow it. A flood of Texas beef would stream eastward to the army of the Confederacy. He felt his excitement stir again. "It might mean all the difference," Jeff's grandfather had said. That flood of Texas beef, streaming east, could mean the difference between winning the war and losing it.

Now, to his right and left, Jeff heard the

others, riding as carefully as he through the brush tangle toward the long wings of the corral they had built earlier. He could hear more cattle ahead, coming clumsily to their feet, listening, crashing away.

This would be the last bunch they'd gather, he thought, before they trail branded the herd and headed east. With any kind of luck, today's catch would bring the gather to eight hundred head, which was the number they had decided upon. Nearly five hundred of these belonged to the Hueston family. Mostly the others belonged to the families of Jack Littlefield and Madison Quinn, who were going along on the drive with Jeff, and to some other neighbors who would give him bills-of-sale for whatever cattle of theirs that he took along.

He heard a steer lumber ponderously to his feet, no more than a dozen yards ahead. He glimpsed the animal through the tangle, shaggy and red-roan colored, with wildly rolling eyes and great horns like daggers curving out two feet on either side of his head and upward toward the sky. Tall and bony and lean, he would still weigh eight hundred pounds. Eight hundred pounds of sinew and muscle and bone. Eight hundred pounds of fury. . . .

This steer did not turn and run on ahead

as the others had done. Instead, it eyed Jeff truculently, head lowered now, snorting and pawing the ground and bellowing.

Jeff raised an arm. *"Hi-yah-yah-yah!"* he yelled, and brought his hand down sharply to slap his brush-scarred leather chaps.

The steer flinched at the unexpected sound, but he stood his ground. He pawed, snorted, and rolled his eyes. He shook his great head and waved those wide-spreading, vicious horns. Jeff yelled again and touched his spurs lightly to his horse's sides.

The horse moved in toward the steer. Suddenly the steer broke to the side, trying to duck past Jeff and away from the trap ahead. Jeff reined his horse aside to head him off, but the steer was faster than the horse. He ran like a deer, the ground shaking beneath his cloven hoofs.

Jeff sank his spurs in earnest now. He yanked the little cow pony around after the running steer, raking his sides angrily. The horse leaped in pursuit. Jeff took his rope, hanging from a thong attached to his saddle horn, in hand and shook out a loop. He could let the steer go, of course. It was only one animal. But it was a big animal, and Jeff didn't intend to let him get away. He was needed in the drive. Besides, to Jeff it was a matter of principle. You didn't let a steer get the best of you. If you let every wild one that tried to break back get away with it, you'd never gather a herd. Not in a million years.

The steer was now a dozen yards ahead, running like a frightened deer. Jeff kept raking the horse with his spurs, and the game little animal gave forth an extra burst of speed in his effort to overtake the steer. Jeff leaned forward, balancing himself lightly in the stirrups. He waited until the way between himself and the steer was momentarily clear of brush and snags.

He made his throw, and the loop, small and slightly oval-shaped, sailed out. It hung over the steer's head for an instant, then settled down over his horns. Jeff dallied the rope around the saddle horn, yanked back on the reins, and braced himself. The cow pony planted all four feet in a frantic, sliding stop and braced because he knew what would happen when the steer hit the end of the rope.

Eight hundred pounds of galloping longhorn yanked the rope taut, and there was a sudden, awful shock. The red steer's head went down. A startled bawl came from the animal's open mouth, to be cut short as one of his horns hooked in the ground and flipped him over, end over end.

Perhaps Jeff's cinch would have stood the initial shock, but it could not stand the second one as well. As the steer somersaulted, the cinch gave way. The red steer hit the ground with a crash that seemed to shake the earth, and the rope went slack. Jeff was somersaulted through the air to land on his back less than ten feet from the downed steer. His saddle sailed through the air after him, landing close by. The rope was still dallied around the horn. The broken cinch dangled.

With the wind knocked out of him, Jeff lay there, gasping helplessly. He tried to draw air into his starving lungs but succeeded only in making choking, bleating sounds. The horse, suddenly free of rider and saddle, free of the rope that had tied him to the steer, trotted away, reins trailing, head turned so that he would not step on them. He disappeared into the brush in the direction of the corral.

Still gasping, still fighting desperately for air, Jeff raised his head and looked around. Dust raised by the falling steer was still settling. Jeff saw that he had narrowly missed striking a gnarled old liveoak tree and now lay close to the base of its trunk. He rolled and forced himself to his hands and knees.

Weakly he stared at the big ugly brute of a steer, also struggling to rise. He suddenly wished that he had a gun. He felt helpless and alone, more so than ever in his life before. He knew what the steer was going to do when he made it to his feet, and he was filled with chilling fear.

He and the steer made it to their feet almost simultaneously. They stared warily at each other for a moment, both too stunned and surprised to move. Then, suddenly, a great bawl of pure fury burst from the steer's throat.

Jeff knew what it meant, and for an instant terror paralyzed him. The steer was going to charge him, was going to try to impale him on one of those savage horns, or trample him, or both.

Wild brush cattle almost never charged a man on a horse, and, even when they did, the horse was usually able to elude the charge. But they would charge a man on foot. And a man on foot was rarely able to get away.

He turned and glanced around frantically for his horse, but the animal had disappeared. He had probably returned to the corral, Jeff thought bleakly. Or he had headed back to the home ranch. In any event, he was gone. He was no use now.

The steer was moving, picking up speed, pounding toward Jeff. Jeff's time was gone. He leaped behind the liveoak. The steer crashed helplessly through the brush for thirty or forty feet before he could bring himself to a stop. He whirled to face Jeff again. He stood there, pawing the ground, raising huge clouds of dust and snorting furiously.

Jeff noticed the rope that still dangled from the steer. The end of the rope had come off the saddle horn and now lay half a dozen feet away from the tree behind which Jeff stood. If he could get his hands on that rope. . . . To forestall the steer's charge long enough to get the rope, Jeff yelled like a maniac. *"Hi-yah-yah! Hey Red, get out of here! Yah!"*

For an instant the steer stood, frozen with surprise. Jeff rushed from behind the tree and dove for the rope. His foot caught on one of the exposed roots, and he was sent plunging headlong to the ground. He turned his head and saw that the steer was coming, coming. . . . But his hand had closed around the rope. He fought to his knees and feet and leaped a second time toward the trunk.

The steer went past him again, missing him. Swiftly now, as swiftly as he could, Jeff ran around the tree. Then, wrapping the rope end around his body, he laid his weight back against it. But the steer did not go to the end of the rope. He whirled and came charging back, head turned a little now so that he could hook Jeff with one of those ugly horns.

Jeff ducked back behind the tree. The instant the steer was past, he took up the slack in the rope and braced himself again. This time the steer hit the end of the rope. It tightened, biting into the bark of the tree, singing like a fiddle string as the steer snapped it tight. The steer hit the ground again.

A grim smile touched Jeff's mouth as he watched the stunned steer struggle to rise. He realized he was shaking and glanced around, hoping none of the others had heard the commotion and come to see what it was.

Before the steer could get up and charge again, Jeff wrapped the rope around the tree trunk two more times. He tied it swiftly and securely, then jumped back as the steer got up and bawled at him.

He watched as the infuriated animal charged to the end of the rope, trying to get at him. He said, soothingly but with mockery in his tone as well: "Easy now, Red. Easy. You stay here a spell and simmer down. I'll bet by the time I come back for you, you'll be tamed down a mite."

Still grinning but shaky, he walked to his saddle and picked it up. It was worn, cracked, and brush scarred. It wasn't much, but it was all he had. Throwing it across his shoulder, he headed away through the brush in the direction he had been going when he first encountered the red steer.

He knew the truculent animal would be known as "Red" until they reached their destination in New Orleans. He also knew there'd be more rebellion before he turned Red over to the Confederate quartermaster there. The steer was a bunch-quitter and a trouble-maker. But he was a big steer. He was eight hundred pounds of meat, and he was going to New Orleans.

II

By the time Jeff Hueston reached the nearest of the widespread wings of the corral, the others had gone on ahead. He could hear the crashing sounds made by the cattle as they milled around in the heavy brush. He could hear them bawling and sometimes the shrill, yipping cry of one of the young drovers.

He trudged on, keeping a wary eye on the thicket ahead of him. He didn't want to encounter another maddened steer today and knew there was a possibility that one or more of them might escape and come crashing back this way.

He stuck close to the wing of the corral, ready to climb over it if any appeared. When he reached the gate, the cattle were all inside, and Jack Littlefield and Madison Quinn were in the act of closing it. Jack turned his head, grinning. His expression was pure mockery, but there was relief in his eyes. "We were just coming to look for you. Your hoss is tied over there to the corral."

Jeff grinned back at him. Jack was a couple of inches shorter than he, stockier, red of face and with long, uncut yellow hair. He wore a straw Mexican sombrero, homespun shirt and pants, and scuffed Mexican high-heeled boots. Jeff had known Jack most of his life. He said: "I tied onto a wild one back there a ways. Busted my cinch. I left him tied to a tree to simmer down."

Jack nodded. Madison, whom the others called Mad, listened without comment, his eyes steadily on Jeff. Mad never had much to say, but he didn't miss much, either. He was wiry and tough and as competent as any man for all that he was only thirteen years old.

Embarrassed by their obvious concern, Jeff walked to the corral fence and stared at the cattle, milling uneasily inside. The corral was built of mesquite poles, twisted and crooked, but adequate if used properly. The posts were also of mesquite, set double in the ground so that the poles had a post on each side of them. Rawhide strips, soaked with water to make them pliable, had then been used to lash the posts together, and, when these strips had dried, they had shrunk and hardened until now they were like straps of iron. This corral, although it had been built hastily, would be here for a long, long time to come. So would the other corrals they had built at various strategic locations in the heavy brush. They could be used again next year and for many years to come.

There were forty-seven cattle in this corral. Twenty-one were cows. Six others were too small to be worth taking on the drive. Only twenty were steers large enough to take. With the red roan steer tied to the liveoak, it made twenty-one. But twenty-one was enough. Twenty-one would bring the total rounded up so far to eight hundred and two.

Jeff turned his head toward the others. He said: "This does it. We'll start trail branding tomorrow and, with any luck, ought to be ready to go by the end of the week. We'll leave these here for a couple of days. By then they ought to have the fight starved out of them."

He crossed to where his horse was tied. He laid his saddle on the top pole of the corral so that he could reach it after he had mounted, then swung to his horse's bare back. Reaching up, he took the saddle from the corral and balanced it in front of him. "I'll fix my cinch when we get back to the house."

He waited for the others to get their horses and mount, staring back at the cattle inside the corral. There were some pretty wild ones in there, some almost as wild as Red. But a couple of days without food or water, a couple of days penned up inside the corral would take the fight out of them. It would take away their wildness and their inclination to break for the brush the moment the corral gate opened and set them free. At the end of two days all they'd want would be water and grass, in that order, and he and the others would be able to drive them the half dozen miles that separated this spot from the home ranch and the herd being held nearby.

He led out. Jack and Miguel Ortiz, the middle-aged Mexican handyman, followed him. Miguel was short, and as lean and tough as a strip of sun-dried rawhide. He had a straggly black mustache. A few black hairs, about a half inch long, grew out of his chin. His hair was almost as long as that of an Indian, falling on both sides of his face but still too short to braid the way the Indians did. Miguel wore a thin cotton shirt and homespun pants. He wore straw sandals on his feet and a straw hat on his head. He rode a sleek brown mule that was as fast as any horse and as sure-footed as a goat. When Miguel smiled, and he was smiling now, a hundred tiny wrinkles appeared at the corners of his eyes and elsewhere on his face. When Miguel smiled, no one could help smiling back. Jeff grinned at him.

He led the others past the red steer he had left tied to the tree so that they would all know where he was. The steer glowered at them sullenly but did not offer to charge again. Jeff said to him: "I said you'd get some sense if I left you tied up here a while." The steer bawled, as if he had understood.

Jeff let himself go limp on the back of his horse, relaxing now that there was nothing more to do. They'd been working like dogs, he thought, for a month and a half, gathering this herd. All of them had lost weight. All of them were tired. Sometimes they were so tired they grew irritable with each other. A couple of days ago Jack Littlefield had gotten into a fist fight with one of the neighbors who was helping hold the herd.

There did not seem to be much likelihood of getting rested up. Not now. Not for another month and a half at least. Jeff didn't know exactly how far it was to New Orleans, but he knew it was a long, long way. There were half a dozen rivers between Goliad and New Orleans, not counting the biggest river of all, the Mississippi.

But Jeff wasn't worried. Not really. He had great confidence in himself, in Jack, and in Mad. They had gathered this herd out of the brush. They had tamed the wild ones, and held them, and nothing would stop them from taking them to New Orleans. Yet, in spite of his confidence, he was a little scared because once away from here, once they had left Goliad and the home ranch behind, they would be strictly on their own.

Slumped on the back of his horse, the saddle balanced on the horse's withers in front of him, he followed the tortuous trail through the brush. At sundown the quartet came out onto a wide, flat grassland on which there were only scattered thickets of mesquite. Here he could see the herd, scattered, grazing in groups of two or three, covering a square mile at least. At the perimeter of the herd he could see the cowboys who were holding them, sitting their horses idly, or dismounted and lounging in the shade of a clump of brush. As long as they had feed and water available, a herd was easy enough to hold. All that was necessary was to keep them loosely bunched.

Jeff headed straight for the house. While still a half a mile away from it, he turned slightly and stopped to talk to one of the cowboys, helping to hold the herd. This one must have been sixty-five years old. He had a wooden left leg and a specially built stirrup on the left side with a hole in it into which the peg leg would fit and turn as he mounted his horse.

Jeff nodded. "Hello, Sam."

Sam squinted at him. His face was seamed and unshaven, but his blue eyes were sharp. "How many did you catch today?"

"Twenty-one, that we can use. If my figurin' is right, that means we've got a little over the eight hundred head we were aimin' for."

"You'll be leavin', then. Soon's they're trail branded?"

Jeff nodded. Cattle to be taken on a long drive were always given a trail brand in addition to their owner's brand, since trail herds usually were mixed, consisting of cattle belonging to as many as a dozen brands in all. It was too difficult keeping track of that many brands. But branding eight hundred cattle for the trail was a drawn-out, dirty job, and Jeff was not particularly looking forward to it. He turned to ride away, but Sam called: "Jeff."

He reined up and turned.

Sam looked apologetic. "I want to go with you, Jeff. I'm too old an' stove-up for soldierin', but I kin ride, and I kin he'p drive them critters." Sam looked as though he expected to be refused.

Jeff hesitated. He was flattered to be asked. Sam could have gone to his grandfather instead of asking him. He also realized Sam might become a burden before they reached New Orleans. But he *did* need help. Two of the boys and Miguel were not exactly an adequate trail crew for driving eight hundred wild longhorn steers. He studied Sam Rhody a moment, then nodded. "We can use you, Sam. You know the way. Thirty a month when we deliver the herd and get paid for it. Nothing, if we lose it, or if we don't get paid. Grandpaw says there's a chance the army will commandeer it and not give us a cent."

Sam nodded gratefully. "Thanks, Jeff. I'll make you a good hand for all I'm gettin' old."

Jeff nodded. "I know you will." He turned his horse and continued toward the house. Jack urged his horse up alongside and asked critically: "Why'd you tell that old sot he could come along? We'll be lookin' after him more than we look after the herd."

Jeff stared at Jack. "Maybe, but I don't think so. You might be glad we've got him along after about a week of driving all day and night, herding half the night. Besides that, Sam's a good hand. He knows ten times more than you and I and Mad put together . . . about cattle, at least."

"How many old codgers you going to take along with us?"

Jeff glanced at Jack irritably. "As many as I think we need. As many as I can get."

Jack scowled, but he did not reply.

Jeff drummed his heels against his horse's sides and pounded toward the house. He dismounted in the yard, led his horse to the corral, and slipped off the bridle. He stood there a moment, glancing at the horses in the corral. Then he hefted his saddle and headed toward the barn.

He could smell supper cooking at the house. There was always the smell of cooking around the house nowadays. With all the hands they had to feed, the women were kept as busy as the men. Mrs. Littlefield was here, helping Jeff's mother. So was Mrs. Quinn. Miguel's wife and two daughters also helped.

Jeff rummaged around until he found a piece of leather from which he could make a cinch. Laboriously he cut a band six inches wide from it, tapering it at the ends so that it would fit through the cinch ring at each end.

He carried it into the blacksmith shop at one end of the long, low adobe barn and here punched holes in the ends so that he could lace in the cinch rings. Then he took it outside where his saddle was, sat down on a chopping block, and began to take the rings out of the old cinch.

With tanned leather thongs he laced the two cinch rings into the ends of the cowhide cinch. He looped the latigo on the saddle through one of the cinch rings and made the end fast with a knot resembling the knot in a necktie. He carried the saddle to the corral and tossed it up onto the top corral pole.

The sky was now flaming from the dying rays of the setting sun, but the edges of the high, thin clouds were turning from gold to purple as the light gradually faded from the sky. The air seemed cool after the burning heat of the October day.

Jeff heard the back door slam and saw his grandfather crossing the yard toward him. He waited expectantly.

The old man was tall and gaunt, and his skin was like cracked parchment that has lain too long in the sun. He had a nose like an eagle's beak, long and sharp and hooked, and the bushiest eyebrows Jeff had ever seen. Old Jake Hueston had fought the British at New Orleans in 1812. He'd fought the Mexicans at Goliad not far from here.

He'd be fighting Union troops right now if the Confederate forces would have him. He'd fought Comanches, and outlaws, and the neighboring cattlemen. His sharp old eyes took in the old cinch lying on the ground by the chopping block and lifted to meet Jeff's glance. "Tie onto a wild one, did you, boy?"

Jeff nodded.

"Git away, did he?"

"No, sir. He's tied to a tree, back there in the brush." There was a pride in Jeff's voice, however hard he tried not to let it show.

"Good boy. You'll get these critters to N'Orleans if anybody can."

"Yes, sir."

Jeff hoped he could some day be as much of a man as his grandfather was. He admired him tremendously. Sometimes he yearned to be close to the old man, the way he might have been close to his father, if he had not been killed. But somehow or other he had never been able to get close to his grandfather. It was like trying to get close to an eagle, or to a panther, or to a wild stallion, standing on some far-off ridge. And yet there *was* a kind of closeness between them. Perhaps it was a closeness of spirit. Perhaps it was there because the same blood ran in the veins of both. It was an unspoken thing, Jeff realized suddenly, and he had a feeling that, whatever he did, the old man would understand. He knew that whatever his grandfather did . . . well, he might not understand, but he'd be behind the old man anyway.

Jeff's mother came out on the back porch and banged the metal triangle, hanging there. Old Jake said: "Time to eat."

"Yes, sir."

Jeff followed his grandfather toward the house. There was a knot of anticipation in the middle of his stomach, an excitement he had never felt before. Right now he was an untried boy. Six weeks from now, he would be a man. . . . or he would be dead.

III

The kitchen was an enormous room, the largest in the house. It had a puncheon floor originally, made by setting short sections of hardwood pole on end and close together. Small cracks and openings between the sections had been filled with adobe mud at the time the floor was made. The whole thing had been worn smooth by countless feet over the years, by countless sweepings, by countless moppings. And worn level, too, except in places where the wear was heaviest. In front of the stove and fireplace and around and under the table there were hollows lower than the level of the rest of it.

The table itself was fifteen feet long. There were heavy benches on both sides, chairs at the ends. Jeff's grandfather took his place at one end. The other would remain vacant unless Jeff's mother decided to sit down.

Jeff took a place on one of the benches not far from where his grandfather sat. Miguel Ortiz sat across from him, next to Sam Rhody. The women brought platters of food, fried side meat, roast beef, hominy, fried potatoes, bread, turnip greens. Jeff loaded his plate and began to eat ravenously.

Nobody talked. Eating was a serious business for these men who had worked so hard today. Most of them had not eaten since breakfast because they hadn't been able to leave the herd or because they had been working in the brush a long way from the house.

When everyone had finished, they got up and silently left the house. They mounted their horses and went out to relieve others who had stayed with the herd. Jeff stayed where he was for the moment, looking at his grandfather. He asked, "How long do you think trail branding is going to take?"

The old man shrugged. "A week. Mebbe a little less'n that, if we're lucky."

Jeff nodded.

Every one of the cattle had to be roped twice, once over the horns by one man, once on a hind foot by another. Backing in opposite directions, then, the horses would pull both ropes taut, thereby dumping the steer to the ground. While he was helpless, men would run from the fires with red-hot branding irons and would burn the trail brand on the steer's hip. The steer would struggle, and he would bawl, but the brand would go on anyway. Afterward, one man would flip his loop off the steer's horns, and, as the animal got up, the other would flip his loop off the hind leg. The steer, released, would trot ponderously back to the herd, none the worse for wear.

A week, Jeff thought as he got up from the table. It seemed a long time but it wasn't, really. The time for leaving was very near.

Jeff's mother came across the room and stood looking down at Jeff's grandfather. "I wish you wouldn't let him go," she said. "He's too young. He isn't ready for this much danger and responsibility."

Old Jake narrowed his eyes as he looked thoughtfully up at her. "The Confederate army would take him, if you'd let him go. They'd give him things to do that're a dam-site more dangerous and responsible than this."

"Don't give me that argument. He isn't going to the Confederate army. And he's only seventeen years old."

Old Jake chuckled. "When I was seventeen, I'd already been on my own four years."

"But you didn't have to drive eight hundred cattle almost a thousand miles."

"Nope. But Jeff's a good, strong, level-headed boy. Reminds me of his father, that he does. Reminds me of the man you married, Martha, nigh onto twenty years ago. This one won't come apart at the seams, Daughter, any more'n his daddy would. Jeff will get that herd through and bring the money home."

Jeff felt flushed and hot, hearing this praise from his grandfather's lips. But he felt proud, too. He was proud the old man thought he could get through.

He knew they'd go on discussing him until the other men came in, so he made a hasty exit and crossed the yard to the corral. He roped out a fresh horse, threw his saddle on, tightened the cinch, and swung astride. He rode out to the herd to relieve someone that had not yet eaten.

It was almost dark by the time he reached the herd. He rode slowly, carefully, singing softly to himself so that the cattle would hear him before he loomed up close to them. They had been held here for some time now. With them were mixed a few tame cattle to steady them. But they were still brush cattle, and they still were wild. If they were startled by some sudden noise, a clap of thunder, a gunshot, even a sudden shout, they might break and run, reverting to their wild state instantaneously.

A soft voice called: "Over heah, son."

Jeff rode toward the sound. A shape loomed out of the darkness, the lumpy, overweight shape of Ted Wilkes. There was a black patch over his right eye. The story was that he had lost it to a thorn, riding in the brush. Ted was well past seventy, Jeff knew. He looked like a shapeless bag of cotton, sitting on his horse. He was always sweating heavily, but he was almost always smiling, too.

Jeff asked: "Have you eaten yet?"

"Nope. But now that you're heah, I'll go on in."

Jeff drew his horse to a halt, but Ted did not leave immediately. He lingered, and at last he said: "I'm an old man, Jeff, an' fatter'n any razorback, but I'd like to go along with you. I'll make you a good hand, boy. You try me out an' see."

Jeff hesitated, thinking about what Jack Littlefield had said about his hiring Sam Rhody for the drive. But he did need men. And he'd never known Ted Wilkes to shirk.

Ted was waiting expectantly. Jeff frowned suddenly to himself. Why didn't he tell Ted he could come along? Because he thought Jack might not approve? His frown deepened. Was he going to make all his decisions only after considering what the others might think of them? Was that the kind of trail boss he was going to be?

He shook his head imperceptibly. They'd never get to New Orleans if he ran the drive that way. He said suddenly: "Sure, I'll be glad to have you go along. We can use you."

A long, slow sigh escaped Ted Wilkes's lips. He said hoarsely: "I thought you were going to turn me down. You ain't going to be sorry, boy . . . uh . . . Jeff."

"I know it, Mister Wilkes. Pay's thirty a month. No pay, if we don't get paid for the cattle. Grandpa says the Confederate army might just commandeer an' not pay us at all."

"I ain't goin' for the pay."

"No. Sure not. None of us is, I guess, although the money will pay a lot of taxes hereabouts."

Ted rode off into the darkness, humming softly to himself. Jeff watched him until he disappeared, then rode the edge of the herd, back and forth, singing softly to steady them.

At dawn the crew was up, eating in the kitchen by the light of homemade candles that sputtered and flickered as they burned. The crew finished hastily as they saw the gray at the windows and went outside.

The corral suddenly became a very busy place, with the hands standing just inside the gate, ropes in hand, waiting as the horses thundered around and around the fence. One after another of the ropes hissed out, each loop settling on a desired horse's head. The cowhands led their horses out of the corral, bridled and saddled, then swung astride.

The air was crisp and cool this morning, and stirrup leathers creaked as the men swung astride. And then the fun began. With few exceptions each horse, as it was mounted, bowed its neck, threw down its head, arched its back and began trying to unseat the rider that had climbed onto its back. The air was filled with sound of hoofs pounding the ground, of creaking leather, of the cowboys' shrill yells, of the slapping of hands on stiff leather chaps.

A cloud of dust was raised, nearly obscuring the bucking animals. Then, one by one, they stopped bucking and lined out, running toward the herd which was now up and beginning to graze. The bucking was a ritual the cowboys didn't even try to stop. It warmed the horses on cold mornings. It took the stiffness out of the men's muscles. It added a touch of excitement to the morning, a touch of excitement that everyone looked forward to.

Once the men reached the herd, they carefully and slowly cut out thirty or forty head, which they drove off to the north of the sprawling ranch house and the buildings that surrounded it. Night herders headed for the house, to get breakfast and a little sleep. Others hauled a wagonload of wood for the branding fires. Still others built fires, half a dozen of them in all, and put the branding irons in to heat.

Stamping irons were rarely used. Most branding stamps were of the kind called running irons with which a man could draw the brand of his particular spread. Today, all the running irons would be making a great, sprawling J D on the gaunt hips of the Texas longhorns here. The J D stood for Jefferson Davis, president of the Confederacy.

Jeff Hueston was with the men who were driving the small bunch toward the branding fires. So were Jack Littlefield and Mad. Jeff smiled faintly to himself. Boys and younger men invariably preferred the riding and roping to the more tedious, dustier work around the branding fires. They liked the excitement of it.

The older hands didn't care. Jeff saw both Sam Rhody and Ted Wilkes with the group at the branding fires.

Then he had his rope on the horns of a black and white spotted steer and was dragging him along toward one of the branding fires while Jack Littlefield, swinging a small, tight loop, made a throw for the steer's left hind foot. The steer felt the loop as he stepped into it and tried to shake it loose, but he was too late. Jack yanked it tight.

Jeff continued toward the nearest of the fires, rope dallied, dragging the bawling steer along behind his straining horse. When they were within a dozen yards of the fire, Jack's horse pulled back, stretching out the steer's rear leg, dumping the protesting animal to the ground.

Jeff lounged in his saddle, waiting patiently. A man ran from the branding fire, a smoking, red-hot iron in his hand. The steer tried to kick him, but he avoided the kicking rear foot with ease. He planted one boot firmly on the steer's back to steady the animal, then bent to apply the iron. A cloud of smoke rose, smoke from the burning hair. There was a sizzling sound as the iron burned through to the steer's thick hide. The man worked swiftly and efficiently, neither burning too shallowly nor too deeply. When he had finished, he straightened, spat, and walked back to the fire. He returned the iron to the fire to re-heat.

Jeff eased up on his rope, but Jack kept his tight so that the steer could not get up. Jeff tried to flip off the loop but could not because one of the steer's horns was dug into the ground. He dismounted quickly. Coiling the rope as he went, he hurried to the steer. The animal raised his head, eyes rolling, tongue lolling out. Jeff grinned and flipped off his loop. "You ain't hurt half as bad as you think you are," he said.

He returned to his horse and mounted. Jack slacked his rope and, when the steer struggled to his feet, flipped off the loop. The animal bawled once with outrage, then turned and trotted back to where the others were being held.

Jeff rode into the milling bunch and roped out another steer. Jack followed, flipping out a loop as he went.

Once more Jeff dragged the steer to one of the fires where he was branded and released. The morning slowly wore away. The sun climbed across a cloudless sky. Dust rose in blinding, choking clouds from the milling animals and men. The bunch of forty or fifty, branded, were driven off across the wide flat and another bunch cut from the milling, uneasily bawling herd. It would simplify the work if the branded cattle were held together in another place and not allowed to mingle again with the herds of unbranded animals.

Noon came and passed. The afternoon dragged away, with the work going more slowly now because of the aching weariness in the men. It was heavy work; it was dirty, dusty, sweaty work. Jeff changed horses half a dozen times. Jack changed almost that many times.

Sometimes the bunch being cut from the herd would break and run, and then the cowboys would have to pursue them, head them, and bring them back. Sometimes a single steer, seeing a rider coming after him, would break and run. And this one, too, would have to be pursued.

They did not quit until the sun was low over the western horizon. A few stayed with the small bunch that was already branded, numbering perhaps a hundred and thirty head. Still others stayed to hold the main herd, which was slowly drifting farther down the valley of the San Antonio River to better grass. The remainder gathered up their gear, killed their fires, and rode back to the Hueston ranch house half a dozen miles away.

IV

The following day was scarcely different from the last, except for the fact that, in late afternoon, Jeff, Jack, Mad, Miguel Ortiz, and Sam Rhody left the branding fires and the bawling cattle and the dust to ride back into the thicket to get the wild cattle from the corral where they had left them two days earlier. As he rode, Jeff Hueston grinned wryly to himself. He was excited, thinking of what lay ahead when the herd was branded and they started for New Orleans. He thought of his grandfather and of the things old Jake had said about him, and he felt warm once more with pride. Then he thought of what had been in the back of his mind ever since the idea of making this drive had been born.

Thinking of it made him ashamed, and, because he was ashamed, he became angry at himself and at his mother and his grandfather. Why should he feel ashamed just because he wanted to serve his country? His brothers were in the army of the Confederacy. He was old enough right now to join.

He was seventeen. The army took boys as soon as they turned sixteen.

His mother and grandfather might have a little trouble keeping the ranch going, but they'd make out all right, even if he was gone. They could hire somebody like Sam Rhody, or Ted Wilkes, men who were too old for the army, or who were crippled. They would get along.

Another chance like this might not come during his lifetime, Jeff thought resentfully. A man ought to be allowed to go off to war and fight without being made to feel guilty because he did. He examined his own feelings reluctantly and admitted his motives for wanting to go were mostly selfish ones. It was exhilarating to think of fighting in the war. It was no less exhilarating to think of wearing a handsome gray uniform with a wide-brimmed cavalry hat. When he thought of it, Jeff could see himself, riding a tall, spirited cavalry horse.

And his imagination put a lot more gold braid on that uniform than would ever be on it in reality. He grinned shamefacedly to himself. He was being a fool. He was indulging in daydreams. The truth was that there was probably nothing more romantic about soldiering than there was about cowboying. You could get killed or hurt doing either one. And both were dusty, sweaty, bloody businesses.

Fact was, Jeff didn't know for sure what he'd do when he got the cattle to New Orleans and sold them to the Confederate quartermaster there. He might enlist. He might come home. In the meantime he guessed he'd go on feeling guilty every time he thought about enlisting against his mother's wishes. He'd feel guilty every time he thought that doing so would be letting his grandfather down. Right now, though, there was this to do. There was today, and there was a herd to be gotten to New Orleans.

It was near sundown when they reached the corral out in the brush. The cattle stood listlessly, staring at them without much fear. Jeff leaned down and opened the gate, then swung it wide without dismounting from his horse. Jack and Mad rode inside, while Sam Rhody and Miguel positioned their horses on either side of the gate. Jeff turned around and rode back into the brush to release Red, the steer that had broken his cinch and dumped him two days ago.

Behind him, as he rode, he could hear the shrill, yipping cries as Jack and Mad urged the cattle out. He could hear the crashing sounds they made as they pushed

196

through the heavy brush and occasionally heard shouts from either Sam or Miguel as they sought to keep the little bunch heading the way they wanted them to head.

Jeff pushed harder, not wanting them to catch up with him before he reached and released Red. And then, suddenly, he saw the steer ahead of him.

Red was more subdued than when Jeff had seen him last. There was weariness about the way he stood. There was dejection in him, but there was still spirit, and there was a flash of wildness in the way he rolled his eyes. Jeff grinned. There was something indomitable about Red, something undefeated. It was the quality that had made Texas longhorns thrive and multiply in such a hot, unfriendly terrain as this brush country was.

He stared at the ground around the tree. It looked as though it had been plowed. There was no vegetation left on it. Only Red's hoofprints. He must have been moving almost constantly for the past two days.

Jeff dismounted a dozen feet from the steer. The animal faced him, head lowered truculently, but not pawing and not straining at the rope. Jeff approached cautiously.

The others were closer now. He could hear the cracking of brush and the yipping yells. He had not much time. And he wasn't sure Red would let him reach the liveoak tree to which he was tied.

Jeff feinted suddenly to the left. Red lunged that way. Jeff leaped instantly to the right, darted past the steer, and reached the safety of the tree.

Red charged at him half-heartedly. Jeff untied the rope. He waved his arms at Red and yelled. Puzzled, the steer turned and trotted a dozen yards away.

With the rope end still in his hand, Jeff sprinted for his horse. He swung into the saddle, wrapped the reins temporarily around the saddle horn, then began to coil the rope, meanwhile urging his horse closer to the steer by the guiding pressure of his knees. When he was only half a dozen feet away, he gave the rope a sudden flip, and the loop came off old Red's wide-spreading horns.

Now Jeff held his horse perfectly still, and the big steer also remained motionless. After several minutes the other cattle came into sight, and Jeff moved his horse aside and out of their way. Red joined the others sullenly and moved along in their midst through the brush. After a moment Jeff joined Sam Rhody on the left flank of the herd. Sam rode watchfully, weaving back and forth in his saddle to avoid the clawing branches of thorny brush, occasionally raising an arm to ward off a low-hanging branch. If the cattle tried to turn toward him, Sam would urge his horse on a little faster to head them off. If they started to turn the other way, he'd slow and drop back slightly to allow Miguel, on the other side, to do the same. And behind the little bunch, in the drag, Jack and Mad moved along steadily, seldom yipping now but occasionally whistling or slapping a chap with the end of a rein.

The sun was down and dusk beginning to creep across the baking land when they came out of the thicket and headed across the plain toward the San Antonio River in the hazy distance. And just at dark they pushed the bunch into the unbranded portion of the herd, being held not far away from the ranch. Silently now, and wearily, they headed for the ranch. Ten minutes after reaching it, they were in their bunks and sound asleep.

Jeff did not help with the branding on the following day. He drove into Goliad with his grandfather to lay in the supplies they would need for the drive to New Orleans. Money came first, Confederate currency, and there was not much of this, but his grandfather withdrew all there was in the little bank in Goliad. After that, they went to the mercantile store and loaded the wagon with barrels of flour and sugar, with coffee, salt, gunpowder and lead for bullets, and a gun for Jeff.

It was the first gun he had ever owned, and, while it was not new, it was in good working order. It was a Colt 1849 Pocket Pistol, having a three-inch octagon barrel and a silver-plated guard. With it there was a powder flask and a small pouch containing percussion caps and another pouch with bullets. There was also a bullet mold. The storekeeper showed Jeff how to load the gun while his grandfather picked out a belt and a holster in which he could carry it.

Wearing it, Jeff stepped out into the dusty street. He felt about ten feet tall with the gun strapped around his waist.

His grandfather came out of the store behind him and stood looking at him quizzically. "Makes you feel big, doesn't it?"

Jeff grinned shamefacedly, and nodded.

His grandfather said: "It's a tool, nothing more, nothing less. It doesn't make you anything you weren't before you put it on. If you'll remember that, you'll get along fine with it."

Jeff nodded. "Yes, sir. I'll remember."

"Good. Then let's get back to the ranch and rig up a chuck wagon for your crew."

They climbed to the wagon seat. Jeff picked up the reins and drove. He could feel the weight of the belt and holstered gun. He could also feel the weight of responsibility it had put on him. He was somehow sobered today and felt older than he had yesterday.

Half way back to the ranch he turned to his grandfather and said: "I've been thinking that maybe, when I get to New Orleans, I'll join up."

He was surprised when his grandfather agreed. "I knew you had that in mind."

Jeff waited and finally asked: "Aren't you going to tell me that I can't?"

"Nope." His grandfather shook his head, staring straight ahead at the team. "You're seventeen. That's almost a man. Time you get this herd to New Orleans, you'll be a man. A man can decide things for himself."

"How about the ranch?"

His grandfather shrugged. "Your ma an' me'll get by all right. Your ma'll be a mite upset, I expect, havin' all three of her sons fightin' in the war. Was all of you to get kilt, I reckon she'd not get over it."

Jeff scowled.

His grandfather glanced at him. "Reckon mebbe you think sayin' that ain't fair. And mebbe it ain't, I just don't know. But it had to be said. It's the truth. It's one of the facts. And a man has to look at all the facts when he's decidin' something."

Thoughtful, Jeff remained silent all the way back to the ranch. He guessed being a man had disadvantages as well as advantages. You didn't have someone telling you what to do and what not to do, but you still couldn't do what you wanted to do, no matter what. There were consequences to consider. There were other people you had to think of, whether you wanted to or not.

Arriving back at the ranch, Jeff's grandfather had him drive the wagon up next to an old two-wheeled Mexican cart that sat behind the adobe barn. He said: "Here's your chuck wagon, Jeff. This old two-wheeled rig'll do you better'n a wagon would. And when you get where you're goin', you can just leave it there."

Jeff stared at the old *carreta* with dismay. Then he got down and began to unload the wagon into it. His grandfather helped him with the heavy barrels and afterward went around the *carreta,* examining the wheels, the axle, the hubs, the tongue, and single-trees. He said: "Drive the wagon over to the smokehouse, Jeff, and load up on lard an' sidemeat an' such. Whilst you're doin' that, I'll get the forge goin' an' do a little fixin' on this chuck wagon here."

Jeff climbed to the wagon seat and drove the team over to the smokehouse where he loaded up the things his grandfather had indicated. He drove back and unloaded the supplies into the cart. He could hear his grandfather in the barn, shoveling charcoal into the forge, working the bellows to get it going. Having unloaded the wagon, he drove it to its accustomed place beside the barn and unhitched the teams. He drove them into the barn, walking behind them, and, when he got there, unharnessed the horses and led them to water in the corral out back. After that he brought them in again, gave them a feed of grain and a little hay.

He could smell the smoke from the forge, and could hear his grandfather hammering on the anvil as he shaped a piece of iron. Jeff went back to the *carreta* and stared at it.

They'd need water barrels, one on each side. He returned to the smokehouse and found two oak barrels with covers that would hold water. He carried them back, one by one, and found a place where they would fit, one on each side of the huge old cart. He put them in place, then found some strips of rawhide which he soaked before using them to bind the barrels securely in place. He knew, when the rawhide dried the barrels wouldn't move until the rawhide was cut.

A cover was needed for the *carreta* now, he realized. The bows were still intact and strong enough, though they were weathered gray and cracked from sun and rain. There wasn't enough canvas here on the ranch, and they couldn't afford to buy it in town. He'd have to use hides, he realized. A rawhide cover would shed water and would outlast canvas. He went to the pile of hides over by the slaughterhouse and selected three.

He soaked them in the overflow from the water trough in the corral and found that the hair slipped out easily. He cut rawhide strips from them to sew them together with, then laid them over the *carreta*'s arched bows, where he trimmed them and squared them so that they would fit. Working laboriously with awl and narrow rawhide strips, he sewed them together tightly so that no water could leak through. He was careful to leave enough slack in the hides so that, when they shrank from drying, they would not pull loose or crack the wagon bows. He worked steadily all the rest of the day, while his grandfather came and went between the cart and his forge, shaping pieces of iron, fitting them in place. At nightfall the cart had been completely covered and repaired.

Jeff's grandfather let his forge die down and stood, staring at the cart. He said: "To-morrow we'll build Miguel a box for his dishes and his gear. We'll put a hinged front on it that'll drop down an' give him a table to work on whilst he cooks." He grinned at Jeff. "Get yourself a horse an' go see how the brandin's goin'. I got a hunch you'll be startin' out about day after tomorrow."

Jeff hurried to the corral for a horse. He was tired from all the heavy work he had done that day, but he was also still more excited than he had ever been.

V

When Jeff Hueston reached the herd, he discovered that his grandfather had been right. There now remained less than a hundred head to be trail branded for the drive. Tomorrow would see the completion of the job.

He returned to the house wearily, almost too tired tonight to eat. But he forced himself to do so, knowing food would make him feel better and would give him strength. After that, he took a bath in an oak tub in the middle of the kitchen floor to wash the stinking odor of rawhide off.

He literally fell onto his bed upstairs and did not awake until he heard his grandfather yell up the stairs at him just before dawn on the following day. He groaned, but he swung his feet over the edge of the bed and sat up straight.

He could not recall ever having been this tired. He grinned wearily to himself. He'd be a lot more tired before they got that herd to New Orleans, so he might as well start getting used to it. Today should be a little easier, though. He and his grandfather were going to build a grub box for the chuck wagon while the others finished branding. Both his grandfather and himself, and the others, should be finished by noon or at the latest by early afternoon. They could then lie around and rest the remainder of the day. They could turn in early so as to get an early start on the following day.

He dressed swiftly, feeling rising excitement again. He could hardly wait until this day would be over with and the drive begun. He hoped nothing would go wrong, that nothing would delay their start.

He hurried downstairs. His mother and grandmother had apparently been up and busy for some time. There was a roaring fire in the stove. Breakfast was cooking on it, beef steak, pork sidemeat, potatoes.

The men were noisier today than they had been before. There was an excitement in them all, a new, boisterous hilarity. The end of the job was near for most of them. But for a few the beginning of another, bigger job was close at hand.

With breakfast over they trooped, yelling, from the house. They caught up their horses, mounted, and rode out the bucking before they lined the horses out for the herd.

Jeff and his grandfather went into the blacksmith shop.

From a pile of used lumber Jeff selected a number of rough-sawed boards. Old Jake got hammer, saw, an augur, and wooden pegs and began to build the grub box to go on the back of the *carreta*.

Once breakfast was over, Jeff's mother gathered up all the metal dishes on the ranch and enough pots and pans for Miguel to cook for a trail crew. She brought them out to the *carreta* and put them beside it on the ground.

Jeff helped his grandfather in every way he could, but he was no carpenter. Therefore, whenever he was unable to help, he watched carefully the things his grandfather did. A man ought to be handy with tools, his grandfather had always said. A man ought to be able to do all the things that needed doing on a ranch. By watching, Jeff could learn.

In late morning the box was finished and installed. Jeff put in the metal dishes, pots and pans, the lard, the salt, and pepper. He put up the cover and turned in time to see a huge cloud of dust, approaching from the direction of the herd. His first startled thought was *stampede*. Then he saw that the dust was being raised by galloping, yelling horsemen, and he knew that they were through. The trail branding was finished. The herd was ready to go to New Orleans.

The excited crew rode into the yard. They clustered around Jeff, slapping him on the back, telling him: "Boy, it's up to you now. It's up to you to see them critters get to Jeff Davis in good shape."

Jeff grinned embarrassedly, nodding. "They'll get there all right. We'll get 'em there if we have to carry 'em."

They bellowed with laughter at that, but there was approval in their eyes.

Jeff's mother beat on the triangle to announce dinner, and they trooped in for it. The air was rich with the smell of fried chicken. Jeff looked at his mother affectionately. She had done her part all along, but now she had done more. She had prepared a regular feast for them. He ate ravenously and after dinner went outside with the men. Those who were sending cattle along with the herd showed him their tally sheets on which their cattle had been counted. They gave him bills-of-sale so that he could legally dispose of them in New Orleans.

Jeff's grandfather brought him his own saddlebags and gave them to him so that he could carry his money and papers safely.

Somehow the afternoon passed, and the

evening. Jeff laid awake a long, long time that night, staring into the blackness of his room. This was the biggest thing that had ever happened to him, maybe the biggest thing that would ever happen to him. He told himself determinedly that he was not going to fail. He was going to get those cattle through to New Orleans. And yet, when he thought of the obstacles — the miles of thicket — the rivers, the Mississippi. . . . Men would try and take the cattle away from them, outlaws that roamed this huge and sparsely settled land. Even if he delivered and sold the cattle, he'd still have to get home with the money.

He slept at last, but it was not an easy sleep. He dreamed that outlaws hijacked the herd, killed all his drovers, and left him for dead, while they drove the herd away. He awoke in a clammy sweat.

Hearing someone moving downstairs, he realized it was time, and he jumped eagerly out of bed. He hurried down.

Breakfast was almost ready. While he was waiting, he went outside, caught himself a horse, and saddled it. He led it back to the house, tied it, and went inside to eat.

Both his mother and grandfather were silent this morning, watching him with worry and concern in their eyes. Each time he caught one of them glancing at him, he would smile reassuringly. But he was growing ever more nervous himself, and he was glad when breakfast was over and he could go outside.

Miguel Ortiz, Jack Littlefield, Madison Quinn, Rhody, and Wilkes clustered around him. He said, trying to make his voice sound as though he was a lot more sure of himself than he really was: "Miguel, the *carreta* is all fixed up as a chuck wagon. I think it's got everything loaded into it that you'll need except for fresh beef. Get a team harnessed to it and start out as soon as you're ready."

Miguel moved away into the early morning darkness. Jeff continued: "Mad, the remuda is your job. I want each man to pick himself five horses out of the bunch in the corral. Turn 'em out. Mad, you bunch 'em an' head 'em north. Stay about half a mile off to the right of the chuck wagon."

Madison Quinn nodded, his expression unreadable in the near darkness. Jeff said: "Mister Rhody, I reckon you know the country ahead of us better'n anybody here. I'd like you to ride point. I'll take the swing and flank. Jack, you'll be drag. We'll keep 'em closed up tight for the first few days. They're still plenty wild, and they'll run for the thicket, if we give 'em half a chance."

He swung onto the back of his horse. He followed the others to the corral. They waited for him to pick his horses, since he was to boss the drive. After that, Rhody picked his horse since he held the choice position, that of point. He would ride ahead of the herd, choosing the route, responsible for finding the safest, easiest one.

Wilkes picked his horses next, since he rode swing on the other side of the herd from Jeff. These two positions were perhaps hardest of all, requiring the most riding back and forth to see that none of the cattle strayed away from the herd. The two swing riders were also responsible for seeing to it that the herd was kept moving at the desired pace. They would wear out more horses in any given day than the others would.

Jack Littlefield picked his five horses, after Wilkes had finished, and cut them out of the corral. Madison Quinn picked his five last, cutting them out, also cutting out an extra team for the chuck wagon and a couple of saddle horses for Miguel because he would stand night guard right along with the rest of them.

When all the horses had been cut out and when everyone had saddled up, Mad rode off to bunch the horses and push them north. Jeff led the three drovers toward the herd.

The men who had been night herding the cattle helped Jeff and his three drovers get them started north. Jeff's grandfather rode out to watch from a nearby knoll, and Jeff's mother drove the buggy out to watch from the same low knoll.

Jeff stood in his stirrups and stared ahead at Sam. He waved an arm and bawled: "All right, start 'em out! Let's go to Noo Orleans!"

They picked up his yell and threw it back enthusiastically. And the herd began to move, crowding, bawling, their great, widespreading horns crashing together, their great hoofs raising a towering cloud of dust.

Slowly north crawled the herd, north and a little east. And, though, he was too busy for much in the way of thinking, an uneasy fear began to grow in Jeff Hueston's mind. It was fear of the river, the great river, the Mississippi. More than a mile wide it would be, where they encountered it. He had talked to his grandfather about the river, and he remembered his brothers' description of it in the letters they had written home.

Were there steamships and ferries that would carry eight hundred wild Texas cattle across? And, even if there were, was it possible to get these wild cattle to go aboard? Jeff doubted it. He doubted if they could be forced near a dock, let alone onto a steamer's deck. Even if they could be forced aboard, what would keep them there? They could sail over a steamer's railings like deer going over a fence.

Perhaps the only way was to swim the herd across. If they could be forced into it . . . ! There was some doubt that they could.

He shook his head impatiently as he raced along the flank of the herd to turn back half a dozen steers apparently bent on making for a small thicket of brush nearby. He had too much to worry about right now to worry more about how they were going to get across the Mississippi River. Maybe they wouldn't even have to go across. Maybe they'd find a Confederate quartermaster on the western bank of the river who would take the herd off their hands. Besides, more than three hundred miles still separated them from the banks of the Mississippi. A lot could happen in those three hundred miles.

He reached the bunch trying to quit the herd and saw that one of them was old Red. "Looks like learnin' comes hard to you, Red. Looks like you didn't learn your lessons too good last time I tangled up with you." Jeff muttered this to himself as he took down his rope and shook out a loop.

The little bunch of cattle was trotting now, heading straight for the thicket of brush. Jeff raced around to head them, waving an arm and yelling at them. All but Red stopped and rolled their eyes warily at Jeff. Only Red kept going, and, seeing him moving ahead in spite of Jeff, the others followed suit.

Jeff raked his horse with the spurs. He whirled the rope around his head once, then threw it out as he came in range of the red roan steer. Again he felt that terrific shock as the steer's eight hundred pounds of galloping fury hit the end of the rope. But this time Jeff's cinch held. The horse stood the shock well, having braced himself, but he did take a couple of steps to regain his balance.

Jeff rode the horse up close to the steer, but he did not shake off the loop. He waited until the steer got up, leaving the rope dallied to the saddle horn. The other cattle, seeing what had happened to Red, now trotted back and lost themselves in the herd. Jeff grinned down at the rebellious steer. "All right, Red. Let's find out who's boss right here and now. Let's get it over with."

As though understanding his words, the steer lowered his head belligerently and pawed the ground. Jeff eased his horse around between the steer and the thicket and waved an arm. "Get on back there, you pig-headed longhorn! Or do I have to dump you again?"

As though he understood, the steer ducked past Jeff's horse and headed for the thicket at a head-down run. Jeff pulled back on his reins, and once more his horse braced all four feet. Red snapped the rope taut and crashed to the ground again.

Coiling the rope as he rode, Jeff rode to him and waved his arms again. The steer had had enough. Switching his great long tail, he trotted toward the herd. Jeff slacked his rope and flipped off the loop around his horns. Red had disappeared into the herd.

Jeff grinned to himself as he rode up the flank of the slowly-moving cattle. Red might not have learned all he had to learn, but he sure had made a start.

VI

Miguel Ortiz sat up on the seat of the *carreta,* driving the team of heavy work horses pulling it, staying well out to one side of the slowly moving herd. Cook for the trail drivers was a position of great responsibility for Miguel, who had never had a position of responsibility before. Always in the past someone had told him: "Miguel, do this," or "Miguel, do that," and, if he did not know how to do the particular thing he had been ordered to do, he would be shown. This was very different. He was responsible for driving the chuck wagon, or cart, to the place of camping where he would build a fire and prepare a meal for the five others who were bringing the herd along behind.

At first, driving ahead and setting up camp was a fairly simple business, since both Miguel and Sam Rhody were familiar with the country ahead, and Sam would only say: "We'll camp at Arroyo Conejos, Miguel," and Miguel would know exactly where that was. But as the drive progressed, as they passed beyond country that was familiar to them both, deciding where to camp began to present problems for Miguel.

Sam Rhody explained it to him patiently: "We drive about twelve miles a day, Miguel. I'll give you a heading around noon every day, and you go around five or six miles beyond, depending on how far we've already driven by the time noon comes. We'll need water at the camp site or near it for the cattle, and it ought to be a place where the brush is not too thick and where there is some grass. You can't hold cattle on a bare bed-ground, and it's hard to hold 'em dry."

"*Sí, señor.*" Miguel grinned widely at Sam, and Sam couldn't help grinning back.

And so at noon Miguel would whip his horses into a trot and go on ahead, the great clumsy *carreta* squeaking along ponderously, with pots and metal dishes rattling around inside the box where some of them were hung on nails and, therefore, free to bang against the box's sides with each lurch the chuck wagon took.

Miguel had solved the problem of how to figure distance. At noon he would ask Sam: "How far I go today, *señor?*"

Sam would say: "Five miles, Miguel. I figure we made better'n seven since we started out."

Miguel would drive away, watching a rag

tied to one of the spokes on the *carreta*'s left wheel. Miguel could count to a hundred in Spanish. He would count a hundred revolutions of the wheel, then drop a pebble into a lard pail hung behind the seat. A pebble represented a hundred revolutions of the wheel. A hundred revolutions was approximately a quarter of a mile. Jeff Hueston had told him that. Four pebbles, then, to the mile. For five miles, twenty pebbles. When there were twenty in the pail, Miguel would begin looking for a suitable place to camp.

Having found it, a place where, preferably, there was water both for the cattle and for the men, Miguel would unhitch and tie his team to a clump of mesquite. Being heavy, the tongue of the cart kept it from tipping up backwards.

Next, Miguel would gather wood and chop it into the right lengths for the cook fire. He would build a fire, having first piled rocks around it on which he could place his skillets and Dutch oven, or, if there were no rocks of the right size in the vicinity, he would rig a pole over the fire from which his pots could be suspended above the coals.

Having built the fire, he would open the grub box Jeff and his grandfather had built. He would get out his huge pan of sourdough, in which some sourdough from the previous day remained. He would add to this and would set it aside to permit the dough to rise.

Next he would get out a quarter of beef, which was always hung out in the air at night and wrapped during the day to keep it cool. From this he would cut chunks, which he would throw into a big cast-iron pot to cook. Sometimes he would add onions or potatoes, since he had a sack of each in the chuck wagon that they'd brought from the Hueston ranch. But not always. He did not know if they'd find farms ahead where they could buy more onions and potatoes, and he planned to make what they had brought with them last.

Coffee came next, made by bringing a huge graniteware coffee pot full of water to a boil, then throwing in a handful of coarsely ground beans that had been parched and browned over the coals of a fire. It was a substitute for coffee that none of them liked particularly, but then real coffee had been almost impossible to get in Texas since the first year of the war. Or, perhaps, Miguel would have put a pot of beans to soak in the morning before starting out. Now he might add more water and put them on the fire to cook for the remainder of the day.

With these things done, there would be

time for Miguel to leave the chuck wagon and cut more wood. Or he might go hunting, if there were signs of game in the neighborhood, being careful always that a mile or two separated him from the herd of longhorns when he fired his big smooth-bore shotgun at a rabbit, at a wild pig, or at a deer. If his hunting was successful, then next day there would be a change from boiled beef and beans.

Long before sundown the herd would approach, its peculiar sound audible from half a mile away. The sound was a strange one, thought Miguel sometimes, a kind of low rumble or thunder in the ground. And in the air there would be another, different kind of rumble, this composed of the mingled bawlings of several hundred cattle, the clashing together of their horns, the crashing sounds they made going through scattered clumps of mesquite or catclaw or other brush.

Sam Rhody would select a bed ground for the night, one that was neither too far nor too close to Miguel's camp. Two men would remain with the herd while the others came in to eat. The horses would be watered, then placed in a rope corral formed by stringing a single rope chest high in a circle, tied to and held up by whatever brush was in the neighborhood. The horses could easily have broken out of this rope corral, but they never did. They seemed to have an unspoken understanding with the men that this rope, for all its flimsiness, was a tight "fence" that they could not break through.

Now, three of the trail crew would eat. As soon as they had finished, two of them would ride out to relieve the guards that had remained with the herd. The guards would eat. They might sit around and talk for a little while. Usually, however, they were just too tired for talk. They would get their bedrolls out of the chuck wagon and lie down on the ground, keeping their horses saddled and tied nearby, so that they could get them immediately, if any need arose during the night.

These men would sleep approximately half the night. They would then relieve the night guards on the herd and would remain with the herd until they were relieved to eat breakfast at daybreak. Miguel, having fed all the drovers, would wash up his dishes and pots, if water was available. If it was not, he would scour his pots with dry sand until they were clean. He would usually mix more sourdough to raise during the night. He might put on another pot of meat or beans to simmer over the coals of the fire throughout the night. Then he, too, would roll up in his blankets and go to sleep.

Miguel was awake at dawn or a little before, while the sky was still dark. Once again, he would build a fire and begin the preparations for breakfast. Then he would call the men. "Rise and shine, *señores*. Rise and shine, and we will go to New Orleans." And, no matter how many times they had heard Miguel call them in exactly this way before, they would get out of their bedrolls, grinning at the peculiar inflections Miguel's Spanish accent gave the words.

They crossed the Guadalupe River near Clinton, getting their first taste here of what would happen repeatedly during the coming weeks each time they reached the bank of some sluggish stream. The water was not particularly high since it was in the fall of the year, but there had been enough heavy rains farther north along its course to fill the river bed with muddy water so that the cattle had to swim.

While they were yet half a mile from the river, Sam Rhody left the point briefly and joined Jeff Hueston on the flank. "We got a better chance of gettin' 'em to take to the water if we bunch 'em fairly tight and push 'em pretty hard, so's they're movin' at a good clip when they come to the river bank. The lead steers'll be shoved into the water by them behind afore they rightly know what's happenin', an' once in the water it'll jest plain be easier to swim on acrost than to turn around an' try goin' back."

Jeff nodded. "I'll drop back to the drag and tell Jack to keep 'em bunched an' moving fast. You go around on the other side and tell Mister Wilkes."

Sam Rhody nodded, then wheeled his horse, and galloped again to the point position. From there he eased back on the other side until he reached Ted Wilkes. After that he returned to the point, dropping back a little behind the half dozen steers leading the herd so that he could drive them along and thus set the pace for the others farther back.

Slowly, ponderously, the herd began to pick up speed. Both Jeff and Ted Wilkes rode like demons, covering both swing and flank positions, pushing the cattle in closer and urging them along. By the time Sam Rhody finally dropped down the cutbank into the brushy bottom of the Guadalupe, the herd had been formed into a great, ponderous wedge, at the point of which was Sam.

Standing in his stirrups, waving his arms

wildly, Sam yelled like a maniac. The lead steers hesitated on the river bank, with Sam crowding them mercilessly from behind. At last, to Sam's great relief, a steer plunged in with a great splash. Another followed, and a third. And then all those ahead of Sam were in and swimming toward the far bank, with only their horns and upper part of their heads showing above the turgid, muddy water.

Sam's horse tried to balk at the bank, but a touch of Sam's spurs changed his mind. He plunged in after the steers.

And now the herd came on behind, closely bunched so that no animal saw the water until it was right in front of him. One by one they plunged in and swam, and, back where Jeff and Wilkes and Jack Littlefield were, a shout of triumph rose. Then Jack, the drag rider, was in the water, too, and after him, Mad, and the remuda, while Miguel and the chuck wagon waited on the western side until all the cattle and horses would be across.

Now, as all the drovers knew, it was vital to keep the cattle closed up, headed straight toward the far bank. If open water appeared between the leaders and those behind, there was a chance some of the steers would turn, thus beginning a milling movement among the swimming cattle. A milling herd in the water was a nightmare for cattle drovers. It meant taking a horse into the midst of them, risking being impaled on one of their sharp horns, or, worse, being dragged beneath the surface to drown because it would be impossible to swim under such conditions or to reach the surface again and breathe. It meant herding them in the water, turning them, heading them straight for the opposite bank once more. More often than not a milling herd would return to the bank from which it had started out. And once a herd has refused to cross a river, it is almost impossible to get the cattle to enter a river again.

Fortunately this herd did not begin to mill but continued swimming until the leaders reached the eastern bank of the Guadalupe and came plunging up out of the water like prehistoric creatures of the deep. The horses followed, and, while Mad stayed with the horses and Jack and Ted Wilkes stayed with the dripping steers, Jeff Hueston and Sam Rhody put their horses into the river once more to return to where Miguel waited with the *carreta* on the western bank.

They got axes out of it and cut two sections of log from dead trees in the river bottom. Using ropes dallied to their saddle horns, they dragged these to where the chuck wagon was. Laboriously they lifted the logs and lashed them, one on each side of the *carreta* with rope and with rawhide strips. Then they mounted and watched, while Miguel drove his team into the river and began the trip across.

The cart settled deeply into the water, but it floated and gradually began to move across. Flour and other provisions that the water would spoil had been piled high on the rawhide cover and lashed down there. Even so, the water was perilously close to them.

Eventually the chuck wagon reached the eastern bank, and the straining horses pulled it up onto dry land. Here, Jeff told the men they would make camp for the night, news everyone was glad to hear. They built fires and began to dry their dripping clothes.

It was almost dark when the stranger appeared, riding out of the dusky grayness in the east. He rode straight to the largest of the fires and sat his horse, looking down at Sam Rhody and Jeff. He asked: "Who's the trail boss, men?"

Sam gestured with his head at Jeff. The stranger glanced at Jeff with some surprise — surprise he didn't express. He asked, his voice hoarse and gravelly: "Mind if I git down, ramrod?"

Jeff said: "Nope. Get down and eat."

The stranger dismounted, and Jeff watched him carefully as he did. The man was about twenty-five, Jeff guessed, of medium height but muscular and strong. He had the quick movements of a cat, and there was a certain wariness about the way he moved that also reminded Jeff of a cat. The man accepted a tin plate from Miguel and squatted on his heels to eat. Between mouthfuls he said: "Name's Cliff Wasson, men. I'm a good hand with cattle, if you're needin' hands, and I'll work pretty doggoned cheap."

Jack Littlefield, watching from the shadows, said: "There's jobs for able-bodied men your age in the army of the Confederacy, mister. How come you haven't taken one of them jobs yet?"

The man glanced at Jack, his eyes narrowing. "That's a fair question, I reckon. Happens I want to do just that, but I want in the fightin', not in some Texas garrison that'll never see a bluecoat or hear a shot. I figure to go east to New Orleans or Vicksburg or some place an' enlist back there. That way, I'll get put in some outfit that'll be in the thick of it."

The answer seemed reasonable to Jeff, and it stopped Jack Littlefield's protest. Only Sam Rhody's expression of suspicion did not change. Jeff looked around at Jack, remembering the way he had protested the hiring of Sam and Ted, then he looked back at Wasson, neither liking nor disliking the man. He said: "Pay's thirty a month when we deliver the herd. If we don't get paid, you don't get paid."

Wasson nodded eagerly. "You got another hand, ramrod."

Jack left the fire, grumbling. Sam stared at the stranger as though trying to see what was going on inside his head. Jeff felt a touch of uneasiness and admitted to himself that he didn't trust Wasson any more than the others did. But he did need hands. He needed all the hands he could get if he expected to deliver this herd to New Orleans. They'd been lucky crossing the Guadalupe. If trouble had developed, they'd have been able to use an extra man — or half a dozen extra men.

He shrugged as he went to the chuck wagon to get his blanket roll. He'd hired Wasson, and that was that. If he had trouble with the man, he'd simply fire him. Unconsciously his hand touched the revolver in its holster at his side.

VII

They drove toward the Colorado River and crossed it near Columbus without incident. They bedded the cattle on the far side since it was already mid-afternoon.

Clouds had been piling up in the east all during the day, great, puffy thunderheads that marched like gigantic sentinels across the sky. As evening approached, Jeff began to hear low rumblings in the distance, the rumblings of thunder in those distant clouds, and occasionally he would see lightning strike down through one of them toward the ground beneath. Something in the air made the cattle roll their eyes, bawl nervously, and switch their great, long tails. Miguel cooked supper silently, often glancing uneasily in the direction of the herd.

Jeff and the others ate swiftly. They did not need to be told there was danger in the atmosphere tonight. Those approaching thunderheads told them that. So did the way the cattle stood, or lay on the ground, not relaxed and easy but tense, as though ready to spring up and run, as though terrified of the night, and the coming rain, and the distant rumblings of thunder along the horizon where the lightning was.

Jeff finished eating, then went out to relieve someone who had stayed with the herd. Before leaving, he told the others: "No sleep tonight until we see what those clouds are going to do. Quick as you've eaten, I want every man out there with the herd. You too, Miguel, soon's you get your gear cleaned up and put away."

"*Sí, señor.*" Miguel began moving about hurriedly, washing dishes and stowing them away. He put more water into the coffee pot and threw in another handful of dried, roasted beans that had been ground as a coffee substitute.

Jeff rode slowly toward the uneasily stirring herd. He had never experienced a cattle stampede, but he had heard old-timers tell of them. He had heard of the static electricity, called St. Elmo's fire on the sea, that in an electrical storm would form at the tips of the cattle's horns like dim, blue lamps, burning there. He had heard of the small things known to have set off stampedes, a sudden sneeze by one of the night herders, a shout, a shot, the unexpected striking of a match, even a tumbleweed blowing suddenly in among the bedded herd.

He looked around him now at this unfamiliar country. He had no idea what lay to the east, since there had been no scouting done after the river was forded this afternoon. But he felt sure it was not much different from the land on the west bank of the stream. It would be slightly rolling and would be cut with arroyos, deep dry washouts into which a man and horse could fall, never knowing the danger was there until it was too late. There would be prairie dog colonies where a horse could break a leg by sticking it into a prairie dog hole, perhaps killing or injuring the rider when he fell. There would be the ever-present brush. . . .

As he approached the cattle, he began singing softly to himself so that they would hear him coming, so that he wouldn't startle them. A shape loomed up ahead, the shape of a man on horseback. Jeff recognized him as the new man and said: "Go in and eat, Cliff, then come back here with the herd. That thunderstorm's heading toward us, and the cattle are edgy anyway. We may all have to spend the night with them."

"Sure, ramrod. Give me fifteen minutes to stuff some grub down my gullet, and I'll be back." The man rode away.

Jeff, still singing softly, frowned to himself. Wasson seemed almost like the atmosphere tonight, he thought. Tense. Uneasy. Strange. His voice had possessed a peculiar quality Jeff had never noticed in it before, a quality he could only define as suppressed excitement. As though Wasson knew something was going to happen tonight. As though the knowledge excited him.

He rode north along the edge of the herd, picking his way carefully, singing softly.

**Oh Susanna, oh don't you cry for me,
For I'm goin' to Louisiana
with my banjo on my knee. . . .**

Another shape loomed up ahead, and this was Sam Rhody. Sam halted his horse and said in a hoarse whisper: "Easy does it tonight, Jeff. Easy does it. All they're waitin' fer is an excuse."

"What do we do if they run, Sam? I've never been in a stampede."

"Run with 'em, Jeff. You run with 'em an' try to head 'em off. You try not to get directly in front of 'em because, if you do an' your horse should fall, you'd be pulp by the time the others came back to pick you up."

"And what if we can't head 'em off?"

"Then they run 'til all the spookiness's run out of 'em. And we gather 'em up the best way we can."

Jeff nodded. He sat there in the darkness for a moment, then turned, and rode slowly back in the direction he had come. A drop of rain stung his face. Lightning flashed, closer now, and after several moments thunder rolled ponderously across the sky. Jeff stared in the direction of camp, wishing the others were already here. The presence of men around the fringes of the herd might tend to calm the cattle down.

Jeff saw something familiar about a nearby steer, something familiar about the way his great horns curved. He recognized Red. He stopped singing for a moment in surprise, staring at the huge, ungainly animal. Red stood with his legs spread, head turned, flared nostrils sampling the wind off the approaching thunder clouds. Every muscle of the longhorn's body was tense, visibly so. Suddenly a faint blue light flared at the tip of one of his great, outspreading horns.

Jeff heard the others coming, and for the moment left the herd and rode to intercept them. There was growing tenseness now in Jeff, growing dread. It was as though he knew the cattle would stampede tonight, a premonition of disaster, perhaps of death.

Rain began to fall in great, enormous drops that kicked up little spurts of dust wherever they struck the ground. Jeff saw Miguel, Cliff Wasson, and Jack loom out of the darkness ahead of him and, when they reached him, said: "Keep singing to 'em and move slow and easy. No talking and for gosh sakes, if you have to cough, cover it up. It wouldn't take much to set 'em off tonight."

Rain was falling steadily now, and in minutes Jeff was soaked. Miguel and Jack Littlefield rode off together downwind, but Wasson rode the other way, going upwind, disappearing almost immediately into the darkness. Jeff himself rode straight back to the herd. Big Red had disappeared, probably upwind in the same direction Wasson had gone. That was the way he had been heading when Jeff had seen him last.

Lightning flashed almost directly overhead. An instant later thunder cracked, rolling ponderously across the sky.

There was another kind of thunder, too, a more ominous kind to the drovers trying to hold the herd. It was the sound of uneasiness in the eight hundred cattle they were holding here. It was the sound made by hundreds of cattle, coming to their feet, stirring, looking around. They needed a leader and a specific thing to make them run in a single, definite direction. At the moment they had only their fear, their dread of the lightning and of the thunder, rolling across the sky.

Jeff rode back and forth, singing a little louder now to be heard above the pound of rain, the rumble of thunder in the distance. He raised his face and looked up at the blackness of the sky, knowing that at any instant lightning might flash again, thunder roll again, and that the next time the cattle might not stand still.

From upwind, the sound came suddenly, sharply, unexpectedly. There was no mistaking it; there could be no doubt. It was a gunshot fired from Cliff Wasson's gun.

Why? thought Jeff in desperation, even as he saw the way the cattle all turned away from the shot, the way they surged into motion, not individually but simultaneously, as though the gunshot was a signal that had been pre-arranged, that they had all been waiting for.

Already Jeff's horse was running wildly, recklessly, as though even he had caught the contagion of excitement. Rain slashed into Jeff's face. Mud thrown up by the hoofs of the racing cattle pelted him.

Lightning flashed now at regular intervals, illuminating the blackness of the night, showing each time it flashed a fearsome sight — eight hundred cattle, maddened by fear, running as though the devil were pursuing them. Horns crashed together. Hoofs pounded the ground, creating a new and different kind of thunder, a steady kind, a hundred times more fearsome than the thunder in the sky.

Washouts loomed ahead. Jeff's horse sailed over two of them, and the sensation Jeff got as he did was the feel of flying through the air, of being suspended above the earth, with only the blackness of the sky around him and beneath. Ride with them, Sam Rhody had said, but not in front of them. Stay with them until there was a chance to turn them, to start them milling, to start them circling. Or, if a chance to start them milling never came, then at least the drovers would be with them when they stopped, when they finally lost the will to run, when their excitement died in weariness.

Jeff wondered where the others were, where the new man, Cliff Wasson, was. He wondered why Wasson had fired his gun. There seemed to be no answer to that puzzling question. There could have been no good reason for Wasson to fire his gun. Either it had been an accident, or Wasson had deliberately started this stampede. But why? Why would a man want to do such an awful thing, unless Wasson expected to profit from what he had done?

It must have been an accident, thought Jeff. *It could not have been deliberate.* He wouldn't think that of any man. Yet, even while his mind cleared Cliff Wasson of guilt for starting the stampede, he could not help remembering the way Wasson had been earlier tonight, filled with suppressed excitement as though he *knew* the cattle were going to stampede.

Then Jeff was forced to stop thinking about it. All his attention was needed just to stay on his horse, just to guide the horse along the fringes of the stampeding herd. He was filled with terror as he thought of the things that lay ahead. He was filled with fear for the other men, and he wondered if any of them had yet been caught by the stampeding herd, if any of them lay back there in the mud, pounded by a thousand hoofs into it until they were no longer recognizable as men.

Again the lightning flashed, and now, in its flashing, Jeff looked around for the other men. One was ahead of him, riding a horse, racing as fast and as recklessly as Jeff's horse was. During another flash of lightning he turned his head, looked behind, and thought he saw another man back there. Wasson? The impulse to draw his horse in enough to let the man catch up was strong in Jeff, but he successfully resisted it. How the stampede had started didn't matter now. What was important was getting it stopped before any of the men were killed.

Suddenly a void opened up in front of Jeff. His horse tried to stop when he saw how impossible it was to jump. He skidded to the lip of the wide arroyo. Then, seeing he could not stop, he made a belated effort to jump. Out into the center of the arroyo he sailed only to fall into it, to plunge into the torrent of muddy water running four feet deep in the bottom of the normally dry wash.

The icy, muddy flood closed over Jeff's head as he was flung from the saddle by the horse's tumbling motion when he fell. But he held onto the reins as though to a lifeline that would save him, if he could but cling determinedly enough to it.

He was fighting now for life, for air, for breath to fill his lungs. He was struggling upward through the icy current, battered against his horse's body, raked by the sharp, curving horns of a frantic steer, kicked by the hoofs of another as it plunged in almost on top of him.

It seemed like an eternity to Jeff that he and his horse fought the water, trying to escape from it. Then they were across, and Jeff's horse was fighting up the other side, dragging him behind, more drowned than not, coughing and spitting and gagging on the water he had swallowed as he fought frantically for breath.

All around him steers were fighting their way out similarly, to go on stampeding across the ink-black plain, but half-heartedly now, as though the icy plunge had cooled their excitement and their fright.

Jeff stayed on hands and knees a moment, his hand still clinging desperately to the soggy reins. He coughed until he thought he would never stop.

At last, though, he was able to breathe normally again. He got to his feet, realizing the cattle had all gone by, realizing, too, that both the thunder and the lightning had stopped at last. He got painfully to his feet, relieved to find that he could walk and move both arms. At least he had not broken any bones.

He led his horse forward several yards, watching to see if the animal limped, if he had broken any of his legs. Apparently the horse had not.

Jeff put a foot into the stirrup and stepped

astride. He reined the horse in the direction the herd had gone. He felt the heavy weight of discouragement and defeat. He had come scarcely a hundred miles from home, and already he had failed. He had lost the herd. Then his eyes narrowed with determination, and his jaw grew firm. He touched spurs to his horse's sides and galloped along in the wake of the vanished herd. But even anger and determination could not keep him warm. He began to shiver violently.

VIII

Jeff rode dispiritedly through the early hours before the dawn, through muddy land and dripping brush, feeling more depressed than ever. Alternately he thought of his brothers, fighting for the Confederacy, of his grandfather and mother, depending on him to bring home the money the cattle brought to pay taxes that otherwise would go unpaid. He thought of Jack, and Mad, and Sam, and Ted, and Miguel, some or all of whom might be lying dead in the pounded wake of the stampeded herd.

He knew there was nothing he could do until it got light. All he could do now was ride along, following the wide trail, as the others would be doing if they were still alive and able to. Gradually, dawn began to lighten the eastern sky. It showed first as a faint gray above the horizon, the vaguest kind of differentiation between land and sky. Slowly the gray became lighter until the horizon was a clearly defined line, and not long after that objects around Jeff began to be visible, a clump of brush, a dry wash, a

242

puddle left over from the rain last night. He strained his eyes ahead, looking for cattle but mostly looking for horses and for men.

Last night's anger was growing again in him, anger at Wasson, who had fired the shot that had started the stampede. He didn't really care if Wasson had fired it intentionally, or if it had been an accident. Either way, it was inexcusable. Wasson had, deliberately or carelessly, risked men's lives and scattered the cattle so that days would be needed to gather them up again, if, indeed, it was even possible to find them all. His hand strayed to the holster at his side. He was both surprised and relieved to discover that his revolver was still there. He withdrew the gun and stared down at it, not knowing if it would fire or not. Probably not, he thought, after the soaking it must have had last night. And yet, it was possible that it would. He raised it in the air, thumbed the hammer back, and pulled the trigger.

The shot was flat and sharp, but it seemed lost in the vast expanse of the Texas plain. Jeff halted his horse that had jumped, then broken into a gallop immediately after he fired the gun. He listened intently but heard only the sound of the horse's breathing and a trickle of running water in some nearby wash.

With a sinking feeling in his stomach he wondered if he alone, of all his crew, had survived the stampede. He wondered if he were all alone out here.

He touched spurs to his horse's sides, and the animal broke into a trot. Scattering clods of mud with his hoofs, he traveled steadily toward the crest of a small rise about a mile ahead. He was only half way there when the first rays of the sun touched the few lingering wisps of high clouds with pink. By the time he had traveled the remaining distance, the sun was poking its blazing golden rim above the horizon in the east.

Jeff sat his horse at the crest of the rise, staring out across the plain. The warmth of the sun was welcome, and his shivering began to abate somewhat. Far in the distance he saw a spot of black, that could be a man on horseback, and relief washed over him like a flood. At least he was not alone. At least someone besides himself had survived. And, if one had survived, perhaps the others had also.

He turned in his saddle and stared behind. Back there, he saw two little small dots, also horsemen, he guessed. And then, suddenly, almost lost because the distance was so

244

great, he heard the faint crack of a gun. Back where the two men were, smoke puffed like a wisp and then was gone. Moments later, Jeff heard the sound of the second shot.

He waited impatiently. He realized they had seen him because they had altered course slightly and now were coming straight toward him.

While they were still a quarter mile away, he recognized them both. One was Sam Rhody. The other was Jack Littlefield.

He rode to meet them, grinning with relief that they were safe, looking them over carefully as he approached to see if they had been hurt. Both were wet and bedraggled, as he was himself, and Sam Rhody had lost his hat. Otherwise, they seemed to be all right.

All three smiled sheepishly at each other, monstrously relieved and reluctant to show how very relieved they were. Jack asked: "Anybody else? Have you seen anybody else?"

Jeff gestured behind him. "I saw someone up ahead."

Sam Rhody growled: "Hope it's that Wasson jasper. I'd like to do a little settlin' up with him."

Jeff said: "Let's go find out."

He turned, and the others followed. At a rolling gallop they went down off the rise and headed toward the speck ahead of them on the plain, now smaller than when Jeff had first spotted it and, therefore, considerably farther away.

They maintained this gait steadily for an hour. Then the man ahead apparently turned his head and spotted them, because he whirled his horse and came galloping toward them. It was Miguel, Jeff saw at once. He was grinning widely at seeing them alive and evidently unhurt. He was covered with mud, and there was a trickle of blood on one side of his face, coming from a large bruise, but otherwise he seemed to be all right. He said: "My horse fell with me, *señores*, but he was not hurt, and neither was I. Have you seen any of the others yet?"

Jeff shook his head.

Miguel said: "I have been following the trail of two horses. Perhaps they are the horses of Madison and Mister Wilkes."

Jeff nodded. He followed Miguel, who turned and resumed the trail he had been following. Sam and Jack galloped along a dozen yards behind.

They rode this way for the better part of an hour before they glimpsed a small wisp of smoke, rising from a brush thicket a little to their right. Jeff glanced around. Sam Rhody had a revolver, and Jack had a rifle. Miguel was unarmed. He said: "Let's surround this thicket. I'll ride in. If it's Wasson, and he tries to get away, grab him."

The others nodded.

"I'd like to get my hands on him," grumbled Sam.

Jeff waited until the other three had positioned themselves on all sides of the thicket in such a way that they couldn't miss anyone leaving it. Then he urged his horse toward the rising plume of smoke. He was careful to keep his hand away from his gun. If Wasson was in here, he wanted to talk to him. He wanted to know what had happened last night. If Wasson had deliberately started the stampede, there was plenty of time later to settle up with him.

But, before Jeff could reach the fire, almost as soon as he entered the thicket, he heard Madison Quinn's shrill yell. "Jeff? Is that you?"

Jeff returned his shout. "It's me!" He turned his head and shouted the others in. "It's all right. It's not Wasson, it's Madison Quinn!"

He continued toward the fire, hearing the crashing as the others entered the thicket on all sides of him. Almost immediately afterward he reached the fire and smelled cooking meat, and his mouth began to water with hunger.

Mad stood beside the fire. Ted Wilkes stood across from him. Both were grinning widely. Over the fire, spitted on a stick, were chunks of beef. Jeff swung from his saddle, hurried forward, and gripped Mad's hand. He went around the fire and shook hands with Ted, feeling a little foolish at this show of emotion, but overwhelmingly relieved that they were alive and apparently unhurt.

Mad said: "We found a steer with a busted leg, so we shot it and cut some meat off to eat."

The others arrived, talking excitedly, with relief equal to Jeff's.

Jeff backed up to the fire so close that soon his clothes were steaming as they dried.

As soon as the meat was done, they took it off the spit, holding the hot pieces in their fingers, eating ravenously. The meat quickly disappeared, but, when it had, all of them felt stronger and in better spirits.

Jeff turned to Mad. "You have any idea where the remuda is?"

"They ran with the cattle, Jeff. Wasson was on the other side of the herd from where I was, so when he fired that dog-goned gun, they came straight toward me. I let my horse run free with the others until I figured I was clear of the cattle, then I pulled aside and tried to go after the herd. I have an idea the horses quit running right after I left them and shaded up in some brush where it wasn't quite so wet."

Jeff nodded. "All right. Backtrack on the cattle until you pick up the horses' trail. Bunch 'em and bring 'em here. We're going to need a lot of horses in the next few days, if we're going to gather up that herd again."

Mad agreed and immediately untied his horse, mounted, and rode away. He disappeared into the brush.

Jeff turned to Miguel. "How about the chuck wagon? Did the herd stampede over it?"

"No, *señor*. They missed it by about thirty yards. The chuck wagon is all right."

"How about horses? You got any horses for it?"

Miguel shrugged expressively. "I don't know, *señor*. They were tied to some brush nearby, but they may have pulled loose and run when the cattle ran."

Jeff said: "Well, go on back there to the chuck wagon. If you've got a team, hitch 'em up and bring the chuck wagon here. Get a meal going right away and keep coffee going all the time. If you haven't got a team, you'll have to stay there. But get some food cooking. We'll need a lot of it, because we've got a lot of work ahead."

"*Sí, señor.*" Miguel grinned, mounted, and rode out of the thicket in the direction Mad had taken a few moments earlier.

"I guess it's up to the rest of us to get that herd gathered," Jeff said. He looked at Sam. "I may be ramrodding this drive, but I can use some advice from you and Ted. How would *you* begin, if it was up to you?"

Sam glanced at Jeff with increased respect. He said: "I'd follow the trail they left as long as there is a trail. Likely, where it ends, you'll find half of 'em or more. Start driving them back this way, breaking away where you find trails leaving the main trail and picking up the bunches that made those trails. That may not be the only way of gatherin' 'em up again, but it's sure the best."

Jeff was glad he'd asked Sam's advice. He supposed he should have been able to figure out that Sam's way was the only logical way, but he had not. The task had seemed so monstrous, so mountainous, he hadn't known where to start. He began to feel a little more cheerful about their prospects as he mounted his horse and led the way out of the thicket of brush. The others followed him, and soon they were all riding in the broad, muddy trail left last night by the stampeding herd.

They held their horses to a trot, saving them because they could not know when Mad would be able to reach them with fresh mounts. This way the morning dragged away.

In early afternoon they reached some low, rolling hills, and here the trail they were following split in all directions. Jeff immediately divided the men, and they made a huge surround, afterwards working back to where they had separated, driving everything they found in front of them. By evening Jeff saw with satisfaction that they had recovered almost half the herd.

He also noted something else with equal satisfaction. The cattle were tired, listless, and subdued. They were easy to handle now, and Jeff was glad they were. He and the others started them back in the direction they had come earlier, knowing that the really hard work wouldn't begin until tomorrow. That was when they would have to start beating brush thickets, looking for the strays that had left the others along the line of flight. There was where the hard work would begin. Gathering up those strays, one or two at a time, might take a week or more.

IX

All the following day they moved the herd slowly back toward the place from which the stampede had started. It turned out that Miguel's chuck wagon team had bolted when the cattle did, but Miguel trailed and recovered them. He hitched them to the chuck wagon and came toiling across the plain the morning of the second day. He stopped, unhitched, built a fire with dry wood he always carried in the chuck wagon, and prepared a meal of sourdough biscuits with honey and boiled beef stew with potatoes and onions. He made prodigious quantities of coffee, and afterward, no matter what time of day or night a crew member came to his fire, they always found the coffee hot and some kind of food available.

In mid-afternoon the second day after the stampede, while they still were half a dozen miles from its starting point, Jeff Hueston finally cut Cliff Wasson's trail. It was heading west, away from the main trail made by the stampeding herd. The trail of Wasson's horse was following a bunch that had separated from the main herd while the stampede was in progress.

Two possibilities occurred to Jeff. Either Wasson had, in the darkness, unknowingly stayed with a bunch breaking away independently, or he had deliberately cut this bunch out of the main herd, intending to steal it for himself.

Jeff's face was grim as he took the trail. Had Wasson stayed with the smaller bunch by accident, he would have returned before this. No, Jeff had to admit it was more probable that Wasson had stolen the cattle for himself. And Jeff meant to get them back.

The trail was already two days old, so Jeff pressed his horse hard, following it. He rode until darkness obscured the trail, then dismounted, picketed his horse carefully where there was plenty of grass, and laid down to sleep. The others would worry about him, he supposed, but they would surely know he was on some trail or other. They'd know he would return as soon as he possibly could.

He slept heavily that night, near exhaustion from the strain of the past two days, but he awoke as usual before dawn and was up and in the saddle as soon as it was light enough to trail. He had no food and no water, but occasionally he crossed a trickle of water in a wide, dry stream bed, and, whenever he did, he would drink, lying flat on the sand.

Wasson had also been pushing hard and had, Jeff realized, encountered difficulties of his own. He did not dare sleep until he had the cattle corralled some place. If he did, they'd be gone when he awoke. It was the realization of this that made Jeff so sure Wasson couldn't have taken the cattle very far.

In mid-morning he sighted a plume of smoke, rising out of a dense brush thicket ahead of him. The trail he was following headed into the thicket along a narrow, rutted road. Jeff halted, frowning to himself. He knew Wasson would kill him if he got the chance. It was up to him to see to it Wasson didn't get the chance.

He dismounted and led his horse deep into the thicket of brush, well away from the narrow road. Then he returned to and followed the road, heading into the heart of the thicket. He was careful to stay at its edge and to stop frequently to listen, so that he could duck out of sight if anyone approached. For all he knew, Wasson had confederates. No telling how many men there were in here.

He traveled this way for the better part of a mile, and at last the plume of smoke was close ahead of him. He picked his way into the thickest brush he could find and worked his way closer to the clearing where the cabin was. It was built of pine logs and roofed with sod. It appeared to have no more than one small room.

Behind the cabin there was a corral. Inside the corral were about fifty of Jeff Hueston's trail-branded steers. Jeff stared at the cabin for a long, long time. A single horse was tied in front of it. No other horses were to be seen. Nor did there seem to be any other roads leaving the clearing where the cabin was.

Jeff wished now that he had brought some of the others along with him. Angry as he was at Wasson's theft, he didn't want to kill the man. But he did want the steers, and he intended to get them back.

Then his worried frown relaxed. He didn't have the others along with him, but there was no reason Wasson had to know. If he could make Wasson *think* two or three of the drovers were here with him, then Wasson might panic and choose to run instead of fight.

Carefully he worked his way around the clearing, keeping himself hidden in the brush. The rear and west sides of the cabin had no windows in them. Concealed behind these windowless walls, he came out of the brush and ran lightly to the corral.

It had no gate. Its opening was closed by poles. Swiftly, and as silently as he could, Jeff took down the poles one by one and laid them carefully on the ground. He glanced frequently and worriedly toward the cabin, but no one came out.

When he had all but the bottom two poles out of the corral opening, he ran around in back of it and ducked into the brush. The cattle began picking their way cautiously out of the corral. Jeff drew his revolver and fired, simultaneously yelling: *"Hi-ya-ya!"*

Instantly then, without waiting to see what had happened in the clearing, he dashed out of sight into the brush. Running, clawing frantically, sometimes falling but never stopping, he quartered around the clearing. Coming into sight of it again, he saw that the cattle had all broken out of the corral. Dust still hung over the place where the road disappeared into the thicket, indicating that they had followed the road going out of it.

Wasson had apparently tried to head them off on foot, knowing he could not get to his horse in time. They had almost trampled him in that rush to escape. One had knocked him down. Others had probably kicked him as they passed. Wasson was just now getting to his feet, disgustedly dusting off his pants with his dusty hat. He was cursing bitterly. Jeff raised his gun. He sighted about ten feet to one side of Wasson and fired. The bullet struck the ground, spraying the man with dust. It whined away into the beyond.

Wasson whirled, yanking out his own holstered gun. Jeff ducked back into the brush and ran again, without waiting to see what Wasson was going to do. This time he struck the road, whirled into it, and ran back to the clearing. Wasson had reached his horse and had the animal untied. He still held his revolver in his hand.

Now Jeff steadied his gun against a tree, sighting very carefully. He fired, and Wasson's horse dropped like a stone. It lay completely still. Wasson turned and fired instantaneously toward Jeff, shooting at the cloud of powder smoke from Jeff's gun, still hanging in the air. Jeff turned and ran as swiftly as he could along the narrow, rutted road he had traveled earlier with such caution.

He had hated shooting Wasson's horse, but he hadn't been able to bring himself to shoot Wasson instead. This way, Wasson couldn't follow him — not until he could get his hands on another horse, and that might be a long, long time.

At the place where the road left the brush thicket, Jeff found the cattle, spreading out but still loosely bunched. They were grazing hungrily, and he guessed they hadn't eaten for a day and night at least. They'd probably been in Wasson's corral all that time.

He circled behind them, back and forth, back and forth, slapping his chaps with the ends of his reins, whistling, sometimes yelling sharply when a steer refused to budge. Getting them started took him quite a while, and he kept looking back over his shoulder occasionally, in case Wasson decided to pursue on foot. Only when a good mile of open country separated him from the edge of the brush thicket did he relax.

Once he got the cattle moving, he kept pressing, quartering his horse back and forth at a steady trot, yelling, slapping his chaps, and whistling. Now that the sharp edge of their hunger had been dulled, the cattle seemed content to reach down only occasionally and crop a mouthful of grass, traveling afterward while they chewed it placidly.

Jeff felt warm now, and good. He grinned with satisfaction to himself. He had outwitted Wasson, a man much older and more experienced than he. Single-handedly he had recovered these fifty cattle, for which Wasson had started the stampede. He had left Wasson afoot, without a horse, without the means of catching one. He couldn't help grinning when he thought how enraged Wasson must be. But it served the man right. He had risked the lives of five other men just so that he could steal from them. He probably wouldn't have cared if they had been maimed for life, or even if they'd been killed.

Jeff kept driving, even when it got dark. Fortunately there was a moon and no clouds in the sky to dim its light. As long as Jeff stayed away from heavy brush, he could see the cattle and keep them bunched. They seemed to have had enough of running, at least for now. Yet Jeff knew that once a herd of cattle has stampeded, it is that much easier for them to stampede again. Like bad habits in humans, the habit of stampeding in cattle is hard to break. He and the others would have to watch more closely after this. They'd have to watch the herd every minute of every day until the memory of the stampede had faded from their memories.

It was light when Jeff reached the place from which he had left the main trail two days ago. There were fresh cattle tracks overlying the tracks made by the herd when it stampeded. These tracks were headed back the other way. Jeff turned his bunch of fifty into that trail. They picked up speed, now, seeming to sense that the others were close ahead. Jeff didn't even have to drive them. He only had to follow along behind.

In mid-afternoon he reached the place where the main herd was being held. Jack, Mad, Rhody, and Wilkes rode out to meet him. The cattle he was driving lost themselves in the main herd, creating hardly a stir.

All four fired questions at him, but suddenly he was ravenous for food. And he felt weak for lack of it. He said: "Later. Right now I can't think of anything but eating. Has Miguel got anything cooking over there?"

"Haven't you eaten since you left?"

Jeff shook his head. He felt almost completely exhausted, so much so he wondered if he could even muster sufficient strength to eat.

He rode to the chuck wagon and slid wearily from his horse. Jack Littlefield unsaddled and unbridled the animal, then mounted and hazed him toward the horse herd a quarter mile away. Miguel brought

Jeff a steaming plate of stew, several cold biscuits, and a tin cup of coffee. Jeff sat down and began to gulp the food. It tasted better to him than anything had ever tasted in his life before. And with each mouthful he swallowed, a little more of his strength seemed to return.

He finished eating at last, refusing seconds from Miguel because he knew his stomach might rebel if he overloaded it now. He looked up at the others, his eyes heavy-lidded. He told them briefly what had happened. Then he answered wearily the questions put to him for a while before getting up and stumbling to the chuck wagon for his blanket roll. He laid down, pillowing his head on his saddle, and, despite the fact that it was broad daylight, he was almost instantly asleep.

X

Jeff slept all the rest of that day and all that night. He did not awake again until just before dawn, since the others had not called him for night duty with the herd. A tally of the cattle, made as they lined them out toward the north and east, revealed that they had lost eighteen head, according to Sam Rhody, not a heavy loss under the circumstances.

Once again, Jeff took his position at swing, Sam his at point. Jeff noticed that Red assumed a position with the leaders and thought grimly to himself: *Too bad we didn't lose you, Red. I think you're a trouble-maker, and I think you had your part in starting that stampede. You try anything else and I may find I don't care about taking you to New Orleans, after all.*

But each day thereafter Red appeared in the vanguard of the herd, along with half a dozen others who were always there. Jeff grew used to seeing certain other animals in certain positions every day, and one night asked Sam Rhody about it. Sam nodded.

263

"Yep. Cattle are like people in some ways, I guess. They like repetition, and they like things to be the same. By the time a herd's on the trail a while, most of the critters have got their regular places in the bunch. Some like the point. Some like the flanks. Some like to get right smack dab in the middle of the herd, and others like bringing up the rear. But once they get situated, you'll find 'em in pretty much the same position every day."

"Do all of them do that?"

Sam shook his head. "Not all of 'em. Most, though, I reckon. Drovers get to callin' different animals by name, like you an' that Red of yours. They'll call one Fiery because he's got fire in his eye, or they'll call one Smoky because he's a roan. Or they'll call one Snuffy because he's always pawin' the ground an' snuffin' at them."

The days passed monotonously. No more rains drenched the drovers and the herd. Grass was not always plentiful, but it was adequate. Jeff couldn't see that the cattle were losing any weight.

They crossed the Brazos near Richmond, the Trinity River at Liberty, the Neches at Beaumont, and the Sabine near Orange. When they had crossed the Sabine, they were no longer in Texas but in Louisiana and more than half way to New Orleans.

They had been gone almost a month, counting the week that had been lost on account of the stampede. Long days in the saddle had melted much of the fat from Ted Wilkes's huge frame. His clothes hung from his body loosely, making him look like a gaunt skeleton. The others had also lost weight, if not commensurably, then more than they could spare. All looked exhausted with weariness.

At times they passed through low, swampy areas and, at others, across plains similar to those in Texas, except that sometimes the vegetation was quite different. Mesquite gave way to huge liveoak trees, occasionally festooned with moss. Jeff was nearly bitten by a water moccasin riding through a shallow swamp one day.

But they now could have a change of diet, which was very welcome to all of them. Wild pigs were common here, and the meat of the wild pig was very different from the stringy beef they had been eating. It was not as fat as the pork Jeff was used to getting at home, but, roasted over the fire on a spit, it was delicious. Furthermore, they had been able to replenish their supply of potatoes and onions from isolated farmers along the way.

It was a good thing food *was* plentiful, Jeff thought more than once. If it had not been, they would have been unable to go on. They were up each day before dawn, which at this time of year meant about 5:30 in the morning. After a hasty breakfast they usually moved out at six.

The cattle, broken to trail, were willing to get up and move out. Starting them usually presented no particular problem. Even so, it took the great herd half an hour to get lined out on the trail. From the leaders, including Red, to the cattle being brought along in the drag by Jack Littlefield, the distance was usually almost a mile. Covering twelve miles a day meant that a great deal of time was spent by the cattle grazing along the way. Driven faster than that, or in country where the feed was poor, cattle would lose as much as half a dozen pounds a day. Half a dozen pounds multiplied by eight hundred animals meant a loss of nearly two and a half tons of meat each day. On the other hand, if the cattle were carefully driven, in good feed and with plenty of water, they would usually gain a little weight.

All day the drovers rode along with the herd. With the herd well broken to the trail, Jeff Hueston rarely used up more than three horses a day. Even so, for every mile the cattle covered, he rode three or four, sometimes more. Occasionally he would change places with Jack Littlefield in the drag, knowing how hard it is on one man to live in choking dust day after day. Or he would tell Sam Rhody, or Ted Wilkes, to relieve Jack for a while.

There was usually a stop at noon, for the cattle to water or to lie down and chew their cuds. At these stops the men would dismount, unsaddle their horses, and rub their sweaty backs with their horsehair saddle blankets. Then they'd lounge in the shade and eat a piece of cold meat or a few cold biscuits they had saved from breakfast earlier. Ted and Sam would smoke if they felt able to spare the tobacco from their meager hoards. And perhaps at the noon halt Sam Rhody would spin a yarn about fighting the Mexicans, or about sailing a tall merchant ship in the Gulf, or about the jungles of Central America where he had spent time as a youth.

In early afternoon they would go on again, and some time during the afternoon Miguel would pass them with the chuck wagon, heading for their evening camp. Near sundown they would stop the herd and get it to milling, then let the cattle spread out and begin to graze. A couple of them would stay with the cattle while the others came in to eat. After eating, those who had come in first would return and relieve the others so that they could also eat.

Most times, when dark came, at least three of the men were already asleep. But never did they sleep more than six hours before they were called to relieve others, riding night guard with the herd. It added up to sixteen hours in the saddle, or getting ready to climb into the saddle again. The pay was a dollar a day — if and when Jeff Hueston sold the herd — which amounted to, roughly, six cents an hour for their working time. In spite of that none thought of complaining. Money was a rare commodity in Texas, where everything they used, or almost everything, came from the native soil. Nearly all Texas ranchers had a few sheep, which were raised for their wool. It was clipped at regular intervals, carded and spun into yarn, and the yarn was, in turn, made into cloth called homespun, perhaps the most familiar fabric of that time. Each Texas ranch also had a garden plot where vegetables were raised. And meat was, of course, plentiful. A little money, therefore, would go a long, long way. It would pay the taxes on the Texans' land. It would buy calico for women's dresses. It would buy powder and lead for the men's guns. And that was about all it was needed for.

They crossed the Calcasieu River and four days later bedded the herd in a grove of scrubby trees not far from Opalousas, Louisiana. Jeff had just started eating his supper of beef stew and sourdough biscuits when two men rode into camp. They sat their horses, looking down at him. At last one of them said: "We're looking for the trail boss, son."

Jeff stood up. He was a little irritated that they had not immediately recognized him as the trail boss, but he supposed their not doing so was natural enough. "I'm in charge. What can I do for you?"

Both men looked at him skeptically. At last they climbed down from their horses. They approached and stuck out their hands. The tall one said: "I'm Orval Thornsberry, and this is Walt Vasquez. Where you taking these steers, mister?"

"New Orleans. The Confederate quartermaster in New Orleans."

"Where you from?"

"Goliad."

"How many men you got?"

Jeff frowned at him. "You're good at asking questions, mister. Now suppose you answer some. Who are you, and what are you doing here? What do you want from me?"

Thornsberry grinned. He was a big, lanky man who appeared to be in his middle thirties. He wore a beard that was clipped raggedly and a wide mustache. His eyes were blue and sharp. He wore homespun pants and shirt, Texas boots with spurs, and a Mexican sombrero. He also carried a gun that looked like a Navy .36 caliber Colt, although it might have been a copy of that gun manufactured in the south for Confederate officers. Thornsberry said: "Pardon my bad manners, Mister . . . ?"

"Hueston. Jeff Hueston."

"Mister Hueston. I should have explained what I was doing out here right away. I guess someone like you gets kind of edgy on the trail, what with all the outlaws and deserters skulking around in the brush these days."

"I haven't seen any outlaws or deserters." But Jeff couldn't help thinking of Cliff Wasson as he said the words.

"Good. It's a good thing you haven't."

Jeff waited patiently, beginning to distrust these two. At last Thornsberry said: "We've got three hundred head of our own cattle we were figuring on taking east, but we can't hire help hereabouts. All the able-bodied men are off to war. And we can't drive three hundred head anywhere, just the two of us. We'd like to throw in with you . . . throw our herd in with yours. You'd get yourself a couple of extra hands that you won't have to pay wages to, and I reckon our three hundred head ain't going to make your job any harder than it already is."

The other man, Walt Vasquez, was short, thick-set, and dark of skin and hair. His eyes, also dark, bespoke his Spanish ancestry. He flashed Jeff an engaging grin and spoke now for the first time. "You will still be trail boss, *señor,* and we will just be drovers, working for you. We do not want any authority, and we know that, if you have brought this herd of cattle all the way from Goliad, you can take our cattle safely with you to New Orleans."

Jeff began to feel a little less suspicious of the pair, but he had to admit the flattery was partly responsible for his changing attitude. He frowned. "I'll think on it. I'll want to see your cattle first of all. If there are calves and she-stuff in your herd, I don't want any part of it."

Thornsberry was looking at Jeff with increased respect. "No calves and no she-stuff. Get your horse and come with us to

271

take a look, if you'd like."

Jeff nodded. He finished eating, gulped his coffee, then untied his horse and swung astride.

As he left camp following Thornsberry and Vasquez, it occurred to him that, if they did have designs on the herd, one of the smartest things they could do would be to lure the trail boss away from it on some pretext or other long enough for their confederates to raid the herd. Uneasily he looked back over his shoulder toward the camp. Shrugging then, he turned his head and stared at Thornsberry and Vasquez ahead of him. He was getting jumpy, he guessed, after his experience with Wasson. He didn't trust anybody any more. He had no reason to think Thornsberry and Vasquez weren't what they said they were. And, besides, he'd know soon enough. It was almost dark, and their herd had to be close or they would have waited until morning to take him for a look at it.

They struck a narrow, rutted road and turned into it as the sun dipped down below the horizon in the west. After traveling for about a mile, they left the road and headed straight into the brushy woods. The high clouds in the sky flamed pink and orange and began to fade before they reached a corral in which a good-size herd of cattle milled.

Thornsberry turned, and Jeff tried quickly to erase his expression of relief. Thornsberry said: "We drive 'em out every morning and hold 'em while they graze all day. We bring 'em back here and put 'em in the corral at night. We've been three weeks trying to figure a way to get 'em east."

Jeff nodded shortly and rode to the corral. He circled it, staring down at the cattle intently. He saw no calves. He saw only two cows, both dry and without calves. The cattle were mostly black, a smaller variety than the Texas longhorn but just as wild and just as mean. He and his men were nearly exhausted from the long drive they had already made from Goliad. A long drive still remained, and there was still the mighty Mississippi to be crossed. He could use two extra men, particularly if what they said about outlaws and deserters was true. Even if it weren't, there were likely to be Union patrols ahead. If they ran into any, they'd lose the herd and probably their lives as well.

He turned, stared at Thornsberry and Vasquez, then nodded his head almost reluctantly. "All right. We'll drive past here in the morning, and you can push your stuff in with ours."

Thornsberry extended his hand and shook Jeff's warmly. Vasquez grinned with wide relief. Jeff turned his horse and headed back toward camp. He hoped he had not made a mistake.

XI

The herd moved out at dawn, now heading almost directly east. They strung out, but Jeff and his drovers held them south of the woods where Thornsberry and Vasquez were keeping their cattle corralled. Drawing abreast of the woods, a stream of wild black cattle came racing out to mingle with the Hueston herd. For several moments it looked as though there might be another stampede. Fortunately, there was some scattered timber and brush here, and the leaders, that might have led a stampede, were not aware of the black cattle until long after they had joined the herd.

Once all the black cattle had mixed with the others, Thornsberry and Vasquez came over to where Jeff was riding on the flank. Each was leading a string of saddle horses, the halter of each successive horse in line tied to the tail of the horse ahead of it.

Thornsberry said: " 'Morning, Mister Hueston. We've brought our saddle horses and our gear. Where do you want us to ride?"

Jeff glanced sharply at him to see if there was mockery in his respectful tone. He couldn't detect any, but he knew that didn't mean it wasn't there. He said shortly, perhaps more so than necessary: "Shove your horses in with the remuda. You'll find it south of here and maybe a little to the rear." Both men nodded. Jeff added: "When you get back, one of you can take one flank and one the other. With more cattle we'll need two men on each side, riding swing."

Thornsberry and Vasquez nodded, turned, and rode away, leading their long strings of remount horses. Jeff stared somberly at the black cattle nearest him. They would weigh only about two thirds what the Texas cattle did, he supposed. They were faster on their feet and could dodge a rope a lot quicker than the Texas cattle could. He doubted if their dispositions were any worse. They couldn't be. But, even if they weren't, the black cattle would create problems anyway. For one thing, they weren't broken to swim the way Jeff's cattle were. If the black cattle balked at the bank of the Mississippi . . . they might make the whole herd balk. That worried Jeff, even though he still hoped ferries or steamers would be available for transporting the cattle across to the other side.

Other things began to worry Jeff now, that had not worried him before. While they had been in Texas, it had been certain they would not encounter any roving Union patrols. Here it was different. Thornsberry told him: "They probe down this way every now and then . . . thirty, forty, fifty men. I think they're just tryin' to make our side keep troops here to watch out for 'em."

So Jeff took to scouting ahead wherever the lay of the land permitted it, watching toward the north from some high point, sometimes even climbing a tree so that he could see. If they encountered a Union patrol, everything was lost, the herd, perhaps their lives as well. They would not be able to escape — not with over a thousand head in their care.

The miles dropped slowly behind, but with each mile, now, they were closer to their goal, closer to the completion of the grueling drive.

It began to rain again, but this time it was a different sort of rain, not the violent thunderstorm during the stampede, but a soft, drizzling kind of rain, scarcely more than a heavy mist, that soaked the men and the horses and the cattle and kept them soaked. In this gray drizzle one morning the cattle in the lead abruptly stopped. Behind them others stopped, and others, as the drag kept coming on. Muttering angrily to himself, Jeff Hueston spurred his horse toward the point to find out what was happening.

Before he saw Sam Rhody, he saw the soldiers, and for an instant his heart seemed to stop beating in his chest. There must have been at least forty of them, slickered, sitting their dripping horses in the steadily drizzling rain.

Jeff halted his horse and sat frozen for several moments before he realized that their hats were gray instead of blue. When he did realize it, a tremendous feeling of relief washed over him, turning him almost weak. He began to grin and touched his horse's sides with his spurs. The animal moved forward, to stop again a dozen feet from the Confederate officer in charge of the patrol. Jeff's grin widened as he rode close and stuck out his hand. " 'Mornin', sir. I'm Jeff Hueston from Goliad."

The man did not return his smile, but he did extend his hand. He was a tall, lean man, a tired-looking man with a two day's growth of graying whiskers on his face. There were deep hollows underneath his eyes. His mouth had a tight, firm set to it as though his patience with this whole business of soldiering was nearly gone. He said:

"I'm Captain Ireland, Mister Hueston. Where are you headin' with this heah herd?"

"New Orleans, sir. We're headin' for New Orleans. And by golly, we're almost there."

"Not yet, son," the officer said grimly. "Not yet. But I'm condemned if I understand your cheek. You're under arrest, suh, you and all your crew!" He turned his head and barked an order to his men. They moved forward, faces grim, rifles at ready now. Some of them moved down along the flanks of the uneasily stirring herd. Others circled Jeff and Sam.

For an instant it looked as though Sam might try to draw his gun, but Jeff said sharply: "No, Sam! They're our troops. It must be some mistake."

Captain Ireland said coldly: "Sergeant, get their guns!"

Jeff meekly handed over his gun and cartridge belt. He wouldn't have used it anyway. Not against Confederate troops, no matter what they did. But suddenly he thought he understood. These were not Confederate troops at all; they were Union soldiers in Confederate uniforms. That had to be the explanation.

Jeff's heart felt like a chunk of lead, hammering in his chest. He had lost the herd; he had failed. After all the miles, and all the work, and all the sweat and misery, he had failed and his friends had failed. Instead of helping the Southern cause by delivering this beef to the Confederacy, they had helped the Union cause by letting the Union capture it. He stared at the gaping muzzles of the guns trained on him. He gazed at the grim face and set mouth of Captain Ireland. He considered putting up a fight and then discarded the idea. Ireland and his men would kill him if he resisted them. They would kill any of Jeff's men that resisted. Besides, how could a handful of men fight forty or fifty seasoned cavalrymen?

Jeff asked miserably: "What are you going to do with us?"

"First of all, we're going to confiscate your herd. Secondly, we're going to court-martial you. If you're not shot, at least you'll be imprisoned for a long, long time."

Jeff stared at him unbelievingly. "What for? Why? Even if you are Union soldiers, you can't blame us for trying to drive beef to New Orleans."

Ireland stared at him puzzledly. "Union soldiers? What the devil are you talking about?"

Jeff said: "You've got to be Union soldiers in Confederate uniforms. Otherwise you wouldn't arrest us for driving cattle to New

Orleans. It wouldn't make any sense."

Ireland stared at him, scowling angrily. "It makes sense, all right, and we're not Union troops. We're Confederate troops, First Louisiana Volunteers. The Union troops are in New Orleans, mister. And you've got the gall to sit there on your hoss an' tell me you're drivin' these cattle there to 'em."

For an instant Jeff was speechless. New Orleans in Union hands? It seemed impossible. If New Orleans had been captured, then the war must already be lost. He stammered: "How . . . ? Have we lost the war?"

Captain Ireland stared at him suspiciously. "Your act don't fool nobody, son. The Union captured New Orleans from the sea, not from the land. And we ain't lost the war, neither, suh. We ain't lost it, and we ain't goin' to lose it."

Jeff whispered hoarsely, "How long . . . how long has the Union held New Orleans?"

"Since April, suh. So don't tell me y'all didn't know about it. Even in Texas, news travels faster'n that."

Jeff nodded. He knew it was no use. He'd never be able to convince anybody that he hadn't known about the capture of New Orleans. It just didn't make sense that such an important piece of news would remain obscure for more than half a year. Even in Texas. Or in Opalousas, where they had picked up Thornsberry and Vasquez.

The other troopers now began to return with Thornsberry and Vasquez, Jack, Mad, and Ted Wilkes. After several minutes still other troopers returned, escorting Miguel and his chuck wagon.

Captain Ireland gave his orders crisply. "Sergeant, query your men and find out if any of 'em has experience herdin' stock. Put 'em to herdin' these. I'll hold you responsible if any of these cattle get away."

"Yes, sir." The sergeant saluted and turned away. Jeff heard him asking the troopers which of them were experienced with stock. Half a dozen replied in the affirmative.

At least, Jeff thought, the cattle would help the Confederacy. Even if he and the others were shot or imprisoned, even if no money ever reached Texas, the cattle would go to the Confederacy. And that was the really important thing.

Those who had been selected rode away to surround the cattle and hold them in this approximate area. The captain looked coldly at Jeff. "Move out, mister. Tell your men to fall in behind. I'd tell 'em not to try anything, too, if I was you. My men will shoot to kill if any of 'em tries to escape."

Jeff looked at the others. "I don't know why we hadn't heard, but the captain says the Union has held New Orleans since last April. He thinks we knew and were planning to traffic with the enemy. We're going to be court-martialed unless we can convince him that we're telling him the truth."

Jack and Mad looked scared. Thornsberry and Vasquez, if they were scared, were concealing it well. Sam Rhody was mad and so was Ted Wilkes. Miguel looked as though he didn't understand what was going on. Jeff said: "We know that what they say isn't true. We know we're right, and I guess that's the most important thing."

Sam Rhody growled: "Not if they stand us up against a wall and shoot us, it ain't. What good is it to be right if you're dead?"

Jeff said: "We're not going to be dead. None of us. When we tell our story, they'll have to let us go." He tried to sound convincing, but it was difficult when he was not convinced himself. He had told his story to Captain Ireland, and he had not been believed. Why should he think he could make some other officer believe him when he had failed with Captain Ireland?

Gloomily he touched his horse's sides with his spurs and followed the captain south through the scattered brush. His men fell in behind, and the sergeant took a position on the other side of him. Behind the drovers came the remainder of the soaked and dripping troop of cavalrymen. Miguel turned his head and looked back at his chuck wagon, almost longingly as though he were wondering if he would ever see it again. Then, frowning, he put his eyes on Jeff and followed through the dripping brush.

This way, speechless, they rode through the gray drizzle for about an hour and a half. At last they reached a small settlement, consisting of a single street in which the mud appeared to be at least six inches deep and was constantly being stirred up by wagons or ambulances or caissons.

There were, perhaps, a dozen store buildings along the single street. Behind the store buildings there were fifteen or twenty houses, ranging from three-story ones to one-room shacks. Beyond, on the other side of a narrow, muddy stream, there was a bivouac area for the troops.

Jeff and the others were herded along the muddy street and told harshly to dismount in front of a dun-colored sandstone building. On the front windows in gold letters were the words: **Jonesboro Bank, est. 1789.**

Inside, a tired looking trooper with a

broom was waging a losing battle with the mud. He glanced up at them resentfully as they came in through the door. Captain Ireland disappeared up some stairs on the right of the tile-floored room.

The sergeant ordered: "All right, down the cellar, you." He gestured toward the rear, toward a stairway leading down.

Jeff went down the dismal-looking stairway first. There was a corridor at the bottom of the stairs and a trooper sitting on an overturned keg.

The sergeant said: "Some more prisoners for you, Nate."

The air smelled moldy and damp. Jeff felt a tingle run along his spine and down his arms. Suddenly he was not as cheerful as he had tried to appear a while ago. Gloom settled down over all his thoughts. They could rot down here until the war was over, he thought. Or they could be taken out into that drizzle and shot. Everybody, from the captain down, seemed to have made up their minds that they were guilty of trying to give comfort to the enemy. Any trial they got would probably be a farce.

The trooper produced a ring of keys and unlocked one of the doors along the corridor. He went in, struck a match, and lighted a single coal-oil lamp. He stood aside while

Jeff and the others filed into the room. Then he retired hastily, slamming and locking the door behind.

Jeff heard the low murmur of the trooper and the sergeant talking for a moment, then the clumping of the sergeant's feet as he climbed the stairs. After that there was no sound but the scurrying of rats in the pile of straw on the far side of the musty-smelling room.

XII

A feeling of hopelessness overwhelmed Jeff. Perhaps the rats scurrying in the straw were the cause of it. Perhaps it was caused by the dank smell here in their cellar prison. Or perhaps it was caused by the cold way they had been treated by the captain and by the men under his command.

The trial — the court-martial they were supposed to receive — was going to be only a formality, Jeff thought darkly. Already the troopers had tried them in their minds and found them guilty of attempting to traffic with the enemy. It was incomprehensible to all of them that Jeff and the others could have remained ignorant of the fall of New Orleans more than six months before.

He stared across at Thornsberry and Vasquez, but they failed to meet his eyes. He said: "You knew, didn't you? You knew New Orleans was in Union hands."

Thornsberry looked up. He shook his head. "No, we didn't know. How could we know? We been busy gatherin' up this herd for the last six months . . . just the two of

287

us. We ain't been to town, and we ain't talked to anybody that *has* been to town. So how would we get the news?"

Jeff didn't believe the man, but he decided it didn't matter anyway. The harm was done. What was important now was how they were going to convince the court-martial board they had told the truth.

They had nothing with which to prove their story. The best they could hope for was that the board would let them write letters to Goliad, asking for confirmation that they hadn't known about the fall of New Orleans. But the way letters traveled nowadays that might take months. In the meantime they'd rot in this cellar, sharing their dirty bed of straw with rats.

Jeff felt like crying at the hopelessness of it. His eyes smarted and burned, but he blinked back the tears angrily. He was trail boss even if he was only seventeen years old. If he let himself break down, the others would break down, too.

He got up and began to pace nervously back and forth. As he did, he examined the cellar, looking for possible ways of escape. There didn't seem to be any — at least none that he could see. There were no windows. The walls were heavy blocks of stone. The best they could hope for would be to tunnel out, after removing enough rocks to permit their bodies to squeeze through. Yet, even if they did succeed in escaping, what good was it going to do? They wouldn't dare to try recovering the herd, or they'd be recaptured immediately. They'd have to slink home and admit to everyone that they had failed.

Jack Littlefield put into words the question all of them were asking in their minds: "Jeff, what're we going to do?" His voice sounded loud and unnatural in the confined space.

Jeff glanced at him and grinned ruefully. "Well, we can't escape unless we're prepared to leave the herd and admit that we were trying to traffic with the enemy. I don't think any of us wants that." Nobody spoke, even though Jeff stared long and hard at Thornsberry and Vasquez. He went on: "We can't write home to prove our story that we didn't know New Orleans had fallen, unless we want to rot here for weeks or even months while the letter's going to Goliad and an answer coming back. So it looks to me like the only thing left for us is to go before that court-martial and *make* them believe we're telling the truth."

"How're we going to do that?" Jack asked.

Jeff frowned. "I don't know. I guess there

isn't any sure way of convincing someone you're telling the truth. I guess you just have to tell it and hope whoever you're telling it to has sense enough to recognize it."

Jeff went back to pacing nervously. He had no way of knowing when the light faded from the sky, but after a long time had passed he heard footsteps on the stairs. The door was unlocked and opened.

Outside, the troopers stood with leveled rifles as a third came into their cell, carrying two large pots. One contained coffee substitute. The other contained stew. The man put both pots down in the middle of the floor, then backed out, and disappeared. After several moments he returned carrying metal plates and cups and a spoon for each of the prisoners. He put these down beside the two pots and retired again.

Jeff waited until the others had filled their plates and cups, then filled his own. The coffee was bad, but the stew was palatable, and he ate enough to fill him up.

The night, though, was miserable. None of them slept much because of their fear of being bitten by one of the huge rats with which they shared the room. And matters did not improve. Night and day became blended into one endless period that was neither night nor day. Their meals came, and the empty pots and dirty dishes were taken away. Sometimes fresh straw was brought to them. Sometimes they were given water with which to wash, but they were not allowed to shave. Jeff supposed their jailers were unwilling to trust them with razors in their hands.

Jeff tried to keep count of the days. He thought it was five days after their incarceration that they were told their court-martial would convene immediately. Again they were given an opportunity to clean up as best they could, but sleeping on a bed of straw that you share with rats is not particularly conducive to cleanliness. Jeff washed and combed his hair with his fingers. He smoothed down his light-colored whiskers as best he could. He brushed his clothes with his hands without improving their appearance much.

The others followed suit. After about an hour had passed, their guards came and marched them up the stairs and out into the fresh air.

The rain clouds had gone. The sky was the brightest, most incredible blue Jeff had ever seen and was filled with light, puffy, drifting clouds. The sun made him blink and squint like a mole coming up out of the ground. Its blinding rays actually hurt his eyes, but he knew that soon would pass.

The others were similarly blinking. Jeff looked at them. Unshaven, their clothing filthy, squinting at the brightness of the sun, they were as villainous-looking a crew as he had ever seen. Suddenly he felt his hope begin to die. Nobody would believe men who looked like this. Nobody *could* believe them. They would either be sentenced to long prison terms, or they would be shot.

For a moment Jeff hesitated, on the point of breaking away now and fleeing toward the brush that surrounded this little settlement. He knew there was little chance of his making it. He might be shot down like a wolf, but wasn't that better than being stood against a wall and shot? Or better than being imprisoned for months, perhaps even years?

He looked at Jack and at Mad and then at the other men. He knew that if he broke and ran, they would also run. He'd be responsible. He felt himself relax.

The guard said: "All right, you. March."

The little group began to move. They walked down the street, through mud that was drying now, and entered another store building farther down the street. This one was large and open. There were chairs for the prisoners. There was a long table at one end of the room, and chairs behind it for the members of the court-martial board. Jeff and the others stood before their chairs. After several minutes a group of officers filed in and took their places behind the table.

The one in the center was older than the others. His hair was gray, and his eyes were incredibly tired looking, as though he had not slept for days. He wore a major's insignia.

The officers sat down, and the sergeant barked: "Sit!"

The prisoners sat down.

The major ruffled through some papers, then glanced up at the shaggy, dirty prisoners with some distaste. He said coldly: "I'm Major Doolittle. You are charged with treason . . . with giving aid and comfort to the enemy. Have you anything to say?"

Jeff was scared. His chest felt as though a steel band were tightening around it. His heart seemed to have stopped, and his throat was drier than it had ever been before. He got to his feet and licked his lips.

The major's cold eyes fixed themselves on him. "Speak up, young man, speak up."

Jeff said: "We're loyal Southerners, sir . . . from Texas. I got two brothers that are fightin' for the Confederacy. We got the idea that the South could use some beef, so we set out to drive some here. We didn't know New Orleans was in Union hands. We don't get much news in Goliad. We ain't had but one letter each from my brothers in the last six months, and neither of 'em said anything about New Orleans. Maybe they didn't even know." He stopped, realizing he was out of breath. He'd done the best he could. He didn't know what else he could do. He'd said what there was to say.

The major looked at the others. "Anybody else?"

Sam Rhody stood up. He said: "Major, seems to me it'd be a mite strange was we to tell a Confederate officer we was drivin' cattle to New Orleans if we knew it was in Union hands. That'd be like tightenin' the noose around our own necks, now, wouldn't it?"

The major asked: "Anybody else?"

Jeff looked straight at the major, meeting his eyes as though he was already feeling the bullets of the firing squad thudding into him. He said: "We've told the truth, sir. We've told you the exact truth." He sat down. There was nothing more that he could do. It was up to Major Doolittle now, up to him and the other officers who sat on the court-martial board with him.

Major Doolittle spoke to the guard. "Take them away, Sergeant."

Jeff and the others rose. They filed from the room into the street. They were marched back the way they had come, back into the Jonesboro Bank building and back down into the rat-infested cellar where they had spent the last several days.

The sergeant acted as though they had already been convicted. Jeff supposed their defense had been weak, if, indeed, it could even be called a defense. And if the sergeant had not believed their story, then it was doubtful if the major and the other members of the court-martial had.

The door slammed. The single lamp flickered weakly. Coming down here had been ten times as hard this time as it had been the first time, perhaps because today they knew what their cell was like, perhaps because the sun had been so bright up there in the street. Or perhaps it was because coming back down here intensified the gloominess of all of them. None thought they were going to be freed. All thought they would be convicted and either shot or imprisoned.

Sam Rhody said: "When they take us back up to hear the verdict . . . I say we'd better make a break for it. I'd rather be shot trying to escape than be stood against a wall."

Ted Wilkes said: "That's because you're an old fool, Sam. What about these boys? They ain't as old as we are. They got more to live for than a couple of old duffers like you an' me."

Sam looked at Jeff. "What about it, Jeff?"

Jeff said thoughtfully: "I think we ought to wait and hear the verdict before we do anything. Maybe they'll decide we told the truth." Thornsberry snorted, but Jeff didn't look at him. He continued: "If they find us guilty . . . well, I guess then it's time to decide what we ought to do."

"Too late then," Sam Rhody growled. "If they convict us, they'll be expectin' us to make a break."

Jeff nodded. "I suppose you're right." He stared around at the others. "I'm going to take a vote. How many of you want to do what Sam Rhody says? How many want to try and escape before we even hear the verdict of the court?" Several of the men started to raise their hands. Jeff added quickly: "Wait a minute before you vote. If you vote to try and escape, we're throwing away what little chance we have of getting freed and of getting the cattle sold and the money back to Texas. If we try and escape, we probably won't make it anyway, but one thing's sure. They'll figure for certain we're guilty, and those of us they don't kill outright, they'll stand against a wall." He waited a moment for what he'd said to sink in. "All right. Let's have the vote. How many of you want to try and escape?"

Thornsberry and Vasquez raised their hands immediately. So did Sam Rhody, although there was now some doubt evident in his eyes. Ted Wilkes, Miguel, Jack, and Mad held back, waiting to see what Jeff would do. When he did not raise his hand, they refrained from raising theirs.

Jeff said: "Three for escape. How many against?"

Now Ted, Miguel, Jack, and Mad raised their hands.

Jeff also raised his. He said: "Escape's voted out. I guess we'll wait and see what the verdict is."

Scarcely had he finished speaking when he heard the footsteps of the guards coming down the stairs outside their door. The door opened, and the sergeant beckoned them. "Come on. The board's ready to give their verdict."

Scarcely daring to breathe, Jeff followed the sergeant up the stairs. The others followed him. They walked in a column up the street and into the room where the court-martial was being held.

The major waited until they were all in place. Then he stood up and said: "You have been found. . . ." — he hesitated, as though wondering if the verdict he was about to announce was the right verdict in this case, then at last continued — "not guilty of the charges brought against you in this court. You are free to go. But pick yourselves another destination, boys. Pick a town that's held by the Confederacy next time."

Jeff began to laugh almost hysterically. The others joined him.

The sergeant, whose manner had miraculously changed, now said: "I'll have your hosses brought here, boys." And he added beneath his breath: "I'll have a few other things brought to you, too. Seems to me you got somethin' coming for all you been through the last few days."

Jeff could think of only one thing. He asked: "The cattle . . . are they all right?"

The sergeant nodded. "Little heavier, mebbe, for gettin' a week on good rich grass. But otherwise just the same." He grinned at Jeff and put a friendly hand on his shoulder. "Good luck to you, son. Good luck to you."

Jeff nodded gratefully as he watched their horses being led toward them up the street.

XIII

Their leaving created very little stir in the town of Jonesboro where the Confederate troops were bivouacked. The sergeant brought them a large burlap bag. When, after leaving the town behind, Jeff opened it to look inside, he discovered it contained coffee beans, nearly twenty pounds of them.

He yelled at the others. "Hey, it's coffee! Real coffee! How long since any of you tasted that?"

Sam Rhody said: "Bet he stole it from the officer's mess. I'll bet he figured the captain owed us something for arresting us, and this was his way of seeing the debt got paid."

Jeff nodded. He realized suddenly that he was breathing more deeply than ever before in his life. He was drawing the winy, clear air into his lungs as though each breath was going to be his last. And he was reveling in the warmth of the bright sun, beating down upon his back. Simple things like air and sun, he thought, are too much taken for granted by men that have never been anything but free. It took a little imprisonment below ground really to appreciate them.

When they reached the place they had left the cattle with the troopers, the herd was gone, but there was a plain trail leading east. They followed this and, after an hour, reached the edges of the herd, which had been moved a little every day to better grass.

The troopers with the herd turned it over to them, grinning and shaking hands. "Glad they turned you loose, boys," one of them remarked. "Where will you go with the cattle now?"

Jeff responded: "Mobile, I reckon." He grinned at them. "Provided it's still held by the Confederates."

"Last I heard it was. Good luck to you."

Jeff waved as the troopers rode out of sight into the brush. Then he turned to the men. "Get going, all of you. We can cover half a dozen miles before the sun goes down."

Once more the herd moved out, ponderously and slowly today because they had remained practically stationary for days. Mad bunched the horses and kept them moving along the southern edge of the herd.

Miguel hitched up his chuck wagon and trailed the herd eastward. Near sundown, however, he pulled ahead and made camp for the night. When the others arrived with the herd, he had a fire going, a huge pot of stew waiting, and best of all a pot of real coffee brewing, coffee whose aroma they could smell more than a hundred yards away.

There was much hilarity and good humor in camp this night. Jack Littlefield occasionally broke into a snatch of song. The others laughed often, at things that were not even funny. They drank coffee as though they had never tasted it before. They shaved, washed, and put on clean clothes, afterward scrubbing, in the nearby creek, the filthy ones they had worn while they had been confined.

Jeff caught himself watching Thornsberry and Vasquez, frowning as he did. He realized he really didn't trust the pair, any more than he believed their story that they hadn't known New Orleans was in Union hands. Probably, he thought, the price of cattle in New Orleans, besieged by the Confederate forces by land, supplied by the Union only from the sea, was double or triple what it was any place else. That would explain the pair's willingness to take their cattle there, even though they knew they would be giving aid and comfort to the enemy. They had known, all right. And they had also known that Jeff and the other drovers would, by their obvious honesty, convince any arresting Confederate troops that they had been ignorant of the fact that New Orleans was in Union hands.

It angered Jeff to feel that he had been used, but there was no help for it now. He had no absolute proof Thornsberry and Vasquez had lied. He could only resolve to watch them more closely in the future.

Right now, there was this herd to be moved on to Mobile. Again there would be the monotony of the trail, monotony that had seemed deadly a week ago and now seemed like a welcome thing. The same leaders had taken their places at point, just behind where Sam Rhody rode. The same steers took their places on the right and left flanks of the herd. The same laggards dropped back into the drag.

Twelve miles had slipped behind that day. The next day saw them move another twelve. As they progressed, Sam Rhody began scouting farther and farther ahead each day because all of them knew the mighty Mississippi could not be far away.

Almost a week after they had been released by the Confederate troops, Sam came riding back at noon to say: "It's fifteen miles ahead of us, Jeff. It looks nigh a mile wide, and it's runnin' like it was forty or fifty feet deep."

This was what Jeff had been dreading ever since they had left Goliad. He nodded and halted the herd immediately. Having done so, he told the crew: "Sam and I are going to look for some way of getting the cattle across. You're to hold 'em right here until we get back." He looked at Ted Wilkes. "You're in charge while I'm gone."

Ted nodded, glancing at Thornsberry and Vasquez, as though he understood what Jeff was trying to say to him. He shifted the holstered Navy Colt revolver at his side as though unconsciously making it more accessible.

Jeff rode out with Sam, and the two caught fresh horses for themselves. Jeff took some of his money out of his saddlebags, leaving the rest in the chuck wagon with Miguel. He led away toward the river, Sam Rhody following close behind.

Once clear of the herd and the drovers' camp, Jeff turned his head. "See any steamboats or barges, Sam?"

"One steamboat is all . . . 'way out in the middle of the river."

"Think we can find ferries or barges to take these cattle across?"

Sam shrugged eloquently. "I don't know,

Jeff. Could be we'd have to swim 'em across. Or sell 'em on this side."

Jeff shook his head. "No market on this side . . . not for that many. We've got to take 'em to a city to get a decent price for 'em."

Sam Rhody was silent.

Jeff asked at last: "*Can* we swim 'em across? Is it possible without losing most of them?"

Sam shrugged again. "I don't know, Jeff. I honestly don't know. I never heard of anybody being stupid enough to try swimming Texas longhorns across a river as wide as that." He grinned. "Not until now, at least."

Jeff said soberly: "We won't try it, if it isn't possible."

Sam studied him. "I didn't say it wasn't possible. We've swum 'em across rivers before. The only difference is the size of the river, an' maybe the size of the old Mississippi is scarin' us more than it's goin' to scare them steers."

Jeff nodded. He knew Sam was right. He touched spurs to his horse's sides and afterward rode without speaking until the two reached the bluff overlooking the mighty Father of Waters. It was a breathtaking sight for Jeff, who had never seen the Mississippi before. It stretched away for what looked like much more than a mile. He could faintly see a green-gray line that marked the eastern bank. He could see islands of débris and logs, drifting in the sluggish current that still managed, he supposed, to move four or five miles an hour.

"Let's split up, Sam," he suggested. "You ride north, and I'll ride south. Cover about ten miles and, if you don't find any barges or ferries, then come back here."

Sam nodded, turned his horse, and disappeared into the brush and trees, heading north. Jeff turned south, staring almost with fascination at the river, flowing toward the sea. It was a light brown color, the color it had gathered in its thousand-mile journey to this place. And it whispered as it flowed along, an almost menacing whisper, as though it were daring Jeff to put his cattle into it and try to swim them across. *I'll kill your cattle, and I'll kill you,* it seemed to say, and Jeff felt an unpleasant tingle in his spine. Then he shook his head angrily. He was letting it defeat him before he ever wet his horse's hoofs in it. He was being a superstitious fool.

After that, he rode farther from the bank so that he would not have to look at the river. But, although he rode more than the

306

ten miles he had told Sam to ride, he saw no settlements. He saw no ferries. He saw no steamboats or indeed even any landings where they could tie up to and load.

Reluctantly he turned his horse and rode back toward the place where he had separated from Sam. He found him waiting when he arrived at dusk, and he did not have to ask Sam if he had found any means of ferrying the cattle across. Sam's face told him he had not.

Jeff shrugged ruefully and grinned. "I guess we swim."

Sam turned and pointed toward the river. "See that floating island of brush and trash?"

Jeff nodded. The island seemed to be literally that except that it was floating, moving along at the river's speed.

Sam said: "If one of them things drifts into the herd, we're done. We'll lose the whole herd and probably drown to boot."

Jeff waited.

At last Sam continued: "It'll take some plannin'. In the first place, we don't dare let them cattle see the river until we put 'em into it. And we've got to be sure none of them floating islands is coming when we do. Looks to me like the only way to do both things is to put a man to watching half a mile upriver. Let him fire a couple of shots when the river's clear. Soon as the others hear the shots, they can start the cattle, moving fast."

"What if they balk on the river bank?"

Sam shrugged gloomily. "Then we're finished. We'll never get a second chance. If they refuse it the first time, they'll never swim, not if we try 'em a thousand times."

Jeff nodded. "Let's get back to camp."

In darkness the pair returned to the place they had left the cattle earlier. The others looked a little scared when Jeff told them how wide the river was and that they would have to swim. He hadn't meant to scare them, but neither did he want them to panic when they saw how wide and swift the water was.

Patiently he explained how it would be done. "Sam's going upstream to wait about half a mile from where we plan to cross. The crossing we've picked is a spot with a brushy trail down through the bluff. The cattle won't see the river until they're right at the edge of it." He drew a breath, took a sip of coffee, and went on. "We'll hold the cattle about a half mile short of the river. When the river is clear of floating trash, Sam will fire a couple of shots, and we'll move out. We'll move 'em fast . . . get 'em running, if we can. We've got to force the leaders into the water before they get a chance to balk. And we've got to keep 'em heading straight out into it until the whole herd is in. We're not going to get a second chance. So put 'em in. Force them. And once the leaders are in, put your horses right in there with them."

Miguel asked: "What about the chuck wagon, *Señor* Jeff?"

"Leave it. Get yourself a saddle horse and help drive the cattle. After we've got 'em across, we'll come back, cut some logs, and float the chuck wagon across."

Mad asked: "And the horses, Jeff?"

"Rope corral 'em. Each of you pick a fresh horse . . . the best swimmer in your string. Then help Mad get up a rope corral to hold the rest of them. We'll come back for them after we've got the cattle on the other side."

"How far away is the river, Jeff?" Ted Wilkes wondered.

"About fifteen miles. We'll drive to within two or three miles of it tomorrow. The next day we'll take 'em across, early, while they're strong enough to swim that far."

He went to the cook fire and got himself a plate of stew. He also got himself another cup of fragrant coffee and sat down to eat. He didn't even know if it was possible for cattle to swim a mile, and he realized that they might have to swim even farther than a mile, if the current worked against them rather than helping. Furthermore, he didn't know if they'd take the river, when they saw how wide it was. He didn't know if he and the others could keep the cattle bunched, could keep them from milling in mid-stream until they all were drowned.

He thought of his mother and his grandfather. They were depending on him. But he was doing the best he could. The cattle couldn't be sold this side of the river. Not eleven hundred of them. There simply was no market on this side.

Sam Rhody came and sat down across from him. Sam was sipping coffee and looked speculatively at him. Jeff felt like asking him if it could be done, if he was doing right in attempting it. But he stopped himself before he put his thoughts into words. Sam wasn't the trail boss. He was. The responsibility was his, and it wasn't fair to shift it onto Sam by asking his advice. Obviously Sam thought the crossing possible, or he'd have tried to stop Jeff from attempting it. And if it was possible . . . they'd make it, that was all. They'd make it, and they'd get the cattle safely across.

He glanced up at Sam again, and this

time he was surprised by an expression on Sam's face that made him feel better than he had in a long, long time. Sam was staring at him with plain approval in his eyes. He grinned at Jeff and said: "We've come a fur piece, Jeff. We ain't goin' to let a little old river stop us now."

And Jeff grinned back.

XIV

They covered a little more than their usual dozen miles the next day and halted for the night no more than a mile or two from the river bank. There was tension in camp. All the men were silent and subdued. No one talked, and no one sang. They sought their blankets early, except for the night guards, who rode back and forth, humming and softly singing snatches of song, but without any real enthusiasm.

Jeff rode the edges of the herd, on guard tonight, frowning, realizing how tense he was. He was afraid of that river ahead of them. He was scared to death of it. And so were the others. Raised in the arid, brushy Texas plains, they had little experience with water. Many of them couldn't even swim, and, if they were separated from their horses, they knew that they would drown.

Jeff was relieved at midnight and returned to camp. He rolled himself in his blankets, but for a long while he did not sleep. Instead, he stared at the sky, remembering how terrible the river had looked, remembering how distant had been the line of green, marking the eastern bank. Several times during the night he considered trying to find buyers for the cattle here on the western bank. Each time he discarded the notion, painfully aware that, if he stayed on this side of the river, it would be because he was afraid. He would, furthermore, take a disastrous loss on the cattle. Whoever bought them would have to take them across the Mississippi himself and would expect to be paid handsomely for the risk he took in doing so.

Jeff didn't know when he finally fell asleep. It seemed only a minute or two before he awakened again to find the eastern horizon turning gray. He got up immediately.

Miguel was already up and had a fire blazing cheerfully near the chuck wagon. A pot of coffee was on the fire, and Jeff poured himself a cup.

The others were now getting up. As soon as they did, each rolled up his blankets and deposited the roll in the chuck wagon along with his possibles sack. Afterward they came to the fire, filled a plate, got a cup of coffee, and sat down to eat. This morning they were silent. Occasionally one would look furtively at another and glance quickly away afterward.

Jeff looked around the fire and said: "Keep your positions, except that I want Ted to move up to point and take Sam Rhody's place. Mad can move up and take Ted's position on the swing. Miguel will help Jack with the drag."

No one spoke or acknowledged his orders, but he knew they would be obeyed. They got up silently, mounted, and rode to the horse herd to get fresh mounts. Jeff accompanied them.

Having caught himself a fresh horse, he and a couple of the others went out to relieve the night guards who, after being told Jeff's orders for the day, caught fresh horses for themselves and went in to eat. Another twenty minutes passed before they came riding out from camp toward the herd.

Jeff stood in the stirrups and waved them toward the Mississippi. "Let's go! Let's move 'em out!"

To the accompaniment of shrill, yipping yells, of the slapping of chaps with reins, of shrill whistles, the herd moved ponderously east. The yells and whistles, that normally would have stopped as soon as the cattle were moving, did not stop today. Gradually, as they traveled, the pace of the cattle increased.

Sam Rhody, who had ridden out earlier, must now be on the bluff, thought Jeff. With luck, they'd hear him shoot very soon and would be able to keep the cattle moving toward the river without the necessity of stopping them. But, if they still hadn't heard Rhody's shots by the time they were half a mile away, they'd have to stop the herd and wait until they did.

Swiftly, swiftly the distance remaining for them to travel decreased. Jeff guessed they were now only half a mile away. He spurred his horse into a run, heading toward the point to order the men to halt the herd. Faintly then, distantly, he heard two close-spaced shots. A grin split his face. Standing in his stirrups, he yelled: "It's clear! Let's go!"

He continued riding toward the point, aware Ted didn't know where the brushy trail was that he and Sam had found last night. When he reached the point, he waved Ted back. "I know where they have to go down! I'll ride point, and you drop back to swing!"

Ted nodded. He had lost so much weight since leaving Goliad that he was now hardly any heavier than average. Ted moved to the

315

right side of the herd and stopped his horse briefly to let the cattle move on ahead. Jeff took his place at point, riding at a fast trot with the cattle keeping pace behind.

What if he missed the trail, he wondered fearfully. What if he missed that brushy trail and took them down at a place where they could see the water before they were forced into it? Scowling, he put his doubts away from him. He wasn't going to miss the trail, and the cattle weren't going to refuse the river when they came to it.

He reached the lip of the bluff at the river's edge. Briefly he glimpsed the river through the trees, wide, brown, stretching away into the distance. He felt a chill touch his spine, and then his horse was plunging down, and the cattle were plunging blindly after him.

The thunder of their hoofs rose as they picked up speed, going off the bluff. The drovers' yells were shrill and sharp, and, if they choked off suddenly as the men glimpsed the Mississippi, they did not remain silent long. Dust rose in a blinding cloud. The hoofs of the running cattle left a wide, trampled swath in the underbrush. Jeff grinned, exhilarated in spite of his fear. This was like a controlled stampede, he thought. And at this rate of speed the leaders wouldn't be able to refuse the river even if they wanted to.

Ahead, he saw the water suddenly, and at the same time he seemed to hear its whisper even over the noise of hoofs, pounding along behind. Then his horse was at the edge, hesitating but crowded on from behind so that he had to plunge into it. Jeff felt the chill of the water. It came as high as his chest as his horse sank deeply into it. But the animal bobbed up almost at once and began to swim strongly toward the opposite bank, which Jeff could no longer see.

He glanced around. Cattle were plunging in, bawling in terror but plunging in. They were swimming strongly, horns clashing together, terror widening their eyes, nostrils flared and held above the water as the huge brutes fought to stay afloat.

So far, this was like any river crossing. So far everything was going well. Sam Rhody had signaled that the river was clear of floating débris, so there shouldn't be any trouble from that. Jeff guessed that what he had to fear most was fear that could paralyze him, keep him from thinking straight, fear that would make him hesitate when it was disastrous to hesitate.

He saw Vasquez plunge his horse into the water with a yell. He saw Ted Wilkes, and the enormous splash he made. He heard their yells. He kept his horse swimming straight for the opposite bank, noticing suddenly how far downstream he had already drifted from the place where they jumped in. They'd be a half dozen miles downriver by the time they made it across, he realized, maybe more.

No matter. Just so they got across. He stared back over his shoulder. Thornsberry was in the water now, and so was Mad, on the other flank. Still the cattle came pouring off the bluff, driven now by gunshots from Miguel and from Jack Littlefield who were desperately trying to keep them closed up so that they could not see the river too soon and refuse to jump into it.

Jeff held his breath momentarily as he saw the cattle still on the bank begin to split, half going right, half going left, refusing the river at the instant they came to it. He saw Miguel and Jack come into sight, saw them look out questioningly across the river toward where he was. He raised an arm and beckoned them into the water. He saw them hesitate, looking after the cattle that had turned back. He thought desperately: *Come on! Come on! If you don't come in, some of those swimming are going to turn back!*

As though they understood his thoughts

and the urgency of them, both Jack and Miguel suddenly plunged their horses into the river. They began to swim strongly after the last cattle that had entered it.

Jeff turned his head and stared toward the eastern bank. They were in this now, all of them. They were in it, and they could not back out. Perhaps a hundred cattle had refused the river, and they would have to be sold for whatever they would bring on the western side of the Mississippi. The others . . . ? All they had to do now was survive getting across.

It seemed almost quiet after all the noise of the past two hours or so. The gunshots were stilled. So were the shouts. There were only muted sounds now, the occasional clash of horn on horn, the harsh breathing of the swimming cattle, the sibilant whisper of the river itself. It was like being in another world, a brown, smooth, wet world that went on and on . . . into infinity. It might as well be infinity, Jeff thought, as he looked behind at the bank they had just left. They had not yet gone a tenth of the way.

He heard a sudden shout from his right and turned his head in time to see Ted Wilkes's horse suddenly overwhelmed by a bunch of cattle turning downstream into him. Instantly Jeff reined his own horse aside, even though he knew leaving the point was exceedingly dangerous. He saw Mad urging his horse on faster behind Ted, but he knew Mad could never reach him in time to do any good.

Horns gouged both Ted and his horse. The horse began to fight, panicking. His head went under, and Ted slipped from the saddle to relieve the horse of his weight. He clung to the saddle horn, trying to keep the horse between himself and those viciously sharp horns.

Jeff's fear was no longer something only in his mind. If that downstream turning of the herd was not halted immediately, the whole herd would begin to mill. And here in the Mississippi they'd mill until they could swim no more. They'd drown, horses and cattle and men, and be swept out to sea.

Jeff reached Ted. He yelled: "Back in the saddle. Your gun, man, your gun! We've got to turn them back!"

Ted climbed back into his saddle, dripping, weak and looking sheepish. He drew his gun. Jeff, moving out into the river again, staying downstream from the cattle but crowding them, yelled: *"Yah! Yah! Yeeeiii!"* He fired his gun, holding it close to a swimming steer's face. The animal reversed his direction and began battling the others as he tried to swim upstream. Jeff yelled and fired again, and another steer turned.

Behind him, Ted was also firing and also turning steers, one at a time, slowly, too slowly perhaps. . . . Jeff had no time to be afraid now. He had no time to think. He only knew that if he didn't turn these steers, all of them were going to die. But it was slow . . . slow. Suddenly another gun began firing, and another voice joined Jeff's and Ted's. It was that of Madison Quinn, who had overtaken Ted. And suddenly, as quickly as the cattle had begun to turn downstream, they turned back again. Jeff urged his horse on ahead, gradually assuming the point position once more, gradually swimming out in front of the foremost steers. Madison Quinn fell back, yelling continuously. Ted also kept yelling, as he checked his gun to see how many loads were left.

Jeff felt weak. He realized that despite the wet condition of his clothes, he was sweating heavily. That had been close, as close as he ever wanted anything to get.

He glanced behind again, and was surprised to realize that the western bank was almost as far away as was the eastern bank. He studied his horse's head. The animal was swimming gamely, but it was time to help him out. Jeff slipped from the saddle on the upstream side and let his body sink into the water, leaving only his head above the surface and his hand, clinging to the saddle horn.

The horse seemed to be swimming more easily now, he thought. And unless the cattle started to turn or unless a snag threatened them. . . . Suddenly he saw it, almost upon him when he did. It was a tree, an entire huge cottonwood tree, almost completely submerged but drifting down upon Jeff with deliberately frightening speed.

He raised himself out of the water a little, staring at it, trying to calculate the way it was drifting in relation to the herd. If he could slow the herd, even a little bit, it would drift on past harmlessly. But if he failed. . . . It would overwhelm him and his horse, dragging them under the surface. And it would turn the cattle, would head them downstream and begin again the milling he and Ted and Mad had stopped only a few moments before.

He pulled himself back into the saddle, tightening the reins, turning the horse first upstream and then down as he forced the horse to swim a zigzag pattern in front of the wedge of swimming steers. The tree was closer, closer. Jeff suddenly yanked back on the reins as though he could stop the horse in water the way he could on land. He let out a startled yell.

Branches brushed his face. Something raked the horse, turning him half way around. Another branch struck Jeff on the back, nearly knocking him from the saddle. And then the thing was past, safely past and drifting away downriver.

Jeff didn't even look at any of the other men. He didn't want anyone to see how white his face was, how scared his eyes. He was shaking as though he had a chill. Gritting his teeth, he stared straight ahead while the horse fought steadily toward the bank, which now was drawing near.

Cattle and horses and men dragged themselves dripping from the mighty Father of Waters nearly an hour after they had entered it. Men and horses moved off to one side, the men sprawling out on the ground while the horses stood with wearily hanging heads. The cattle bunched in the brush, too tired even to eat. They had done the impossible, Jeff thought. They had swum a herd across the Mississippi, and he doubted if they'd even lost a steer.

XV

The herd was across, but the task was by no means done. There still were about a hundred head of cattle on the western bank, animals that had refused to plunge into the river when the others did. They would have to be gathered and driven to the nearest settlement where they would have to be sold for whatever they would bring, not much probably under the circumstances. The chuck wagon had to be floated across, and the remuda swum across. After that, the men would need some rest.

Jeff and the others sprawled out exhaustedly for nearly an hour, some dozing, some just staring at the clouds, drifting in the sky. At last Jeff roused himself and began to gather firewood. Before long he had a fire going, and his clothes were steaming as they dried. It seemed silly to dry his clothes when he was going right back into the river, but it wasn't. At least he'd get warm before he did.

The horses finally raised their heads, and the cattle began to spread out and graze.

Jeff said: "Ted, you and Jack and Thornsberry stay here and watch the herd. The rest of us will go on back. I expect Sam Rhody has gathered up the cattle that wouldn't swim, and he's probably holding them for us."

He walked to his horse and swung astride. Miguel, Madison, and Vasquez followed suit. Jeff headed his horse back toward the river and, when the animal tried to refuse the water, he spurred and forced him in. Again the water came to Jeff's chest as the horse sank from his plunge. Then the animal's head broke the surface, and he began to swim.

This time Jeff had no assurances from Sam that the river was clear of floating débris, and he could not forget his horrified fear as the floating tree had borne down on him earlier. Therefore, he kept a watchful eye upstream. Floating débris was not nearly as big a problem to four men and horses as it was to a herd of a thousand cattle. It could be avoided with relative ease, but Jeff didn't intend to be surprised.

As soon as the horse was lined out toward the opposite bank, Jeff slipped from the saddle on the upstream side and, clinging to the horn, let the horse carry him along. He wondered briefly if he'd make it to shore were the horse to play out in midstream. Probably not, he thought. He could swim, but not very far. He'd better do everything he could to help the horse and make sure the animal made it safely to the western shore.

Their horses did make it and in early afternoon climbed, dripping, from the river, too tired to shake themselves, too tired to do anything but stand with hanging heads. Again Jeff allowed them to rest for nearly an hour, then mounted, and led the others north. He knew they must have drifted several miles downriver with the current going across with the cattle earlier, and they had probably drifted an equal distance downriver on the return trip. So their original starting point must be six to eight miles upriver from where they were right now.

It was late afternoon before they finally found the place, and the first thing they did was to rope out fresh horses for themselves. Jeff left Madison Quinn to turn the horses out of the rope corral to graze and to keep them loosely bunched, and with the other two continued north, following the trail of the cattle that had refused to swim. He guessed, from their tracks, that there were close to a hundred head, and he found the tracks of Sam Rhody's horse overlaying theirs.

He caught up with him a couple of miles farther on. Sam grinned at him. "Looks like you made it, all right. I'll bet you're the first man that ever swum a herd of Texas longhorns across the Mississippi, but I'll bet you won't be the last."

Jeff nodded, too worn out even to return Sam's grin. He asked wearily: "Do you have any idea where we might sell this bunch?"

Sam replied: "There's a big farm a couple of miles north of here. I saw it when I was scoutin' the river day before yesterday. Maybe we can unload 'em there."

Jeff assented. After a while, when he saw the white buildings in the distance, he circled the herd and rode directly to the farm.

He didn't haggle long; he knew he hadn't time. He sold the cattle for four dollars a head and took payment in Confederate currency. Even so, it was dark by the time he and the others headed south again.

They camped this night on the western bank and could see the fire on the opposite side but downriver where the cattle were. They turned in early, knowing tomorrow would be as hard as today had been.

At dawn they were up again, eating the

breakfast Miguel prepared. Jeff took an axe out of the chuck wagon and found two trees large enough to float the chuck wagon across. He and the others cut them, working in shifts with the single axe, and trimmed their branches, then, with their horses, dragged the logs to the chuck wagon. They lashed them to the two huge wheels. Miguel drove the chuck wagon into the river, the wheels skidding because of the logs lashed to them.

With a tremendous splash, the chuck wagon plunged in. Water raised perilously close to Miguel's dry foods, which he had lashed down on the top of the rawhide cover. Jeff rode his horse into the river and swam him out until he was ahead of the lead team, pulling the unwieldy cart. He stayed in this position, giving the teams something to follow, thereby lessening their fear. Behind the chuck wagon Mad, Vasquez, and Sam Rhody drove the remuda into the river, with a tremendous splashing and nickering, and began to swim the horse herd across.

This trip was easier than the first had been and without incident, except that once a floating log nearly collided with the chuck wagon. In mid-morning the chuck wagon labored up out of the river at a place where there was a shallow bank, and the logs, used to float it across, were cut loose and allowed to drift away. The horse herd climbed out, and the horses shook themselves, rolled, and began almost listlessly to graze.

Jeff let the men and animals rest long enough for Miguel to prepare coffee and a meal, then waved them on, encouraged and full of hope now that the river had been crossed.

The steady monotony of the drive was welcome. They covered nearly eight miles before they stopped at dusk. The next day they covered twelve. And the day after that another twelve. They worked together like the veteran drovers they had become, and Jeff's suspicion of Thornsberry and Vasquez began to evaporate.

Forty miles from the Mississippi, however, they were stopped again by another troop of Confederate cavalry. It was just before noon. Jeff saw them, coming from the south, and rode to intercept them so that they would not stop the herd.

A lieutenant rode at the head of the troop, which numbered sixteen men. He was younger than Captain Ireland, but, like the captain, weariness showed plainly in his bloodshot eyes. He nodded shortly at Jeff. "I'm Lieutenant Frost, suh. Who are you and where do you think you're taking all them steers?"

Jeff said: "I'm Jeff Hueston from Goliad, in Texas, sir. We brought these steers from there, and we're takin' 'em to Mobile." He added quickly: "That is, if Mobile is still in Confederate hands."

The Lieutenant's eyes were cold. "And what makes you think Mobile is *not* in Confederate hands?"

"Nothing, sir. Nothing at all. We just. . . ."

"You just what, suh?"

Jeff hesitated. If he told this cold-eyed lieutenant that they had been arrested and court-martialed before, it might result in another arrest and another trial, but he had to tell the lieutenant something. He said: "We originally started out for New Orleans, sir. News travels slow in Texas, and we didn't know the Union had captured it. When we found out they had, we turned north again and headed for Mobile."

"How did you get across the river, suh?"

"Swam, Lieutenant. We swam."

The lieutenant's eyes widened with disbelief. He said: "Surely you don't expect me to believe a story as wild as that?" Frowning, he studied Jeff for a long, long time. "Know what I think, suh? I think you brought this herd up from New Orleans. I think you're takin' it to the Union army north of here. I think it came into New Orleans by boat."

Jeff said: "No, sir. You're wrong. I. . . ."

The lieutenant didn't seem to be listening. He said: "Take him into custody, Sergeant. Take his gun away. Then arrest the others and detail some of your men to hold the cattle here."

The sergeant saluted. He stared at Jeff. With weary resignation Jeff withdrew his revolver from its holster and handed it to the sergeant. He waited with the lieutenant while the sergeant and the rest of the troop galloped toward the herd to halt it and arrest the other men.

Jeff said angrily: "Lieutenant, we've been through all this before. We were arrested at Jonesboro on the western side of the river and court-martialed there. We were cleared and released. Do we have to go through it all again?"

"Why didn't you tell me you'd been arrested before?"

Jeff said: "I was afraid you'd arrest us if I did. But now that you have, I guess there's no use keeping quiet about it any more. If you'll just telegraph Jonesboro. . . ."

"The wires are down, young man, and I

can't spare a dispatch rider now."

Jeff knew when he was licked. He knew he couldn't fight this lieutenant or his troop of cavalry. No matter how wrong they were, he could never fight Confederate soldiers and neither could his men. They'd have to let themselves be arrested, let themselves be thrown again into some rat-infested jail until someone got around to court-martialing them. He thought, almost desperately, that the war might very well be over before he got this herd of cattle delivered anywhere.

The troopers came back with the dis-armed and disgruntled drovers riding ahead of them. The men looked at Jeff. Sam Rhody said disgustedly: "Here we go again!"

Jeff stared at the men's faces, one by one. He noticed Thornsberry, whispering to Vasquez, but he could not hear what was said. Then they all were riding south in the direction from which the cavalry troop had come, muttering angrily underneath their breaths.

They were not taken to a town this time but to a cavalry bivouac on the bank of a clear, slow-running stream. The guardhouse here was an abandoned icehouse built of logs and filled with damp sawdust that had once been used to keep ice from melting when summer came. There was another tallow lamp that was lighted before the heavy door was slammed and locked. Then there was only silence, the damp smell of sawdust, and the men's disgust that was almost as thick as the silence and the sawdust smell.

Madison Quinn asked: "What are we going to do, Jeff? We might not be as lucky this time as we were last time they court-martialed us."

Jeff said: "There isn't anything we can do but wait."

Jack Littlefield said: "I'm beginning to think patriotism doesn't pay. After all we've been through to get them cattle to the Confederacy. . . ."

Jeff interrupted: "There have been times when I would agree with you. I keep holdin' onto the thought that they're only doing what they think is right."

The others lapsed into silence. There were a few cracks between the logs so they could tell when it got dark outside. Shortly after it did, the guard brought their food to them. Thornsberry, who was close to the door, caught the guard's sleeve and whispered something.

When the guard had gone, Sam Rhody asked suspiciously: "What'd you have to say to that guard, Thornsberry?"

"I just asked him if he knew what they

were going to do with us."

"Why'd you have to whisper, then?"

Thornsberry laughed nervously. "I guess I've been in jail so much lately that whispering is getting to be a habit with me."

Sam snorted his disbelief. He edged to where Jeff was and said beneath his breath: "I say we'd better watch them two."

Jeff nodded. He ate hungrily and put his plate on the stack of plates the others had placed beside the door.

Half an hour passed. At last the guard came to the door. Behind him was another guard who beckoned to Thornsberry. Thornsberry followed him outside. The first guard gathered up the plates and withdrew, locking the door behind him.

Sam stared at Jeff, an angry scowl on his face. "I told you. I told you Thornsberry was up to something."

Jeff nodded. "Looks like you were right."

Sam said: "I say we beat it out of Vasquez. He knows what Thornsberry is up to, if anybody does."

Jeff glanced across the sawdust floor at Vasquez. The man was staring at the floor between his feet, and he would not look up. Jeff said: "What good would it do? If Thornsberry is making some kind of deal, I don't see what we can do about it, anyway.

Nobody seems very inclined to believe the things we say."

Sam scowled furiously at Vasquez, who still would not look up. He said threateningly: "If them two do make a deal, I'll cut their black hearts out. I swear I will!"

Jeff grinned wryly at the man. "If they've made a deal to sell us out, I'll hold 'em for you, Sam."

XVI

An hour passed. At last Jeff heard voices outside the icehouse, muffled because of the thickness of the walls. The lock was removed, and the door swung open.

There were two guards outside. One held a rifle, leveled and cocked. The other held a lantern. The one with the lantern said: "Vasquez? Come on out."

Vasquez got to his feet. He glanced furtively at Jeff, then at Sam Rhody. He scuttled for the door as though he expected to be murdered before he could get to it.

Nobody tried to stop him. Everybody seemed too stunned to move. Jeff scowled at the guard. "What's the big idea? First Thornsberry and now Vasquez? Why are you taking them out of here?"

"You'll find out soon enough. Your court-martial's scheduled for tomorrow."

The first guard slammed the door, and the other one snapped the lock in place. The voices of the two retreated and faded away.

Jeff said angrily: "You were right, Sam. They've made a deal. I don't know what kind of story they told, but, whatever it was, it worked. They've been released. You know what they'll do now, don't you? They'll take the cattle, sell them somewhere, and disappear with the money."

Sam nodded gloomily.

"And there isn't a single dog-goned thing we can do about it. That lieutenant has his mind made up that we drove those cattle up from New Orleans. Thornsberry and Vasquez have probably admitted it, but they've likely made up some kind of story to clear themselves. Maybe they said they threw in with us after swimming their little bunch of black cattle across the Mississippi without knowing who we were."

Sam said: "That's about it."

"We've got to stop them. We've got too much work and sweat in those cattle to just let them get away from us."

Jack Littlefield said: "Maybe we could loosen one of these logs and get out. Or maybe we could dig down under this sawdust and tunnel out. If we only had some tools. . . ."

"It's no use, Jack," Jeff disagreed. "What good would it do to escape? We'd have that lieutenant and his whole troop of cavalry on our backs. We'd have to scatter and run. . . ."

Jack put in: "Maybe we could stay out of sight and just follow along behind Thornsberry and Vasquez and the herd."

Jeff shook his head. "We don't know the country. They'd catch us. And, even if they didn't, I don't see how we could get the cattle back."

Sam said: "Right now the thing to do is get some sleep. We got one thing to be grateful for . . . they're going to court-martial us tomorrow. If we get acquitted, we can still catch up with them two thieves."

Jeff nodded. He stretched out in the sawdust and closed his eyes. It seemed ironic to him that all their trouble had come from the Confederates. They hadn't seen a Union trooper, and they probably wouldn't ever see one now. He laid awake for a long, long time. He knew he shouldn't give up hope. They'd been acquitted by the previous court-martial board. But this time things were different. This time Thornsberry and Vasquez had lied about them, confirming the things the arresting lieutenant already believed. Jeff didn't see how they could get off *this* time.

He slept at last, not because he had stopped worrying, but because he was too exhausted to stay awake. He was aroused by the door being opened and by the guard's harsh voice: "All right! Come on out of there!"

Silently Jeff and his drovers stumbled out of the icehouse. They were covered with sawdust. It was even in their hair. Brushing themselves off, as best they could, they followed the sergeant toward some fires in the bivouac area. Two guards with rifles at ready followed them.

At one of the fires they were given coffee substitute and a plate of cornmeal. All of them ate hungrily. When they had finished, they were marched to the creek and told that they could wash. With no soap, towels, combs, or razors, their clean-up was not noticeably successful, and it did not make them feel better. Combing his wet hair with his fingers, Jeff followed the sergeant toward a building that looked like an abandoned barn. There were four guards following them now, all with ready rifles. The guards and the sergeant stared at them coldly, as though they had already been convicted of treason and espionage.

There was a long bench inside the barn that smelled of hay and dry manure. The sergeant motioned toward it, and the drovers sat down gloomily. They waited, then, almost listlessly, as though they had no hope.

Jeff looked around at them. "Maybe it's not as bad as it seems. Maybe we can send word to Goliad. Or maybe we can persuade them to send a courier to Jonesboro and get the record of the other trial. There are lots of things we may be able to do, so don't get down-in-the-mouth about it yet."

Jack grinned weakly at him. Mad nodded without conviction. Ted just stared vacantly at him, and Sam scowled. Miguel nodded hopefully and smiled what he obviously thought was a cheerful smile.

Jeff heard voices approaching the barn. Turning his head, he saw Lieutenant Frost, accompanied by a colonel and several enlisted men. The colonel seemed to be studying them as he walked past, and Jeff wished fleetingly that they looked a little more presentable.

The two officers sat down at a table, facing the prisoners. Now Thornsberry and Vasquez came into the barn and took places on another bench at one side of the table where the officers were.

The colonel hit the table with his fist. "Court is convened. Lieutenant, I would like to hear the charges against these men."

An enlisted man began to write swiftly in

a dog-eared ledger book. Writing the pro-
ceedings down, thought Jeff.

The lieutenant stood up. "Colonel, we
caught these men driving a herd of cattle
north of here. They say they swam 'em
across the Mississippi and were driving them
to Mobile, but I think their story is ridiculous. It's impossible to swim a thousand
dry-country cattle across the Mississippi, so
obviously they lied. I think they came from
New Orleans. Likely those cattle were
shipped into New Orleans by boat from
Mexico, and these men are trying to take
them north to Union troops."

The colonel asked: "I understand you
have two witnesses to support your charge?"

"Yes, sir. They say they joined the others
this side of the river after bringing their
smaller herd of about three hundred cattle
from Opalousas, Louisiana. Thornsberry
and Vasquez are their names, sir. They're
sitting over there." He waved his hand toward where Thornsberry and Vasquez sat.

The colonel looked at the pair. He said:
"Thornsberry? Stand up."

Thornsberry stood up.

The colonel asked: "Where did you join
these men?"

"About forty miles back, sir. We'd just
swum our cattle across the river . . . they're

small cattle, sir, and able to swim a long, long ways. We met this herd of larger cattle coming north and asked their drovers if we could join them. They said we could. We had no idea they were from New Orleans then. When we found out later, we were afraid to try leaving them, for fear they'd kill us to keep us from informing on them. There was only two of us, sir, and there's six of them. We wouldn't have had a chance."

Sam growled savagely: "Liar!"

The colonel glanced reprovingly at him. "Quiet. You'll get your chance to be heard."

"Oh, sure!"

Jeff gripped Sam's arm. "Be quiet. You're not helping us by making that colonel mad."

Sam grumbled something unintelligible.

The colonel had Vasquez stand up and listened to his story, which was substantially the same as Thornsberry's had been. Then he looked at the prisoners. "Which of you is in charge?"

Jeff got to his feet. "I am, sir."

"Let's hear what you've got to say."

Jeff answered: "We started out from Goliad for New Orleans, sir, not knowing it was in Union hands. News travels slow in the Texas brush country." He paused a moment and then went on. "We got along all right until we came to a place called Jonesboro, west of here and across the river. We were asked where we were going. When I said New Orleans, they arrested us. They court-martialed us and afterward turned us loose. You can get in touch with Jonesboro, sir, if you don't believe that I'm telling you the truth."

The lieutenant and the colonel conferred for a moment, whispering. At last the colonel nodded for Jeff to sit down. He called Sam Rhody, who told substantially the same story, but it was obvious that neither the lieutenant nor the colonel believed a word either Jeff or Sam had said.

At last the colonel banged the table again with his fist. "I find you guilty . . . on a lesser charge than treason because of the ages of some of you. I find you guilty of attempting to give aid and comfort to the enemy and sentence you to be confined in the nearest army prison for a period not to exceed five years or until the cessation of hostilities. Your herd is hereby confiscated by the army of the Confederate States of America." He turned to look at Thornsberry and Vasquez. "I'm making you responsible for delivering it to the army quartermaster in Vicksburg, Mississippi, sir, as soon as possible, but you will have to hire civilians to help you drive it there. I can't spare any of my men."

Thornsberry was grinning, and so was Vasquez. The two scurried from the barn and disappeared. Jeff clenched his fists angrily. He wasn't used to talking back to his elders, but neither was he used to being treated the way he was being treated here. He shouted: "Colonel, you've turned property belonging to loyal citizens of the Confederacy over to a pair of thieves."

The colonel said: "Get them out of here! Put them back in that icehouse until tomorrow."

The guards moved in to surround Jeff and the others, their rifles leveled. Jeff looked at his friends and shrugged helplessly. There was nothing they could do. The herd was lost, and so was their liberty.

Trudging back toward the icehouse, he tried to imagine what it would be like to be confined to prison for five long years. He glanced around at the guards, feeling almost reckless enough to break and run in spite of them. Wasn't it better to be dead than to be shut up in prison for five years?

Then he felt Sam's firm grip on his arm. "Easy, Jeff. Easy. Gettin' yourself kilt ain't goin' to help nobody."

"How can they be so stupid? How can they believe those two thieves instead of us?"

Sam grinned sourly. "Looked in a mirror lately, Jeff?"

"How would I . . . ?" Suddenly Jeff was seeing Sam and his friends as others saw them. He was imagining what he himself looked like, dirty, unshaven, burned almost black by sun and wind. His hair was almost as long as an Apache's, and it hadn't felt a comb for days. He was still carrying sawdust from the icehouse on his clothes, and he could probably be smelled from twenty feet away.

They reached the icehouse and filed inside. The door was slammed and locked. Jeff sank down wearily on the sawdust floor. He was seventeen years old and a man, but suddenly he felt like he was going to burst into tears. He clenched his fists and jaw and sat, staring angrily straight in front of him.

XVII

The remainder of the day and the night that followed were long. Jeff's mind was like a squirrel in a cage, going around and around, frantically seeking a way out of their predicament, but there was no way out. There was no solution. They had been falsely accused and unjustly convicted, but they were going to have to serve their sentences — unless they risked everything, even their lives, by trying to escape.

He realized the others were desperate enough. He was almost desperate enough himself. A plan was what they needed before they could do anything, yet all of them seemed too shocked and numb to come up with anything that might be workable.

This time there were four guards with the trooper that brought their breakfast to them. And again breakfast consisted of coffee substitute and corn meal. Jeff looked at it and asked: "Don't you ever have any meat?"

The man grunted sourly: "A little once in a while."

Jeff said: "There's a million cattle in

Texas. If I don't get back, they'll stay in Texas, and you'll never have meat."

The man stared at him patiently. "Don't tell me about it, son. Tell the colonel. He's the one that sentenced you."

"When are we leaving?"

"This morning . . . soon's you eat." He slammed the door.

Jeff squatted down with his back against the wall and began to eat. Faintly he heard shouting outside the icehouse, but he could not make out the words. The shouting continued for a long time, but finally it stopped. After that, there was silence for an equally long time. When the door opened again, Jeff stared, blinking with disbelief. Standing in the doorway was his brother, Tom, and directly behind Tom was his brother, Luke. Both were squinting, trying to see into the semi-darkness beyond the door.

Jeff howled: "Tom! Luke!" and rushed at them, nearly bowling them over in his eagerness.

Tom was hugging him, and then Luke was hugging him, and then both of them were hugging him, while Jack, Mad, Sam, Ted, and Miguel stood in a circle, slapping them on their gray-clad backs.

At last Jeff stood back. Tears were running down his face, but he was laughing, too. Both Tom and Luke seemed to have aged. Even laughing as they were, they looked beat. Both wore beards and above the beards their eyes were bloodshot and very tired. There was a bloody bandage around Luke's head.

Jeff asked excitedly: "How did you find us? How did you know we were here?"

Tom chuckled softly. "Cut a cattle trail no'th of here yestiddy. Hadn't seen a cattle trail since we left home, so out of curiosity we followed it an' caught up. Saw ouah brand on some of the steers an' asked a few questions of the men that was drivin' 'em. We came right heah after that. We rode all night."

"What about . . . ? Have you seen the colonel and talked to him?"

"Sure have. An' you're free, all of you."

"We've got to catch those cattle, Tom . . . before Thornsberry and Vasquez reach Vicksburg, sell them, and run off with the money they get for them."

"Let's get goin', then. That is, if you don't mind Luke an' me givin' you-all a hand."

Jeff couldn't seem to stop grinning at them — he was that glad to see them after all this time. "Mind? You'd just better come along!"

Troopers brought their horses, saddled,

bridled, and ready for them. They brought their guns, which had been taken from them when they were captured by Lieutenant Frost. After that, a trooper came hurrying to them, saluted, and said smartly: "The colonel would like to see you gentlemen before you go."

Jeff said bitterly to his brothers: "Get that! Gentlemen, it is now. An hour ago we were dirt."

Tom stared somberly at him. "Don't be too hard on the colonel, Jeff. He did what he thought was right. He's busy fightin' a war, an' sometimes things ain't too easy on the man that's in command. I doubt the colonel has had eight hours' sleep in the last week, judgin' from the way he looks."

Jeff grumbled a little, but he didn't say anything. He was not yet ready to forgive the colonel for unjustly convicting them. The man had been too ready to believe Thornsberry and Vasquez. Nor could Jeff forget that, except for the brothers' happening upon that cattle trail, they would now be on their way to prison to a five-year sentence for something they hadn't done.

He lined up with the others in front of the colonel's tent. When the colonel came out, Jeff's two brothers straightened and saluted him.

The colonel looked at Jeff a little sheepishly. "I don't suppose you're in the mood to accept an apology from me, and I don't blame you if you're not. But I want to apologize anyway. What you are doing can contribute greatly to our chances of winning the war."

Jeff didn't say anything and was a bit ashamed of himself because he did not.

The colonel added: "I'll detail a troop of cavalry to ride no'th with you and help you to recover your herd. I'm desperately short-handed here, but I feel I owe you that."

Jeff found his voice at last. "It won't be necessary, sir. My brothers and my crew will be enough."

The colonel's hard mouth relaxed in just a suggestion of a smile. He turned to the sergeant, standing at his side. "See to it that both these troopers get passes to Vicksburg, Sergeant. They can rejoin their unit after the herd is delivered there and sold."

The sergeant nodded. "Yes, sir." He walked away.

Jeff straightened. He saluted the colonel, and the colonel solemnly returned his salute. Jeff, his brothers, and the others turned and walked away, leading their horses in the direction the sergeant had gone a few moments before. The sergeant came out of a tent immediately in front of them and handed a paper to Tom and one to Luke.

Jeff mounted and the others followed suit. Jeff glanced up at the sky, breathed the clear morning air, felt the warmth of the sun on his face, and he grinned exuberantly at his brothers. He said: "Let's go. Let's go get ourselves a herd."

Galloping, he led away, with his brothers following closely. Someone — one of his brothers, perhaps — loosed a high, shrill, yipping cry. Others took it up as they rode out of the Confederate army camp.

It was a cowboy yell, but it was something else. It was known to the soldiers of the Union as the Rebel yell. The colonel stood before his tent, watching them as they disappeared into the trees. There was a faint smile on his face.

XVIII

All the rest of that day Jeff and the others rode steadily north. At dusk, they stopped and ate the field rations one of the troopers had given them when their horses were brought to them. They drank water from a clear-running stream and, after that, laid down for an hour to give the horses a chance to rest.

In the first full dark they rode again, staying on the trail easily with only the light of the stars to illuminate it for them. At dawn, they stopped again, this time for two hours, but it was a cold and hungry camp with neither coffee nor food to strengthen them.

Again they went on, encouraged because now the trail of the herd was very fresh, and they knew they would catch up well before noon today. Jeff's two brothers rode beside him, and the three talked incessantly. Tom and Luke seemed to want to talk only about home. They wanted Jeff to tell them every detail of the roundup. They wanted to know the name of every man who had helped, of every neighbor whose cattle were included with the herd. They wanted to know how their grandfather looked, and they wanted to know if their mother was well, and, also, if she was worrying about them too much.

Jeff, on the other hand, wanted to know what his brothers had done. He wanted details of the battles in which they had participated. He wanted them to tell him where they had been last and where they were going now, and he wanted to know how Luke had been wounded and how serious it was. But Jeff's two brothers wouldn't talk about the war. So Jeff told them about the roundup, about the drive, about the stampede, and the swimming of the mighty Mississippi. He told them about the first court-martial, the second, and thus brought them up to date.

The dust of the slow-traveling cattle became visible to them up ahead, and they stopped on a wooded ridge from which they could see and stared at the plodding cattle, so near their destination at last.

Jeff said: "We don't have any quarrel with the drovers that Thornsberry and Vasquez hired when they were released. They have no idea they're helping to steal a herd."

Luke said: "Then let's play it straight. We'll ride up to the remuda first and relieve the man that's driving it. If he's one of the hired drovers, we'll just let him go. Then we'll ease up to the drag and do the same with the man that's riding it. After that, we can split and ride up both flanks of the herd. That's where Thornsberry and Vasquez will be . . . one of them, at least. The other's probably riding point."

Jeff nodded. It was the simplest idea and depended only on surprise. But if Thornsberry or Vasquez looked behind and saw what was going on. . . . He hoped they wouldn't. He didn't want anyone to get hurt, and he had the feeling that, if this came to a fight, his brothers would be much more efficient about it than Thornsberry and Vasquez could ever be.

Jeff's brothers looked at him expectantly, and he understood that they wanted him to lead out. He felt suddenly warm and a little embarrassed. His brothers were telling him that he was in charge. They were saying that he had brought the herd this far successfully, and there was no reason for them to think he needed their help now.

He grinned gratefully at them. Then he touched his spurs to his horse's sides and galloped down off the wooded ridge toward the drag of the slow-moving herd. He tried to stay concealed in woods wherever possible and to keep to low areas where there were no trees. They reached the remuda first and surrounded the man who was driving it before he knew what was happening.

Jeff said easily: "Just keep your hand away from your gun and nobody will get hurt. Drop back and go on home. This is our herd, and we're claiming it."

The man seemed about to protest, but a look at the grim faces of Jeff, his brothers, and his crew changed his mind for him. Nodding, he reined his horse aside and rode back in the direction he had come.

Jeff said: "Mad, take over here."

Madison nodded and stayed with the remuda while the others rode away.

In the rising dust of the herd they were able to get within fifty yards of the drag rider before he noticed them. Again Jeff said softly: "We're taking back our herd, mister, so just keep your hand away from your gun and everything will be all right."

"How about my pay?"

Jeff shrugged. "I'm not going to pay you, if that's what you mean. Was I you, I'd hang around and see where Thornsberry and Vasquez go if they decide to run. You can try getting your pay from them."

The man nodded and turned back.

Jeff glanced at Tom. "Why don't you take half the men and ride up the right flank?

Luke and I will take the rest and go up the left side."

Tom nodded.

Jeff warned: "I want you to let them go, unless they make a fight of it."

Tom grinned at him. "You're the boss, Jeff."

Jeff nodded. Followed by Luke, Jack Littlefield, and Miguel, he rode up the flank of the herd toward the swing rider, almost obscured by dust, a quarter mile ahead. As he rode, a strange tension began to build in Jeff. It reminded him of the tension he had experienced as he stalked Cliff Wasson in the thicket where Wasson had corralled the cattle he had stolen during the stampede. It was the tension, the nervousness that preceded a fight, not exactly fear but a quickening of all the senses.

The man, riding swing on this side of the herd, turned his head and saw them coming toward him. Recognizing Thornsberry, Jeff dug his spurs into his horse's sides. The animal leaped ahead, and behind him Jeff heard the others thundering.

His hand started toward his gun, then hesitated. He wanted no gun play, if it could be avoided. He wanted no one hurt, not even Thornsberry. All he really wanted was to get back what belonged to him.

Thornsberry yanked his rifle from his saddle boot, the scabbard that hung from the saddle at his side. He raised and leveled it, and a cloud of black powder smoke billowed from the muzzle. The bullet whined like a bee as it went past, less than a yard from Jeff's head. Behind Jeff, Luke's rifle roared. Thornsberry's horse, stung by Luke's bullet, shied violently to one side, almost unseating his rider.

Jeff turned his head. "No! Let him go! He won't shoot again!"

Luke's face was disappointed, but he nodded grudgingly. Jeff glanced at Thornsberry again. The man had veered away from the cattle. He had sunk his spurs and raked his horse's sides with them at every jump. He held the reins in his left hand, his empty rifle in his right. He did not look behind.

Jeff grinned triumphantly. There was a flurry of shots from the other side of the herd, and then silence over there. The cattle, spooked by the shooting, began to trot, and then to run.

Jeff roared: "Head 'em! Head 'em, or we'll have a stampede on our hands!"

He spurred his own horse toward the point, turning steers back into the herd as he did. Behind him came the others, crowding ahead of the running steers, yelling, slapping their chaps with their hands.

Slowly, slowly the running animals turned into the herd. Crowded in this way, their pace slowed to a trot, then to a walk.

Jeff began to gain ground, and at last reached the point. No one was here, but a moment later he saw Tom and those with him, riding through the billowing dust toward him. He grinned at Tom, and his brother yelled: "Vasquez took off like a scared rabbit, Jeff. Looks like clear sailin' from here on in!"

Jeff nodded.

Miguel rode his horse close and grinned widely. "I saw the chuck wagon tracks back there, *Señor* Jeff. I'll go follow them."

Jeff yelled: "Take a man with you."

Tom shouted: "I'll go, Jeff!"

The two disappeared into the dust. Jeff let his horse ease out a dozen yards in front of the leading steer. Behind him, the other men dropped back to take their places on the flanks. There was a warm feeling in Jeff now that the end of the drive was so very near. Vicksburg lay ahead, impossible to miss because all they needed to do to find it was to follow the Mississippi north.

Thornsberry and Vasquez were gone and could make no trouble now. Jeff's brothers were with him and would, by their presence, prevent any further arrests by Confederate troops. All that could conceivably give them trouble would be an encounter with a Union patrol, and that was a very remote possibility.

Jeff kept going steadily until sundown and bedded the herd in a large clearing, surrounded on all sides by brush and woods. And this night he and his two brothers sat around the fire and talked like boys, of the past and of home and of the time they would be returning to it. It was midnight before they went to sleep, but they were up again at dawn and driving on, knowing that today might conceivably be the last.

Vicksburg came into sight in late afternoon, and Jeff bedded the herd immediately, going on into the city afterward with his two brothers, riding at his side. After searching aimlessly for a while, they finally questioned a trooper with sergeant's stripes, and the man directed them to an ancient brick building where the army quartermaster was. Jeff and his brothers climbed the rickety stairs. Jeff could scarcely believe their long journey was at an end.

His brothers saluted.

Jeff said: "Sir, we've got nearly a thousand Texas cattle just outside that we'd like to sell to you."

The man stared at him unbelievingly.

Tom said: "It's true, sir. He drove 'em all the way from Goliad. You can use 'em, can't you, sir?"

The captain leaped to his feet. "Use 'em?" he shouted. "Use 'em? I can use 'em and a hundred thousand more! There's practically no meat of any kind to be had in Vicksburg, and it's the same everywhere." He grabbed his hat up off the desk. "Let's go take a look!"

He strode to the door and down the stairs, followed by Jeff, Tom, and Luke, and at the bottom of them bawled: "Sergeant, my horse!"

The four went out into the street, and, a few moments later, a sergeant came from the rear of the building, leading the captain's horse. All four mounted, and Jeff led out toward where the herd was bedded down.

Riding, the captain studied him. "How old are you?"

"Seventeen, sir."

"And you brought a thousand cattle all the way from Goliad?"

"Well, less than eight hundred from Goliad. There's one or two hundred of them that belong to a couple of men named Thornsberry and Vasquez. I'd like you to hold their share of the money until they come for it."

The captain nodded almost impatiently. "How in the world did you get them across the Mississippi?"

"We swam 'em, sir. Or most of them. There were about a hundred we had to sell on the west side of the river because they refused to swim."

The captain whistled. He pushed his hat back on his head and stared at Jeff with sheer admiration. "And what are you going to do now?"

Jeff glanced at Tom and then at Luke. He said: "I want to join up, sir."

"Join up? Don't be ridiculous, son! You go on back to Texas and bring us another herd of beef. And another after that. You can do a hundred times more for the Confederacy that way than you can in uniform."

Jeff felt his spirits sag.

The captain noticed his face. "Look at your two brothers, son. Look at their faces and talk to 'em. They'll tell you about the war. I'll bet they'd swap jobs with you anytime."

Jeff stared at his brothers, seeing the weariness in their eyes, seeing the discouragement and the defeat. And suddenly he understood something he had not understood before. The Confederacy was not winning the war. Its people were hungry, and its soldiers were very tired.

Jeff realized that every man in the South had to do what he could do best, if the Confederacy were going to win. Another untrained young soldier would be of little value to the South, but an experienced trail boss who could bring thousands of cattle to feed their hungry troops. . . .

He forced himself to grin at the captain and at his brothers, riding just beyond. "I'll go to Texas and get you another herd, Captain. You can count on it." Then he touched spurs to his horse's sides and rode on ahead so that they wouldn't see the sudden tears of disappointment in his eyes.

About the Author

Lewis B. Patten wrote more than ninety Western novels in thirty years, and three of them won Golden Spur Awards from the Western Writers of America, and the author received the Golden Saddleman Award. Indeed, this points up the most remarkable aspect of his work: not that there is so much of it, but that so much of it is so fine. Patten was born in Denver, Colorado, and served in the U.S. Navy, 1933–1937. He was educated at the University of Denver during the war years and became an auditor for the Colorado Department of Revenue during the 1940s. It was in this period that he began contributing significantly to Western pulp magazines, fiction that was from the beginning fresh and unique and revealed Patten's lifelong concern with the sociological and psychological effects of group psychology on the frontier. He became a professional writer at the time of his first novel, MASSACRE AT WHITE RIVER (1952). The dominant theme in much of his fiction is the notion of justice, and its opposite, injustice. In his first novel it has to do with exploitation of the Ute Indians, but as he matured as a writer he explored this theme with significant and poignant detail in small towns throughout the early West. Crimes, such as rape or lynching, are often at the center of his stories. When the values embodied in these small towns are examined closely, they are found to be wanting. Conformity is always easier than taking a stand. Yet, in Patten's view of the American West, there is usually a man or a woman who refuses to conform. Among his finest titles, always a difficult choice, surely are A KILLING AT KIOWA (1972), RIDE A CROOKED TRAIL (1976), and his many fine contributions to Doubleday's Double D series, including VILLA'S RIFLES (1977), THE LAW AT COTTONWOOD (1978), and DEATH RIDES A BLACK HORSE (1978).

The employees of Thorndike Press hope you have enjoyed this Large Print book. All our Large Print titles are designed for easy reading, and all our books are made to last. Other Thorndike Press Large Print books are available at your library, through selected bookstores, or directly from us.

For information about titles, please call:

(800) 257-5157

To share your comments, please write:

Publisher
Thorndike Press
P.O. Box 159
Thorndike, Maine 04986